# LIGHTNING
## of GOLD

Center Point
Large Print

Also by Max Brand® and available from Center Point Large Print:

**This Large Print Book carries the
Seal of Approval of N.A.V.H.**

# LIGHTNING
## of GOLD

# Max Brand®

CENTER POINT LARGE PRINT
THORNDIKE, MAINE

This Center Point Large Print edition
is published in the year 2017 in conjunction with
Golden West Literary Agency.

"Lightning of Gold" first appeared as a six-part serial
in Street & Smith's *Western Story Magazine* (8/22/31–
9/26/31). Copyright © 1931 by Street & Smith Publications,
Inc. Copyright © renewed 1958 by Dorothy Faust.
Copyright © 2012 by Golden West Literary Agency for
restored material. Acknowledgment is made to Condé Nast
Publications, Inc., for their co-operation.

The text of this Large Print edition is unabridged.
In other aspects, this book may vary from the original edition.
Printed in the United States of America
on permanent paper.
Set in 16-point Times New Roman type.

ISBN: 978-1-68324-491-2 (hardcover)
ISBN: 978-1-68324-495-0 (paperback)

Library of Congress Cataloging-in-Publication Data

Names: Brand, Max, 1892–1944, author.
Title: Lightning of gold : a western story / Max Brand.
Description: Center Point Large Print edition. | Thorndike, Maine :
    Center Point Large Print, 2017.
Identifiers: LCCN 2017019380| ISBN 9781683244912 (hardcover : alk.
paper) | ISBN 9781683244950 (pbk. : alk. paper)
Subjects: LCSH: Large type books. | GSAFD: Western stories.
Classification: LCC PS3511.A87 L46 2017 | DDC 813/.52—dc23
LC record available at https://lccn.loc.gov/2017019380

# LIGHTNING of GOLD

# CHAPTER ONE

Honesty is accepted as the best policy, but it turned out the worst policy for Bill Ranger, who was famous for his integrity and as a dog puncher from Dawson to the Arctic Ocean.

Lefty Ranger, as he was sometimes called, had had bad luck—the bad luck to arrive in Circle City, on this mail trip, on the very same day that Menneval reached the town. That could not be put down to anything other than an unkind fate, for Menneval flew as the swallow flies, on swift wings, dipping through the white, silent land as the swallow dips through the vast, free bosom of the sky. He paused in Circle City as a swallow pauses on a branch before it swings off again for the horizon, and in that brief pause he met Lefty Ranger and changed the course of his life.

Lefty had made good time. He started from breakwater with six dogs, and he got to Circle City with five, which was a tribute both to his luck and to his management. The last day, in a sense, was the hardest. There had been little food for men or dogs during the last three days, and on this last day of all there was none at all. So, though the trail went over easy levels, the labor told heavily. Men in Alaska are burned so thin by their labors and their privations that there is little fat for them to burn up when the pinch comes. In time of need, where softer peoples live on the fat that covers their sleek ribs, the north man has to eat and work on surplus nerve energy. If he lacks that, privation kills him like a bullet through the brain.

Lefty's last march on this trip was made difficult further by a steady fall of snow. There was not a touch of wind, but the snow fell down in a steady mist out of the shadow of the sky. On the ground it lay not in the broad, soft, spongy flakes that are familiar to dwellers in more southern climates. Rather, it disintegrated into tiny crystals as hard as rock, and the steel-shod runners of the sled, instead of sliding with an easy hiss over the surface, grated and ground as though running through sand. The dogs leaned hard against their harnesses, and the man helped them along. Another forty-eight hours of expectation would almost have killed Lefty, but he knew that Circle City was close at hand.

At length he entered the town. Through the snow mist he saw lights dimly; the rays shattered as they came through the white fog. They split into reds and blues and yellows, as though cast from a prism of glass. And there was no sound. It was a silent city. It did not seem an empty place; it seemed rather a figment of the imagination, or a city of eternal sleep.

Lefty Ranger was not dismayed. He had been

here before, and he knew how the snow muffles footfalls, muffles voices. Once a great dog came out of the mist and stood there on the edge of Ranger's vision, bristling its hair, snarling silently. He merely smiled and went on. He was very cold. He was hideously tired—that weariness that goes deeper than the muscles and finds the heart and numbs it.

At length a brighter light struck at him from the left, and then came an actual murmur of human voices. This was the place. This was Spooner Joe's saloon, of course.

He halted the team. The light showed him the frame of a door with the snow softly furring it all over, particularly in the corners. This door he threw open, and thought that he saw heaven. Then he took three paces forward.

The frightful cold entered with him, dissolving into a mist like the breath of cattle on a frosty morning. In the center of the room there was a big stove, with a fire that roared in it and kept its chimney trembling. He looked at that stove as a miser looks at gold. He had not been warm for six weeks; he had not escaped from a deep-seated chill for a month and a half, and yet the other men in the room were not hugging the stove. They were scattered here and there. They were standing at the long bar where Spooner Joe presided, lofty as a mast and ugly as a death's-head. They were scattered at the tables, playing poker. They were betting gold dust at the roulette wheel. The night was still young.

"Hey, you, shut the door!" yelled one or two.

Lefty Ranger merely stood where he had halted and laughed thunderously through the mist that he had brought in with him. That mist began to dissolve, falling away from his head and shoulders, from his body, as though it were a heavy gas. Then it slid out along the floor. He waved to the crowd, right and left, shouting: "Mail!"

There were some who knew his face. Others knew his voice. They greeted him with a great roar of welcome. They laughed and sang. They rushed out and tore the heavy mail sacks from the sled. They carried them into the room. They opened them; they spilled the contents along the bar. Names were shouted.

Some of the men were busy opening their own mail. Others hurried out and roused the town. Circle City began to pour into the saloon of Spooner Joe.

It was a great night for Spooner. Those who had letters bought drinks to celebrate the great occasion. Those who had good news set 'em up for the entire house. Those who had no mail and no message drank to forget their disappointment.

As for Bill Ranger, he went to the sled team, carrying out a quantity of dried fish. They should eat before he did, and eat they did, while he stood grinning at their joy and their appetite, throwing the fish to them, one by one, and watching those experts snatch their meals out of the air. Their hunger was a bright light that showed them what was coming. He fed them well, almost dangerously well.

Still he had something to do before he ate. He could not subdue his appetite until that other thing was accomplished. So now he strode into the saloon, again bearing with him a small but ponderous canvas sack that he put down upon the bar with a thump.

For a time he looked around him at the faces of those who were opening mail and celebrating along the bar. The room was filled with the blue-brown shadows of tobacco smoke. Through that mist it was difficult to make out features. His own face, as he pushed back the hood, was masked with a grizzled covering of uncropped beard and whiskers. His smile, beneath that growth of hair, was a distorted grin, strange to see. There was starvation in his eyes, but there was a smile in them, also.

At last, tired of searching with his eyes, he called in a loud voice: "Doc Harness! Doc Harness! Where are you?"

At this, one of the men standing close to him looked hastily, critically up toward the mail carrier. With equal haste he turned his attention down again to his drink. Half a dozen glasses of the same concoction were standing before Bill Ranger, untasted by him. He had this other errand to perform before he could drink, eat, or enjoy himself in any way. Only the starved dogs had taken preference over it.

Trouble and impatience combined in the eyes of Ranger as there was no answer to his call.

"Doc Harness!" he shouted more loudly. "Where's Doc Harness? Why don't some of you fellows go and give him a rouse? Tell him that I'm here and that I got news for him that'll make him stand three inches taller. I got news for him that'll take the kink out of his shoulders for good and all, and . . ."

No one answered. Each man appeared to be busy with his letter or with his drink, and yet, in fact, no one tasted a drop and no one read a word after that cry from Bill Ranger.

Then Joe Spooner, looking more like a death's-head than ever, came down the bar and paused opposite the mail carrier.

"Partner," he said gently, "the kink is already taken out of old Doc's shoulders. You don't need to go on worrying about him any more."

"Just what d'you mean?" asked Ranger, peering at the saloon man as if the face were barely visible at a great distance.

"Bill," said Spooner, "the fact is that Doc Harness up and left us all. We're sorry to have to tell you. Doc has left us, and he ain't never coming back."

Ranger passed a hand over his face. "He's gone and left us, eh?" he said.

"Yes, he's gone and left us. Steady, old-timer."

"I wouldn't've expected it," muttered Ranger. "Not just when his ship came in like that. I wouldn't've thought . . ." He caught firm hold on the edge of the bar, and then drooped in a half faint.

"Grab him, a coupla you," said Spooner, watching the mail carrier closely. "He was old Doc's partner, you know."

Strong hands reached for Bill Ranger. His head had sunk far forward; he seemed to be studying his feet. His knees, also, gave and trembled.

But he shrugged the hands from his shoulders, and gradually, by a great effort of the mind and of the body, he straightened again and stood erect.

"I wouldn't've thought it," he said. "I got onto a hundred pounds of dust in that sack for Doc Harness. That's what I've got for him. I got onto a hundred pounds. Doc, he could've laid back and taken it easy the rest of his days."

"Doc Harness is takin' it easy," said another. "Don't you take it too hard, old son. Doc is takin' it easy, all right. You remember, Lefty, that Doc was always a great hand for sleep. He's havin' the long sleep now. Take a drink, old man. It'll do you good."

Instantly came a deep-throated, murmuring chorus from many voices.

"Take a drink, Lefty. It'll do you a lot of good."

He took a drink. He closed his eyes while he felt the burn of it sweltering down into his stomach. "Just how did it happen?" he asked.

"Why, he just got tired. Got a little sick, but nothing much. He just got tired and give up."

"He never had no luck," said Lefty. "There was no luck laid out for old Doc Harness so far as I could see. But he was never one to give up, not breaking trail, or with a pick, or no way. He never was in the way of giving up a fight."

"Well, Bill, a man only has to give up once in this neck of the woods."

"Aye, and that's true," said the mail carrier. He drank again. His beard bristled fiercely, so that it was plain that he had set his jaw like a rock.

"Well," said Spooner, "it's an ill wind that blows nobody good. Old Doc has got no children and no relatives. He always used to say that all by himself he was father and son, cousin, aunt, and uncle. You're the nearest to him, old son. You get that sack of dust for yourself."

"Me?" said Lefty Ranger. He lifted his grizzly head and stared. "I'd never touch an ounce of it," he said.

# CHAPTER TWO

This announcement caused the others to stare. But they were not greatly astonished. For when one has lived long enough in the great white North, the peculiarities of men are not underlined. They are accepted rather as a matter of course. One takes the exception as the rule, and the perfectly normal man in all his reactions begins to seem the freak.

So they stared at Lefty Ranger, and not a word was said. Merely they watched him critically, nodding a little, as people do when they expect something interesting to follow.

There was only one person who stirred. This was a man of middle height, rather slenderly made, if one could judge his bulk under the heavy coat that he was wearing, the collar turned up so that the lower part of his face was shielded. This man rose from a chair where he had been sitting in a far corner of the room. He laid aside the newspaper of ancient date that he had been reading, and, crossing to the end of the bar, he leaned there, so that he could stare up the long, varnished pavement of the bar and look straight into the face of the mail carrier. He seemed fascinated. But the shadows that crossed his face were so deep that one could not accurately read his eyes.

"If you wouldn't touch it," said Spooner to Lefty Ranger, "tell us what's the matter with it? Is it blood money, old son?"

Lefty Ranger looked fixedly at the saloon-keeper. "Doc's blood is on it," he said solemnly. "It's soaking in Doc's blood."

"So you won't have it?"

"No."

"Then what'll come of it? Give it to the government?"

"A curse on the government!" hissed one. "What does the government do for us up here? What did the government ever do for old Doc Harness?"

Ranger turned his head a little and looked at the man. "I guess the government has done plenty for us all," he said. "The government is like trees. You can't see 'em grow from day to day, but they're working while you sleep. But this here stuff?" He gave a tap with a forefinger to the canvas sack. The dust was packed so tightly in it that the weight of the stroke made not a dimple in the surface of the canvas.

"Well, you figger on giving it to the government?" said Spooner.

"I'm trying to figure what Doc Harness would want me to do with it." He canted his head. He was like one trying to hear a far-off voice.

"Doc was a good old sport," said one meditatively.

"There was only one of him," said another. "How many down-and-outers has he staked?"

"That's just it!" exclaimed Lefty Ranger. "How many down-and-outers has he staked? A thousand, just about. That's where his pile always went. Roulette didn't get much out of him. Faro didn't . . . nor the booze. He never wanted much. Two or three times he had enough stake for him to want to pull out of the country and go south to the cattle ranges. He wanted to buy a place and get to work on it. That was always his idea."

"He'll never see the cattle that sack buys, nor the range that they run on," said Spooner.

"He never will," agreed Ranger. "Twice before he had nigh onto this much. Though when he gave that claim to Dummy Miller for half the dust that come out of it the first year, I never thought that Dummy would play so straight. But straight he was. He turned this over to me to bring on to Doc. And now Doc is gone when he sure had his chance to start south instead of west.

"Well, God knows the meaning of these things, if meaning they have. But Doc always gave his chances away. He couldn't say no, no matter what a loafer the gent was that asked him for a lift. I reckon that's the way this pile oughta go, too. I dunno any more likely way that Doc would've spent it."

"Maybe you're right," said one of the men.

"Well, I've made up my mind," said Ranger. "I'm gonna leave this sack in Circle City. It's to be sieved out to those that need it the most."

"Who'll you trust that to?" asked one.

"I dunno. Spooner is always around here, and Spooner can tell a straight man from a thug, I reckon."

There was a sudden, hungry flash in the eye of Spooner. "I dunno about that," he said. "I reckon I could tell a straight man from a thug, all right. I'd take charge of that for you, son."

Lefty Ranger looked wistfully at him. Then he drank again. "Spooner," he said at last, "you're about as hard as they make 'em. There ain't a man under the sky that you're afraid of. Not even a ghost. How'd I trust this to you if you had a need of dipping your hands into the bag?"

The insult made the saloonkeeper neither flush nor pale. He merely smiled. "I'm afraid of Menneval," he said.

"What . . . him?" exclaimed Ranger. "Yeah. I reckon you're afraid of Menneval. I reckon that everybody else is. But is Menneval gonna come here to Circle City and check up what you do with that money?"

"Menneval will never be seen in Circle City again," said one.

"Not while we got any guns with us," declared another.

"How can he live out there by himself?"

"He ain't by himself. He's got his dogs."

"And they's a pet demon in each dog."

"I'm like to turn over this here money to you," said Ranger. "You could do a lot of good with it, giving the boys a drink when they're feeling down and low, and passing out chow to them that are hungry, whether they're honest or not. But I'd like to have somebody put a guarantee on it and a check on you. I don't mean you no slander and no insult, Spooner. Your drinks is honest enough, anyway."

Spooner Joe seemed totally unaffected by these remarks. In fact, his record was so notoriously black, and had covered so many crimes—from petty larceny to murder and bank robbery—that the words of the mail carrier had a little less sting than might have been supposed. Besides, how could he vent any spite on the person of Lefty Ranger, who was middle-aged or more, one of the best-liked men in the North, and, above all, one who notoriously went unarmed all his days and all his ways.

So Spooner Joe merely smiled a little. "I guess you'll wait a long time before Menneval shows up here," he said.

"No, not a moment," said a voice at the farther end of the bar.

Everyone looked with a start in the direction from which the words had come, and there they saw the middle-aged, slender man who was leaning on one elbow against the foot of the board. He pushed back his hood a little, and the staring eyes of the others saw a clean-shaven, lean face. It was very brown. It was as brown as the face of an Indian almost, not with the reddish, weathered look familiar in those travelers over the snows of Alaska, but a deep mahogany. So dark was the color of his face that the blue of his eyes shone with an electric brightness against that background.

It was more than the mere contrast of color. Certainly those eyes had meaning for almost every man in the room. They did not shout the name, but the mere whisper of it clove from wall to wall: "Menneval."

Spooner Joe grew rigid. He was half turned toward the man, and a covert hand, slowly, softly, drew a Colt revolver from the shelf beneath the bar.

"I'll put my guarantee on that sack of gold," said Menneval. "I'll guarantee that Spooner will spend it fairly and squarely on the right people and never put an ounce in his own pocket. Why should he when most of it will go right back over his own bar again?" His voice changed a very little. "Spooner, put down that gun. Don't be a fool."

The bartender, with a gasping sigh, restored the gun to the shelf.

"Now, boys," said Menneval, "as long as I'm here for a few minutes, we might as well liquor together. Spooner, throw us some glasses and a few bottles, will you?"

Drinks of the so-called whiskey at the Spooner bar were 60¢ apiece—at that time the current rate in Circle City. Afterward the prices were to soar again.

Menneval threw out a small poke, solidly filled, but, when the bartender, coming out from his trance, spun the bottles down the bar and the clinking glasses after them, the men who stood in the long, irregular line touched neither the glasses nor the bottles. They looked before them as men in a dream, seeing strange visions.

Menneval filled his glass without appearing to give it a glance. Then, slowly, he raised the glass toward his lips. "Boys," he said, "here's how. And who says no to Menneval?" His glance ran up and down the line.

"I'll drink with you!" exclaimed Lefty Ranger. He pushed his hood clear back. His bald head glistened like a pale, polished rock. And, snatching up the bottle nearest him, he filled his glass.

"Nobody else? Nobody else?" said Menneval.

One by one, sullenly, as the quiet pressure of his eyes fell upon them, they filled their glasses, and in silence they raised them to their lips and swallowed.

"And you, Spooner Joe?" called Menneval.

There was still no anger in his voice. But under that quiet challenge Spooner broke out into a profuse sweat that made his face shine. He poured out three fingers and swallowed them like a man who needed the stimulant, not the pleasure of the drink. Then he measured out the gold dust from Menneval's bag.

"That's better," said Menneval. "That shows that we're all friends. All friends here together. Now some of you are free to hurry off and tell the authorities that I'm here. Run along. Any of you are free to go. I won't follow you. And I'll be here when the crowd gets back. Spooner, you heard my guarantee on that sack of gold. If I hear that you've gone crooked with any part of it, I'll drop in and give you a call. Now send some food into the back room. Ranger needs a meal, and I'm going to watch him eat it. I'll be in there, you can tell the fellows who pack the guns. I'll be in there sitting between the door and the window, waiting for them. That's all."

He restored the poke to his belt, and, turning on his heel, he walked slowly out of the room, without even a glance over his shoulder.

Spooner Joe reached again for the gun, now that the back of Menneval was turned, but the fingers seemed to freeze on the handles, and he could not raise the weight of the heavy Colt. Another man, with a faint snarl, actually jerked a weapon from under his coat and leveled it at the retreating form. But he did not fire. Enchantment seemed to make his forefinger helpless, and Menneval walked, undisturbed, out of the room.

# CHAPTER THREE

No one stirred, aside from Spooner and the other who had drawn the gun, until Menneval was out of the room.

Then a weight seemed to be taken from every mind. Suddenly they turned their heads to one another. And yet few words were spoken. One or two turned and looked suddenly toward the door.

The man who had drawn the gun hastily swallowed another drink. Then he muffled himself in his parka and went straight to the outer door, opened it, and leaned against the whirl of snow that blew about him, for a slight wind had risen.

He closed the door after him, and again the men at the bar looked at one another solemnly and with meaning.

"It ain't right," said Lefty Ranger suddenly. "It ain't right. He's said where he'll be. It ain't right to take advantage of him. It ain't fair. You wouldn't fight dogs a hundred against one."

"You'd fight wolves that way, though," said Spooner coldly.

"Well," said another, "are you gonna go back in that room with him, Ranger?"

"Why not?" asked Ranger. "I dunno what he's done that's so bad."

"Murder ain't much, I guess," said someone with a forced casualness.

"I dunno how much murder he's done," said Ranger. "Maybe he's all right. I'm gonna go back and talk to him, anyway."

"You got a nerve," said a friend. "Don't you go and be a fool. You keep away from Menneval."

"What's he done?" said the mail carrier. "I don't see any reason. I been inside as long as any of you, I guess. What's he done that you look at him like he has leprosy?"

"Oh, he ain't done much," said Spooner. "He ain't done much." He laughed soundlessly. Then he gave an order to a waiter. Food was to be taken into the back room. Menneval had ordered that this be done.

"He's had four partners," said a man who was older than anyone present. He was a hardy old prospector with a face like a mangy squirrel—the gray hair grew only in tufts on it.

"And where are them four?" someone asked.

"I'll tell you," said the old prospector. "He's had four partners. There was Charley Harmon, first. Charley was the cleanest kid that ever got this far north. There was no better than Charley Harmon. Everybody knows that. Well, he was the first, and he just disappeared. Got pneumonia, they said."

"There was that fellow that we called Chuck Spenser, or Tiny for short," one in the group said. "What become of him?"

"Oh, he got pneumonia," said the prospector sourly. "There was Garry O'Day. He had a terrible accident with a gun, it turned out. Menneval said that was pneumonia, too. But Shamus and Terry March found the body of Garry O'Day in the ice, and there was a bullet hole right between the eyes."

"The last was Lew Pollard," said Spooner.

"Pollard was a thug, a thief, and a hard-boiled egg," said the prospector. "He wasn't no help to have around. The only reason that he took on Menneval as a partner was because he figgered that no matter how tough Menneval was, he was a little tougher himself. Well, nobody has heard of Lew Pollard for quite a spell. And nobody is gonna hear of him again." He raised his hand high and dropped it soundlessly upon the bar. His voice softened to the greatest gentleness. "And nobody," continued the old-timer, "is ever gonna get anything good out of Menneval . . . because he ain't like us. He ain't a bit like us . . . he is plumb different."

"All right," said Ranger. "Let him be different. I'm gonna eat my meal, and I'll take my chance with Menneval."

Straightway he left the room and went to the little apartment at the rear that was often used by gamblers who wished to escape from the disturbance of the crowd.

At the door of this room Ranger paused, shocked to a standstill. On a small table at the side of the room, between the door and window, stood a tray heaped with food. A vast platter of steaming beans particularly fed his eyes. But near the table sat Menneval. He had taken off his outer garments. He sat bareheaded, in a light, closely fitting jacket. It showed the slender, trim body of a boy, but in actual years he might be forty-five, or closer to fifty, even; there was in him a potential age that was incalculable. His hair was perfectly white, close-cropped, and so sleek and thin that it fitted him like a smooth silver cap, but it was not the white of the hair that gave the sense of years to that face. There was hardly a line upon that face. But it looked as though it were hammered out of a metal, delicately and carefully, by the infinitely small hammers of time.

Ranger, after that hesitation, nerved himself. If he had seen without being seen, he would have turned about and gone back to the bar, or actually fled from the building. But he had been seen, and shame supplied the warmth of a courage that had failed him. He went on to the table and sat down before his tray of food, clearing his throat. From the big barroom there was not a sound. In place of the usual riot—particularly the riot of a mail arrival—a waiting silence filled Spooner's saloon.

"Ranger," said Menneval, "don't be afraid. I mean you no harm."

"Afraid?" said Ranger. He was about to deny it, but then he felt that it would, indeed, be foolish to try to deceive those keen, steady blue eyes. "Yes," he admitted, "you threw a scare into me when I come into the doorway. But I'm over it mostly."

"Good," said Menneval. "Go ahead and eat your meal."

It embarrassed Ranger for a time to eat with that eye watching him. But presently a great surge of hunger overcame all sense of place and time. He ate like a starved wolf, and, looking up once or twice, he saw that the other was watching him with the faintest smile of amusement, like a father watching a child at the table.

And yet he was the full age of Menneval, or very nearly so. He knew that mere years are no measure, however. If he had fifty full lives, he never could pour into them what already had poured through the blue eyes of Menneval. What they had said in the barroom was right. The man was simply different.

He went to the kitchen, got himself a second cup of coffee, and looked hard at the Chinese cook. The latter merely shrugged his shoulders. "They are all around," he said.

Lefty Ranger went back to the table. He felt much better. There was vital warmth in him now. It seemed as though a comfortable fire was glowing right under his heart. It seemed as though he never could be cold again. The fumes of the coffee were in his nostrils, and the fumes of the whiskey were in his brain.

"Menneval," he said, "they're all around the place, waiting for you."

"Of course they are," said Menneval. "They're all around the place, with their trigger fingers growing numb. That's why I'm waiting in here. And now, Ranger, I want to speak to you for one minute." He laid the poke from which he had paid for the drinks upon the table. "I want six months of your time," he said. "In this poke there are not quite twenty pounds of gold. That means six thousand dollars. Will that pay you for six months?"

Ranger stared. "What you want me to do, Menneval?" he asked finally, and he swallowed hard. It was high pay. It was the highest pay that ever had been offered to him, and for what?

"I want you," said the other, "to go outside. I want you to go clear down to California. I want you to go up into the hills to the town of Tuckerville. In the country near Tuckerville you'll hear of a man named Peter Crosson. He lives on a small farm. He's half scientist, half farmer, half hunter, half Nature lover. With him there's a lad of twenty-one or -two. That's his son. His name is Oliver Crosson. I want you to find those people, and I want you to talk to them. I want you to find out everything you can about both of them. You're not to tell them who sent you. You're not to tell them that you're interested in finding out about them. You're to act as though you simply chanced on them. When you've found out everything about their occupations, their habits of mind, their entire character, you'll come back here to Circle City and tell me all that you know."

The mouth of Ranger fell agape with wonder. "What's it all for?" he asked.

"I'm curious. That's all. I offer you six thousand dollars. Will you take the pay?"

"Is it gonna bring harm to the Crossons?"

"Harm?" said the other. He became thoughtful. "No," he said, "I really think that I could not possibly harm them in any way." He said it quite solemnly.

"Will you tell me why you should pick me out for a spy?" asked Ranger. "There's plenty more here that you could send that are twice as foxy as I am."

"I'm sending you because you're an honest man," said the other. "And there's nobody else in Circle City that I'd trust . . . as you trusted Doc Harness, and as he was right in trusting you." He got up from the table. "That's all," he said. "Will you go?"

"Yes," said Ranger. He was bewildered. He could not escape from the will of his table mate.

"Good bye, then," said Menneval. He left the poke on the table. He enclosed himself in his furred coat and drew the hood over his head. Then he jerked wide the door just beside the table. He jerked it wide, and stepped quickly back as three rifles rang out in rapid succession beyond the door, and three bullets humming through lodged with separate, heavy shocks in the logs of the opposite wall.

Menneval laughed, and now he glided through the doorway into the whirling of the white snow dust, light and rapid as the shadow of a bird.

Other rifle shots followed; they diminished in the distance. And Ranger heard a hoarse shouting pass away. But he was not disturbed. The laughter of Menneval was still in his ears, and he knew that the man had escaped unharmed.

# CHAPTER FOUR

Alaska was so in the blood and in the bone of Lefty Bill Ranger that he could not get it out of his mind. Even after he arrived in Tuckerville, he would still awake with a start in the middle of the night, with a nightmare dread that he was freezing to death because there was not a sufficient weight of blankets upon his body. But he was not freezing. On the contrary, he was sweltering with heat. Even when the cold wind blew down from the snows of the Sierras, Ranger could go abroad in his shirt sleeves, so powerfully was the resistance to cold built up in his blood and in his nerves; exposure that would have given another man pneumonia was to him no more than a comfortable coolness.

He did not stay long in Tuckerville, with its pleasant peach and plum orchards and genial sense of well-being in the air. He only waited there long enough to find out about the Crossons. As a matter of fact, it seemed as though Tuckerville hardly knew that the Crossons existed. It was only from the owner of the general merchandise store that he could pick up any facts of importance. To that store, as to the only port within many miles, all the outlying people through the hills and mountains near Tuckerville and Tucker Flat had to come sooner or later. The half-wild trappers, the still wilder and more lonely prospectors, the sheep-herders, loneliest and wildest of all, now and again had to come to the general merchandise store—once a year, let us say. And Sol Murphy, who ran the store, kept these vagabond peoples charted in his mind as a ship's chandler keeps a reckoning of the various tramp freighters that have made his port and taken supplies from him.

So he remembered the Crossons, but even he remembered them vaguely. Nevertheless, he said several things. One was that the Crossons were queer. Queer is a word that may mean almost anything out West. It may mean strange. It may mean spiteful. It may mean dangerous. It may mean half-witted. Queer is the term of last resort for people whose vocabularies are short, and, when Sol Murphy attached the words to the Crossons, he both shook and scratched his head.

"What d'you mean by queer?" asked Ranger.

"What makes you wanna know about 'em?" asked the storekeeper.

"Oh, I just heard somebody speak of the Crossons. What d'you mean by queer?"

"Wait till you see Peter Crosson and you'll know what I mean. He ain't like other folks. He don't care."

"He don't care?"

"No," said Sol. "He don't care about nothin'. You'll see. He runs his cows in the hills. Suppose that a bear comes down and raids him . . . why, he don't care. Suppose that a mountain lion, it comes down and slaughters a few colts and calves . . . why, he don't care. He don't hardly bother to go and set traps for 'em."

Sol continued to shake and scratch his head, so that Ranger began to feel that the heart of the mystery was about to be exposed to him. He waited patiently, on the watch, and suddenly Sol Murphy broke out, leaning a little across the counter. "I'll tell you something . . . you're a trapper, ain't you?"

"Yeah," said Ranger.

For that was the character that he had assumed, and he had gone so far as to buy a few traps from Sol. In fact, he had done a little trapping in the old days, the days divorced by more than time from his present self, which had been made by the white Northland.

"If you're a trapper, you get into the hills by the Crosson Ranch and you'll find that the dog-gone' animals ain't got no fear of you hardly. Seth Thomas, he was up there in them hills a year or two back, and dog-gone me if a grizzly didn't come right out and give him a run."

"Charged him?" suggested Lefty Ranger.

"Charged him? Yeah. Hunted him down and charged him, and didn't care shucks about his rifle. He put Seth up a tree, and Seth dropped his gun, and that bear, he batted that rifle to rags and then went off, and Seth come back to town mighty mad and swearin' he was gonna go back and lift that bear's hair. But he never went back for some reason or other." He laughed a little at the thought, but instantly he grew serious again. "Look here, stranger," he said to Ranger, again leaning across the counter.

"Well?" said Ranger, pretending indifference, although the lowered voice of Sol Murphy made the beat of his heart quicken.

"Fact is," said Sol Murphy, "there ain't a gun on the Crosson Ranch." He stared as he named the hidden mystery, and, keeping his face a blank and his eyes wide, he waited for similar astonishment to possess the listener.

Ranger did not need to pretend or to act a part. He gaped in turn. The two men presented perfect pictures of the same emotion.

"Yeah," said the storekeeper, "it's a funny thing."

"Funny?" said Ranger. "I dunno that I see much that's funny about it. Those hills back there look pretty wild to me. Looks to me like a real wilderness where a man could find some pelts. That's why I want to trap it."

"Of course they're wild, those hills. And got some wild men in 'em, too."

"What do the gents up that way say about Peter Crosson?"

35

"They don't like him," said Sol Murphy with decision.

"Don't they? And why not?"

"Well, he ain't neighborly," said Sol.

"Ain't a friendly kind of a gent, eh?"

"No, he ain't," said Murphy with quick decision. "There ain't no friendliness in him. Not that he's a mean man, though," he added hastily, as one who does not wish to be guilty of an injustice.

"What does he do to them?" asked Ranger.

"Well," said Sol Murphy, "that's what I never could find out, but I know that none of the thugs ever bothers him."

"They got a lot of thugs up there, have they?"

"Sure they have. They got a lot of thugs. Why, it's a regular hole-in-the-wall country, what with the cañons and the brush and the woods. You could hide ten thousand men in almost any square mile of that country. If a posse chases a man that far, he stops right there. It ain't anything but a clean waste of time to try to chase into the Tucker Hills. Everybody knows that that knows anything."

The mere thought definitely irritated Sol. He swore once or twice under his breath and glared at Ranger as though he resented the presence of the stranger.

"Why," said Ranger, "I wouldn't think that anybody would wanna take up a holding right up there among them thieves."

"Would you? No, you wouldn't," said the store-keeper. "You wouldn't think so at all, and neither would I. But there they be. Right up there."

"Maybe the Crossons are thugs themselves?" suggested Ranger.

So Murphy shrugged his shoulders. "How do I know?" he asked with the petty anger of a man who dislikes a question that he already had often asked of himself. "Nobody knows nothin' about the Crossons. All I know is that nobody visits the Crossons twice."

This information jarred suddenly home in the mind of Ranger. "Why, that's kind of interesting," he said.

"I think that it is," agreed the storekeeper.

"Nobody ever gets to see 'em up there on the ranch?"

"No."

"How do they drive strangers away . . . them not having any guns?"

"Dog-gone it!" exclaimed the irritated Sol Murphy. "How do I know? Wouldn't I give my front teeth, and my grinders, too, if I could find out what they do to strangers? All I know is that when Charley Moore come back from a hunting trip up that way he had a scared look that didn't wear off for mostly six months, and every time anybody mentioned the Tucker Hills he lost most of his summer's tan and got up and left the room. Nobody knew what to make of it.

But I reckon that he run into the Crossons."

The hair began to prickle along the scalp of Bill Ranger. "It sounds sort of ghostly," he declared.

"Yeah, don't it?" said Sol Murphy. He went on slowly: "There was Jerry Hanson, too. He heard something about the Crossons, and he said that he didn't believe that there was any such kind of people around there in the hills. He said that he was gonna ride right up there and have a look at things. And Jerry Hanson, mind you, is a fightin' man."

"Real one, eh?"

"Well, they say that he's killed three. I dunno nothin' about it, but that's what I've heard. I know that I don't want no trouble with Jerry Hanson. Anyway, I seen Jerry start. He had a horse and a pack mule. He had a good Winchester, and a pair of Forty-Fives that the triggers and the sights was filed off, that bein' the kind of an *hombre* that Jerry Hanson is. He don't trifle none at all. Well, he started off like that, not sayin' nothin' to anybody but me, because Jerry ain't a talkin' man. But he went up there to find the Crossons, because he told me so. And Jerry was the kind that would either do or die, I'll have you know." Sol Murphy paused.

"And what happened with him?" asked Ranger, itching with uneasy curiosity.

"Well," said Murphy softly, "I didn't see nothing of Jerry Hanson till about six months later when I was down at Hampton Crossing, and there I seen a freight train go by, and one of the doors of the boxcars was open, and settin' inside was a man, cross-legged on the floor, his head in his hands, his face lookin' sort of cadaverous and sick. I wouldn't swear to it, but I would've said that that poor, starved-lookin' gent, that a Chinaman would've had the nerve to go up and punch the nose of, I would've said that that was Jerry Hanson."

"You don't say," breathed Lefty Ranger. Then he added with a rickety laugh: "I reckon that I'd better keep away from them hills."

"Oh," said Sol Murphy, "outside of a coupla dozen thugs and yeggs, them hills are safe as can be. You can trap all the mountain lions that you want, and get a good bounty for 'em right down here in Tuckerville. But don't get no foolish ideas. Don't start to trap no Crossons."

"Tell me one thing," said Ranger. "Why don't people talk about 'em more around Tuckerville?"

The storekeeper frowned heavily upon him. "Stranger," he said, "does folks likely talk a good deal about yaller fever and the smallpox?"

# CHAPTER FIVE

When Lefty Bill Ranger packed his roll and left Alaska, he had felt that Menneval's offer was the very height of romantic generosity—$1,000 a month for nothing more than travel, together with a little information to be picked up at the end of the trail.

But when he drove his loaded burro out of Tuckerville and steered his course for the ragged Tucker Hills, he felt that Menneval probably had driven a shrewd bargain with him. He was more excited than ever he had been in Alaska, whether fighting a storm or striking gold. There was danger ahead, and there was mystery ahead. And although he carried with him a good Winchester and an excellent Colt revolver as well, and although he was a master of both weapons, yet mere powder and lead seemed a very small comfort to Ranger.

Other men had come up here into the hills. They had possessed arms equal to his; they had possessed skill greater than his, no doubt, and yet none of them had seen the Crossons without becoming changed men. A mark had been put upon them—a mark about which they would not talk. A horror so great that it was beyond speech had closed over them, and now he was to put his foot upon the threshold of the same mystery, and the very thought of it sent cold prickles up his spine.

The Crossons might be madmen, able to overwhelm the minds of others by the insanity of their fury, their strength, their animal cunning.

The Crossons might be clever, hard-headed exploiters of something that the rest of the countryside knew nothing about. They might, for instance, be working quietly at some rich digging, piling up gold month by month, extracting a fortune that they guarded as dragons guarded hoards of old.

The Crossons, on the other hand—and this seemed the most likely case of all—might really be the capable chiefs who controlled a number of the outlawed men who took refuge in those hills. In that case, it meant that they controlled the exploits of various robbers who issued from the fastness of the hole-in-the-wall country and went down into the rich lowlands for pillage, returning to the safety of the district where the Crossons lived. If this were true, no wonder that men found it dangerous business to approach the Crosson homestead, for twenty armed hands might be raised against any intruder.

Lefty Ranger swallowed hard, but could not get rid of the lump that had formed in his throat. But he plugged away. The honesty for which he was famed in the white North drove him forward. He had undertaken a task. No matter how frightened he might be, he could not withdraw until the thing had been accomplished, or disaster had overtaken him. No doubt that was the very reason why Menneval had selected him, instead of choosing far more cunning and sharp-edged wits for the work that lay ahead.

He rose out of Tucker Flat and its orchards. He pushed back through rolling country where cattle grazed here and there on the good grass. He passed through a borderland of rocks that glistened and blazed in the sun and sweated with cold in the nights.

And so he came into the hole-in-the-wall district.

It was well worthy of that name. Dry draws, only running with water in the height of the rainy season, and cañons, in the palm of which at least a trickle ran all the year long, cut up the face of the country. Around them rose hills as irregular in shape and abrupt in slope as waves in a choppy sea. Rocks grew more than grass on the sides of those hills. There was better pasturage for goats than for cattle. If, here and there, a meadow appeared and a bit of almost level grazing land, it was sure to be fenced away by almost impenetrable rubble of rocks where no road could be made.

It was a country where the pack horse alone could make headway, and even a sure-footed burro could not steer a straight course. Ranger had to climb heights repeatedly and take his bearings, and pick out a way across the wilderness ahead of him, a winding way, sticking to watersheds and small divides.

All grew wilder as he penetrated into the district. He found trees—forests of mighty spruce and pine untouched by the lumberman for the good reason that there was no way of hauling the treasure out to town or city. There were brakes and dense growths where fire had cleaned out the old giants and allowed a crowding second growth to spring up about the scarred and blackened knees of the old forest monarchs.

There were extents of hardy brush, tall enough to cover man and horse, and frightfully difficult to force a way through. Here the cattle, in places, had broken meager trails through growths so dense that there was no turning from the path on either hand. Once committed to one of these green tunnels, a man was as securely hemmed in as though walled in by rock, and Lefty Ranger never entered upon one of them without misgivings.

It was a vast checkerboard of difficulties.

No sooner was a spacious forest left—a forest in which directions were lost with a dizzy speed—than he came into a frightful brake of brush, and when this was passed he would find himself in a tangle of intercrossing cañons and ravines with precipitous sides. Many of these were box cañons. He never knew, when he entered the mouth of one of them, when it would end up in a sheer cliff, with fine spray over the brim of the wall.

He worked farther into the region. Above him rose the loftier heads of the upper mountains, and upon their sides white streaks appeared, like veins of marble, through the cuts of the ravines. White cloaks and caps were on their shoulders and their heads. The dark veil of the forest marched up them to a point where all trees ceased. And he could see timberline marked along the sides at a regular height. Sometimes he felt as though this dark veil of the forest was a symbol of the mystery that he pursued, towering above him unknown, yet leading him on.

He was not a lonely man. He had been too many years in the Far North, and there he had learned to be his own company, not allowing his brain to become too active, and not asking too many questions of the landscape around him. But he fought against a dreaded sense of helplessness in these hills. It was different from the white North. The warmth of the sun, the song of the many birds, and the pleasant sound of the streams should have made this a terrestrial paradise to one so long among the snows. But instead they made it seem like a dream to Ranger. And the dream was all of fear.

He had not really been homesick since he was a child. He could hardly remember the home for which he had been ill at heart then. But he was homesick now.

He told himself that he would walk ten miles and swim a river for the pleasure of talking to an Indian in a tongue that the Indian could not understand. He used to listen to the chattering of the squirrels with a peculiar envy, and the bright flash of a blue jay overhead made him follow the beautiful and evil little creature with longing as it skimmed across the treetops, bent on mischief.

As he worked his way slowly into the country, his eyes were more often upon the ground than upon the natural features around him. It is said by seamen that Satan himself would make a sailor if he would keep his eye aloft. But a wanderer by land can never be at home in any country unless he learns to keep his glance upon the ground.

On the great page of that book he reads most interesting signs. The second day out, for instance, he found the trail of a timber wolf with a spread to the forefoot as great as the broad palm of his own hand. A hundred pounder, that one, if it weighed an ounce.

After that the trails of the wolves grew thicker and more frequent. And most of them were big— astonishingly big. Along with them went the more dapper marks of coyotes, the cunning scavengers and thieves of the wilderness. And even these footprints were greater in size than most that he had seen in his other wanderings. Sometimes he could hardly tell whether the signs were that of a big coyote or a small female timber wolf. But everything was big.

Just as the spruce and the pines overtopped almost anything that he ever had seen, so all the animal life seemed large. The squirrels that scampered on the branches were unusual in size and looked in their fluffing fur as big as Persian cats. The wildcats had nearly the foot-spread of a lynx. And when he found the trail of a mountain lion, he gazed at it in amazement, for it was as the trail of a lion indeed. The sign of the deer were as those of oxen. And the cattle that he came across here and there—long-legged, gaunt-bodied creatures—seemed to have grown beyond their ordinary proportions.

An elk came out of the woods, and, seeing him in the trail not fifty yards away, it stamped its forehoof and shook its head, less frightened than annoyed by his presence. When he reached for his rifle, it turned a little, but paused to look back at him over its shoulder. He could have shot it ten times over, but a certain awe restrained him. What made the wild creatures so fearless?

When he started from his camp on the third morning, he found the sign of half a dozen timber wolves about the place. Some of the tracks came up within three feet of the place where he had slept—and he shuddered at the thought of the great white fangs that could have slit his throat at a single slash.

On the evening of that very day, as he came through the dusk up a small draw, he saw through the blue of the evening a huge gray outline standing on a boulder with the cliff behind. It was a lobo, a king of its kind, and, when Ranger came close to it, instead of bounding away from the rifleman, the big beast merely snarled—a hideous apparition, lighted by the flash of its own long white teeth and the glistening red of its gums.

Ranger gasped. He had been over much of the western world. He never had seen animals react like this in the presence of armed men. If there were thugs, yeggs, bad men among these hills, what kept them from teaching the creatures of the wild better manners?

For his own part, he did not fire a shot at the grinning monster. He had found, in fact, that from the time when he entered the wilderness, he was loath to use a gun. He killed one young fawn that supplied him with plenty of meat. But after that the memory of the echoes that the report roused and brought heavily booming back on his ears depressed him and sent a chill through his nerves.

Instead of firing at this timber wolf that so impertinently challenged him, he went slinking by, and then for quite a time kept throwing frightened glances over his shoulder to see if the beast were following him.

# CHAPTER SIX

In the early morning, Ranger came into view of the Crosson Ranch. He came over the crest of a high hill, and the place was below him, spread out like a map. To understand the panorama, in fact, a map was needed as soon as one removed one's eyes from it. For the Crosson place was simply an elevated and fairly level plateau that had been slashed to ribbons by many creekbeds and the basins of draws. One might have called it a little kingdom of one elevation. It spread out from a central and fairly large acreage that was cut by the channels that water had worn into many crooked fingers that wandered here and there toward the sides of the higher hills. The ravines were dark with trees and shrubbery, or else the naked rocks in them blazed in the morning sunshine.

The level upper land was a solid sheet of green, pleasant to the eye as cool lake water to the thirsty traveler. And in the center of the main body of the green lake there was a shrouding of lofty trees, true monsters from the primeval forest; inside of that harborage rose a plume of smoke, and although the habitation was entirely sheltered from the eye of the most curious, Ranger guessed that this must be the place where the Crossons lived.

Only men who loved solitude could have selected such a site. Within ten miles on all sides of them there was hardly a cultivable or grazing patch of land that amounted to five acres in a solid piece. Here they had some hundred acres of good ground, and the reds and golden browns and whites of the feeding cattle made pleasant resting places for the eyes of Lefty Ranger.

If one loved solitude, one could hardly pick out a better place. No rustler would ever undertake the terrible drive through the badlands that surrounded this island of prosperity for the sake of the few cattle that he could herd before him in the drive down the narrow, dangerous cañons. The ranch itself was very largely a maze. The surrounding entanglement of ravines made a true labyrinth. And the greatest wit would be helpless in such a place, unless he understood perfectly the lay of the land. That was the kind of knowledge that one could pick up by growing into the ranch and growing up with it. It was not something to be studied out of a book. The peculiarities of the formation of that ranch were as singular as the varying characteristics that will show dimly in the face of a man.

And what did they do with their cattle? Did they drive them off in small herds, every two or three years, toward the nearest railroad—far, far away as that was—or did they butcher them on the place, render the fat, and take the hides and horns for sale?

Ranger was much intrigued. He could not tell what they might be most likely to do, but he was rather inclined toward the second viewpoint.

Well, now that he had found the position of the ranch, he could not help feeling that the major portion of his work had been accomplished. Already, in fact, he knew from hearsay that the Crossons were most odd, and even the character of their oddities had been told him during his stay in Tuckerville. If only he could now scratch the soil a little.

That problem of getting in touch with the Crossons was a difficult one, and neither by day nor by night was a solution revealed to him. In the meantime, he had the task of laying out his traps. He selected for that purpose a looping line that ran eight miles along the hills, so arranged that at every place where the ground rose up it looked down upon the ravine-cut flat in which lay the Crosson Ranch. The work of laying out the trap line and of putting up his meager scattering of traps here and there occupied him during two whole days, and occupied him so thoroughly that each night he went to sleep a very tired man, to waken in the dawn hardly ready to resume his work. For the warmth of the climate was as yet far too much for him. He perspired over the slightest exertion, and sweat streamed off him as he toiled over the slopes in the full blast of the afternoon sun. When he got up on the morning of the third day, he found a mockery of his trapping efforts awaited him. For the burro, which he had hobbled loosely and turned out to graze, lay on its side hardly a hundred yards from his camp, with its throat torn open.

The signs of timber wolves were all around it, but not a morsel of the kill had they touched. Pure malice had led to the murder of that inoffensive little beast. Its open eyes were as bright and living as ever, while the dawn light glittered far into their depths. Only the red slash at the throat told him that the burro would never stand up and wag its ears again.

To get the nuisance of the corpse away from his camp, he rolled it to the lip of the nearest ravine and watched it tumble away far below him, plunging into the brush, from which it knocked up a great cloud of dust, almost as though it had set off a charge of powder in striking the shrubbery.

Lefty Bill Ranger went back to his camp with a grimly set jaw. If there were no other men in that district of the world capable of showing beasts of prey how they should behave and whether or not a grown man should be feared and respected and his habitat left in peace, he, Bill Ranger, would now start giving lessons broadcast.

With this resolution strong in his mind, he

had barely got to the little lean-to out of which he was making a home among the rocks when a gray head and shoulders rose from a nest of boulders near him and a lordly lobo grinned its teeth hatefully toward him.

Was it imagination or did he indeed see a splash of blood staining the broad, white vest of the brute?

At any rate, out came his revolver with a slash of light, and he fired straight at the lobo. It seemed to wince as his finger pressed the trigger, but he knew that the wincing came after rather than before the bullet was launched, and, as the wolf dropped among the rocks, out of sight, Ranger knew that he had sent the shot home.

He hurried to the place, near the edge of the hill's shoulder, to finish the business in case the single bullet were not enough, and with a beating heart he told himself that he had done well indeed, and in the cause of justice rather than of himself.

But when he got to the nest of rocks and cautiously entered among them, he found that the wolf was gone.

A few large drippings of blood caused him to hurry on outside the rocks again, and, dropping his eye down into the flat of the Crosson Ranch, he saw his quarry again. It had been hit and wounded, as its flinching and the bloodstains proved, but it was able to run as hardly a lobo ever had run before. Its huge frame humped like a frightened rabbit. It doubled and then stretched, and made no more than a gray streak as it shot in and out among the boulders, and then began to shoot across the open green grasslands.

This amazed the trapper. For he knew that the gray wolf, when it is hurt, runs, of course, but rather for covert than for its home. And here was this evening prowler, speeding out into the open, and heading, in fact, toward the habitation of man.

Perhaps it was a young wolf. No, from its size it appeared fully mature, and therefore in full possession of its senses.

Perhaps it was struck by the bullet somewhere about the brain? No, for it did not stagger about, and its wits hardly could be affected so long as it ran so straight.

What was the goal of its running, then?

It had a den, perhaps, on the farther side of the green sea that made the central part of the Crosson Ranch.

Ranger pulled out his field glasses. They were strong, and the lenses in them were as good as money could buy, but just as he focused upon the wolf, it disappeared into a flashing mass of greenery. He lowered the glass with a muttered oath. The wolf, in fact, had actually entered the plantation of trees around the Crosson house. In a moment it would be issuing on the farther side, continuing its headlong flight for its den. Ranger put this down as a marked freak in wolf behavior, and one well worth noting to its end. It might be a female, perhaps, returning to its young. He told himself that he never had seen a female so high in the shoulders or possessed of such a lordly, shaking mane. However, that was the handiest explanation, and he repeated it to himself as he swept the region of gently rolling grass on all the farther sides of the trees.

But the wolf did not appear again.

No, though he focused the glasses with the greatest care and studied every inch of the features of the landscape, he could not see a token of the big fellow again. Male or female, it had disappeared among the woods of the Crosson place as though it were entering its own home.

Ranger shook his head. He knew much about the impertinence and the cunning of these wild rovers, but he never would have suspected one of them of denning up among trees where man was so close a neighbor. It was almost too much to be given credence.

He lowered the glasses at length, when he had waited a full quarter of an hour vainly, and he went off, shaking his head as many another trapper has shaken his over the antics of the overwise timber wolf.

So he went about his work of the day, visiting his trap line. His catch was good, very good indeed. It was the sort of a catch that a man would expect to snare in a country so filled with tracks.

He got two red foxes in successive traps, then a pair of coyotes in the next two—a catch in every trap, and in pairs, as it seemed. Then there was a bobcat, and three empty traps in a row. He found in the next an idiotic rabbit whose head had been torn off by a mousing hawk or eagle, and the body left secured in the trap. In the last trap of all, as he completed the round and neared his home, with the pelts born on his shoulders, there was another coyote, and such a huge one as he never had seen. It must have weighed close to sixty pounds, and it was in the very pink of fat condition. Much flesh went to coating the sleek ribs of that rascal, to be sure.

He came back to his lean-to very well satisfied with himself. He had been a hunter and an independent roustabout so much of his life that a successful day of shooting or of trapping had its own significance, quite apart from any ulterior motive that led him to remain in this region of the hills.

He had already made the beginnings for several frames, and now he stretched the skins upon them, finished the cleaning and first dressing, and ranged them aside for drying. A month of such trapping as this—this and better, as he learned the ways of the animals and the tracks they frequented—and he would have a whole wagonload of spoils.

He was thinking over this as he went out with the small hand axe to chop wood for the supper fire, but, as he went, a sudden deep chorus of baying came to him out of the Crosson valley.

What dogs were out at this time of day, beginning a hunt?

Then he stopped in mid-stride, for he recognized the fresh outbreak. It was not the chorus of a dog pack. It was the yell of a stream of wolves following a blood trail straight toward his lean-to on the hillside.

The nerves and the brain of the trapper congealed for an instant with cold.

# CHAPTER SEVEN

He ran to the edge of the hill, and with his glass he looked down upon the flat of the Crosson Ranch, the smooth sweep of beautiful green, spotted here and there with groves, and above all, with dense places of shrubbery.

Across the open he saw a mountain lion bounding at full speed, and well behind it came the wolves. And such a pack!

The lobo is a solitary brute as a rule. It prefers to work alone. Sometimes there will be a couple, followed by three or four half-grown cubs, but this is the great exception. Again, in a winter of great famine, half a dozen may band together for more efficient hunting. But this was no season of famine; all of these animals were full grown. And yet there were more than a dozen of the monsters racing after the puma.

It was a sight to dream of, not to tell, for no words could reproduce the ghoulish howling of the timber wolves as they fled on the trail with the quarry in full view. The race had hardly begun, for the puma was putting the wolves behind him almost as though they were standing still, but with such a short-breathed animal as the mountain lion—made to start like an arrow from the bow and to fail almost as quickly—a creature designed for stalking and a single lightning attack, the deep-lunged wolves were sure to gain rapidly after the first burst of sprinting.

But neither the puma nor the lobos were what started Lefty Bill Ranger so greatly.

Behind the mountain lion, behind the wolf pack, appeared a single man on horseback—an Indian, doubtless, for his bronzed body was naked to the waist, and he wore trousers and leggings of the old Indian deerskin fashion, and moccasins on his feet, so far as the glass could tell. Like the Indians of another day, also, he rode without a saddle, and therefore without stirrups. And in place of a bridle he appeared to have a rope noosed over the head of the horse.

A wild mustang that horse appeared to be, with a shaggy, flying mane, and a tail blown straight out by the wind and by the speed of its running. Now it bounded across a little ditch, now it shied violently from the flashing face of a rock that reflected the sunset light, but the rider sat on the bare back with perfect ease.

He was young. He was straight and lithe. The blowing, black hair whipped and snapped behind his head. And as he looked from side to side, he seemed interested in the blue colors that were filling the cañon like ghostly water, or in the rose and gold of the upper lighted mountains, rather than in the strange hunt that was taking place before him.

What was he doing there? Why did he follow the wolves? Was he hunting them as they were hunting the puma? Or did he wish to shoot the puma and scatter the wolves when the time came for the great cat to stand at bay?

If there was any shooting to be done, it would not be with a rifle, at least, for there was no sign of one borne by the young cavalier. There was no token of a revolver, either, but only the sheath of a knife at the right hip, fastened to the belt. The strong glass showed these small details quite clearly, but it showed no sign of a firearm of any sort.

And then the trapper remembered what Sol Murphy had told him. No guns were ever allowed upon the Crosson Ranch.

Was this one of the Crossons, then? Was this one of the men into whose lives he had been sent to peer and listen like an eavesdropper?

No. What white man would gallop half naked across the plain in this manner, on an unbridled, unsaddled mustang? It must be an Indian, of course. No white man could be tanned so dark by mere sun and wind, he told himself. Why, the fellow was almost black. If not an Indian, a Negro, or a mulatto. So thought old Bill Ranger as he stared down and studied the scene, which now began to change rapidly.

For the lion, which at first had been covering the ground with enormous leaps, had now slackened its gait suddenly. Its wind was gone. And up on it swept the wolf pack, yelling like deep-throated demons on their course.

The puma almost halted and half swung around, as though it would make its stand out there in the open, desperate as it was, but, when the wolves drove nearer, its cowardly mind was changed again, and it fled for the shelter of a mass of tall, standing brush.

The wolves were on its heels when it entered, but, as they saw the whipping branches close behind the long tail of the fugitive, they fanned out suddenly and formed a circle around the place.

Was that the end of the puma hunt? For certainly, on the part of the lion, the patience required to remain there would be as great as the wolves' in watching and starving the great cat into submission!

But now came the rider on the horse. Right up among the wolves he drove, and before the mustang was stopped he had swung from its back and landed on the ground with a light, bounding stride. He was not a single stride from two of the huge lobos. What monsters they were the watcher could tell by a comparison of their bulk with that of the man. Yet neither of them offered to spring at the human throat. Neither did either of them skulk away. But they turned their heads with red, lolling tongues and glittering eyes toward the boy, as though asking directions from him.

Bill Ranger gaped like one who has seen the end of the world.

The swarthy youth was in no haste. First he took out a cord and bound it around his head, as if to keep the long black hair from sweeping into his eyes. Then he drew his knife and thumbed the edges of it. The glass showed every detail. Ranger grew feverish with excitement. It seemed as though the youngster were actually mad enough to attempt to enter the dusky shadows of that brush.

When the knife had been tested, three or four of the great wolves were gathered about the boy for all the world like children at the feet of a master. They sat down in a semicircle before him and waited. And from all that circle of watchers around the brush not a single yell went up.

The man now pointed to right and left. Perhaps he gave a spoken command as well, though the glass could not show the movement of his lips. At any rate, the hair of Ranger lifted as he saw two of the big animals enter the shrubbery to the right of the man and two upon the left. The lad himself walked straight forward between the two groups, and all of them instantly were lost in the shadows of the bushes. Here and there the tops of these waved, but not violently.

Then the minutes of waiting began. The heart of Ranger thundered in his throat. It seemed to him hours, yet, when he looked to the west, the sun did not seem to have changed its position. It was as though even the great sun itself arrested its course to look down on the strange scene taking place there in the heart of the brush.

The silence suddenly ended. A loud, screeching cry from the great cat sounded plainly up to the hill shoulder where Bill Ranger was watching, and then the tawny body—head and back and stretching tail—showed for an instant among the top tips of the brush.

Had it aimed at a wolf? Or were these wolf dogs in spite of their appearance? No, it would not have leaped so high at the throat of a dog. A man was its goal, or something as tall as a man.

The thundering heart of Ranger stood still. A terrific series of screeching yells followed from the throat of the monster cat. Then silence followed. It was a silence hideously long, and now the sun began to move. It sank lower. It touched the rim of the western hills. It puffed its cheeks. It sank gradually out of sight, and still no token from the bushes. Ten great wolves lay around the brush. The four and the man who had entered with them had not appeared again. The trim mustang, frightened by the outcries, had run a hundred yards away, and now it was grazing peacefully, a beautiful little bronze-colored horse with a mane and tail of silver.

The sun was out of sight. The fires of the sunset

began to grow dim, and Ranger felt a vast desire to go down and investigate the tragedy of the brush patch.

It would be an easy thing for the mountain lion to dispose of the man with a single stroke of its saber-like claws, tearing out the boy's throat. A wolf could be killed at a single blow, so powerful was the supple, dagger-armed paw of the great cat. Besides, it was in brush tangle, where it would be at home. And Ranger had a picture, horribly clear in his mind, of the four great wolves lying twisted in death, and of the huge cat, with eyes like yellow moons, lying on the body of the human victim and lapping the blood from the hollow of his throat.

Perhaps a wind came over the flat. Perhaps something was moving again in the brush. Ranger focused his glass as well as he could, but uncertainly, because of the dimming light and because his hand was shaking so. But now, out from the brush, tall, erect, unhurt, stepped the lad, carrying draped over his shoulder the flapping, long-tailed pelt of the mountain lion. By what miracle had he, alone and unaided, ripped the hide from the big beast in so short a time? But there he stood, and, as he waved his hand, instantly into the brush leaped the ten wolves that had lain around it in a circle, at watch.

The boy, in the meantime, waved toward the mustang, and a thin, small sound of a whistle reached to the ears of Ranger, who was waiting there in hiding on the shoulder of the hill.

Obedient to the signal, the horse left off its grazing and came at a trot, then a gallop. He stopped short, snorting, pricking his ears as he sniffed at the bloody spoil that the lad was now folding neatly. When folded, he laid it across the back of the mustang, which began to rear and buck, but the raised threatening hand of the master subdued it in a moment. As if from a springboard, the hunter leaped up and sat upon this new-made cushion of lion skin. He sat sidewise, at ease, and waited there patiently while the dusk deepened.

He had not long to pause, for now, out of the brush, in a dark cluster, came the wolves. They went at a slow, shambling trot, like beasts heavy with food, and, forming in a low-moving cloud around the dog-trotting horse, the whole group moved off across the green of the plain, and presently they were more obscure, and at last they were lost to the straining eyes of Lefty Ranger.

# CHAPTER EIGHT

Ranger had no memory, the next morning, of how he had cooked his supper or of what he had eaten. His mind was in such a whirl that he went only automatically about the preparation of his food and the eating of it. The only thing that he could recall with certainty was the care with which he had arranged a circle of large stones that acted as a screen to the fire to shut in its gleaming light.

But when he fell asleep, he had a series of dreams that were clear in his mind the next day and forever after. The nightmare came to him over and over again. It was always the same. He would be sitting on a stone at the bank of a river, fishing, watching the line, that appeared to break at a sharp angle where it fell into the water, and seeing the tiny wake that the broken current made below the string.

Then a feeling of eyes fastened upon him from behind would give him a numbness in the small of his back. He would resist and fight against this foolish sensation, but it recurred with such force that at last he would be compelled, instinctively, to turn his head, when he always saw, stalking behind him, a slender youth naked to the waist, black, shining hair streaming over his shoulders, and his body bronzed mulatto dark by long exposure to the sun. But his eyes were bright and red-stained, reminding the trapper of some wild beast, but what the wild beast might be he never could tell.

The stalking man, when discovered, would straighten and smile and nod ingratiatingly, but, when he was very close to the fisherman, he would suddenly disappear, and in his place there would be a great timber wolf, crouched for a spring, slavering white hate and with red-stained eyes gleaming with hunger. At that point the dream would go out, and poor Ranger, weak with sweat, would awake, turn, and fall asleep again, only to have the same horrible dream over again.

When the morning came, the sun was already up before he awoke and found his head heavy and his eyes dim, exactly as though he had not slept at all throughout the night.

He cooked a small breakfast, and he ate it without appetite, forcing down the mouthfuls. Not once did he look down toward the Crosson place, or toward the break in which the puma had been slaughtered the night before. It was a thing about which he did not want to think. The impossibility of it maddened him. He flushed as he realized that he never could tell this even to an old friend. He would be laughed at as a creator of wild yarns.

What had happened there in the brush? How had the wolves been used by this singular boy to bait the lion? How had the boy himself avoided the lightning spring of the catamount that even wild beasts are not swift enough in reaction to avoid? Had he remained standing, and at the last instant, swerving, buried his knife in the creature's heart as the bulk shot past him with hideous fangs showing and with deadly claws unsheathed and ready? Bullfighters could do such things with the clumsy, blind, charging bull. But a puma is neither clumsy nor blind, and it can think in mid-air as well as when it is on the ground.

But Ranger gave up the problem and refused to be bothered by it. The thing was incredible. It was to be pushed to the back of his mind, together with the fairy stories that amuse a child but cannot occupy a grown man.

The stumbling point here—the sweating point for Ranger—was that he knew something like this must have happened. And now he could believe what he had heard. There were no firearms on the Crosson place. Well, if the evil one had given men such powers as this, what need was there for powder and shot?

He rushed away from his camp to walk the trap line, gritting his teeth and wishing more than ever that he never had committed himself to such a task. Compared with the mystery that gathered around him, Arctic hurricanes with the temperature below zero, a failing dog team, short rations, and a long journey seemed to poor Lefty Ranger as nothing at all. The great white North was a comfortable and familiar land, and he yearned to be back in it. Here in the Southland there were worse things—spiritual torments, eerie problems that no ordinary man could fathom—such as fourteen wolves used as a hunting pack!

So he strode out along the line of his traps, and he took very little pleasure in his catch of the day. It was not large for one thing. He caught three bobcats whose pelts were in such a condition that they were hardly worth the trouble of skinning, and then threw the naked pink bodies onto brush where the buzzards could find them the more readily. The single shrinking fox he looked at more in disgust than in pleasure. But in the last trap of all, that one that was nearest to his camp, he found a prize of another sort. It was a yearling wolf, big for its age, but still not grown to the size of its feet. He looked at it with the strangest of sensations.

It was his. He had caught fairly the cattle killer, in embryo, the butcher of colts and veal and mutton. There was a bounty for the scalp as well. And yet he hesitated. He drew his rifle to his shoulder, and three distinct times he took the bead for the head. And three times he allowed the muzzle of the gun to sink slowly down, overpowered by the thoughts that were his.

At last, with an exclamation, he stepped in toward the beast. It leaped at him, snarling terribly, but he stunned it with a blow from the heavy butt of the gun, and, as it lay limply, he loosed the teeth of the steel trap from the hind leg by which the wolf was imprisoned.

He barely had stood back when the ungainly youngster scrambled to its feet, tucked its tail between its legs, and scampered away as hard as it could go. He watched it curiously. Would it go up among the higher rocks or would it turn and skid away toward the Crosson place? He could not tell. It disappeared among the rocks, and afterward there was no trace of it across the green fields that stretched away toward the Crosson Ranch. Even then, he told himself, he could not regret what he had done. Wolves began to haunt his mind. The short ears and the wise brows of the monsters walked in his thoughts all day and all night. And he could not regret that he had failed to take revenge on this half-schooled youngster. He was thoroughly ashamed, but he was oddly more at ease.

In fact, two thirds of the cloud that had gathered over him seemed to have dispersed. The guilty feeling would not leave him. Neither would the self-satisfaction.

When he got back to the lean-to, however, he had a surprise of another sort waiting for him. As he rounded the rocks and came toward the group of pines that sheltered and shrouded his little camp, he saw two men lolling in the sheds. They sat up as he appeared.

At least, they were not the Crossons, because both of them were armed to the teeth. Each had a rifle close at hand. Each wore at least one revolver. Each had a heavy ammunition belt.

They looked at the trapper, and then they turned their unshaven faces toward one another, as though silently consulting. And such was the ominous nature of their silence that Lefty Ranger took firmly into his mind the fact that he, also, was armed. And that revolver of his he could use, in a pinch.

He halted a few strides from them. "Hello, strangers," he said.

"Hullo," said one of them. The man spoke without real interest, and he stared steadily at Ranger. There was something ominous about the indifference of that man. In this wild country one might have suspected that every human would be glad to see his fellow.

"Who are you?" asked the second man harshly.

"That's my business," said Ranger, and moved his hand a little closer to his revolver.

"It's mine now, though," said the second man. He was one of those hump-shouldered people whose crookedness of back is rather an excess of muscle than the sign of a deformity. His head was thrust out in front on the end of a bulky neck. He looked like a clumsy lump of a man. But as he spoke these words he conjured out a revolver with such flashing speed that Ranger's own weapon was not half drawn before he found himself looking into the round, dark, empty eye of death.

"Now, what's your name?" repeated the other.

His companion was grinning, more of a sneer than a grin. And the gunman's eye glittered in such an uncertain way that Ranger was reasonably certain that the fellow would as soon shoot him down as not. This man already had drunk of blood. The sign of it was in his eye. Therefore Ranger did not hesitate.

"My name's Ranger," he said.

"Yeah," said the other, "and your first name is Forest, ain't it?"

His friend laughed at the jest.

"My name is Bill Ranger," said the man from the Northland.

The gunman moistened his thin lips behind the dark veil of a brushy mustache. "You're too dog-gone' good to talk to strangers, ain't you?" he asked.

Ranger flushed. "You got the drop on me," he said.

"Not that you didn't make a move for yourself," said the other.

"No. I made a move," said Ranger honestly. "Why shouldn't I?"

"You made it, and you lost out. And I got half a mind to make you pay the regular price."

"Aw, have a heart, Wully," said the second man.

"If he was five years younger, I wouldn't have no heart," said Wully. And it was plain that he meant it.

"Now," went on Wully, "what you doin' up here?"

"I'm trapping."

"I see that you got some pelts and you got a trap line. But what you doin' up here?"

"What I told you."

"Don't lie!"

"You show me a place where I can catch more varmints and I'll go there," said Lefty Bill Ranger. "This here place is better than they told me. Look what I've got in this one day's work, will you?"

The other two exchanged glances.

"Well, maybe he's all right," said Wully. And he lowered the muzzle of his gun.

# CHAPTER NINE

He was not through catechizing the other man, though.

"How long you been here?"

"Couple days," said Ranger.

"How you goin' to get your stuff out?"

"I come in with a burro, but the wolves tore its throat out. When I get my pile, I'll buy a mule from down there, I guess. Or a couple of 'em, if I have enough to load 'em. It looks like I have it, all right."

Wully leaned back, his dangerous eyes still fixed carefully upon Ranger. "You give him a go, Sam," he said.

Sam was an opposite type. Thin, almost too cadaverous, light of eye, smiling of mouth. There was still something about him that revolted the blood of Ranger.

"Why, I don't wanna know much," said Sam, "only, what's the name of that ranch down there?"

"It's the Crosson place, I guess."

"Who told you so?"

"They told me back at Tuckerville."

"Who?"

"Sol Murphy."

"He's seen Sol Murphy," said Sam aside to Wully.

"Well, what of it? Go ahead," Wully said.

"You been down to visit the ranch?"

"No," said Ranger.

"Why not?"

"Sol Murphy told me that they were kind of queer."

"Who?"

"The Crossons."

"Queer, are they?" said Wully. "What kind of queer?"

"Like a coin," suggested Sam.

"Shut up, Sam," said Wully roughly. "You talk like a fool. What kind of queer?" he repeated to Ranger.

"I dunno. He didn't say."

"Didn't he?"

"No."

"Well," said Wully, "you haven't found out nothin' about them?"

"About them? No."

"I'm gonna find out about 'em," said Wully, suddenly rising.

"Hold on!" said Sam.

"You yaller dog!" said Wully through his teeth.

"No, I ain't a yella dog. But I don't wanna do nothin' foolish."

"I say you're a yaller dog. You won't take no chances. That's what a yaller dog is, ain't it?"

Sam stood up in turn reluctantly. "I don't like it," he said. "When gents like Jake the Cooler,

75

and Mississippi Slim tell us that the Crossons are dead poison to . . ."

"Shut up!" yelled Wully furiously. "Who you talkin' about?"

"Aw, I dunno. Nobody," Sam said sullenly.

"You ever hear them names before?" asked the savage Wully of Ranger.

"No, I never heard them before."

"A good thing that you ain't," declared Wully. "Well, old-timer, I'm tired of hearin' about the Crossons and what they can do and what they can't do. I'm dead tired of it, and I'm gonna go down and find out for myself."

Sam pointed a skinny arm toward the trees that enshrouded the Crosson house. "Are you gonna hike over to them?" he asked.

"Go get the horses and shut up," directed the formidable Wully. "I'm gonna go down there and find out for myself." He stood closer to the rim of the hill, turning his back upon the trapper. "I'm gonna kill me some beef," he announced. "That's what I'm gonna do. I'm gonna kill me some beef, and then I'll see what those Crossons do about it."

He turned suddenly back upon Ranger as Sam went off to get the horses. "They say that the Crossons don't pack no guns," he said.

Ranger nodded. "I've heard that," he said.

A grin of lewd joy and satisfaction appeared upon the face of Wully. He leered at Ranger, and then licked his lips. "I guess I'll find out about the Crossons, all right," he said.

A warning leaped into the throat of Ranger, but he checked it unspoken. After all, this man deserved all the trouble that his brutal instincts might lead him toward. And yet he almost pitied the bully. Perhaps a little description of how the sun-darkened youth had entered the shrubbery and killed the mountain lion might have dimmed the joy that was in the heart of Wully.

But Ranger said nothing. He was busy looking, now, at the horses that the companion of Wully had brought up. They were a splendid pair, and rough fellows like Sam and Wully had no right to possess such exquisite thoroughbreds, lean and iron-hard of limb, deep-chested, low to the ground, and long over it. They had eyes like stars and the muzzles of deers. And they lifted their proud heads and looked beyond these two men as though they disdained the human hands that controlled them and looked far off to find other masters.

Sam made one further protest before they mounted. "Wully," he said, "we ain't learnin' anythin' by this."

"How do you know," said Wully, "before we've gone and looked?"

"Anyway, we'll get a beefsteak or two out of it."

Straightway they mounted and were off into

the sunset time, running their horses with a speed down the slope of the hill. Ranger looked after them, shaking his head. He did not need to be told that they were a bad pair. No good man would have risked his horse's shoulders to make such a descent as that.

Off across the level green they flashed, and away past the very island of shrubbery in the midst of which the day before the puma had been killed. The nerves of the trapper began to jump.

They went on. They scoured almost out of sight upon the green and then back to the ears of Ranger, very dimly, rang the hammer stroke of a rifle exploding, and then another shot, as though in answer.

Faintly, far away, Ranger saw the animal fall, sinking down behind, and then dropping.

Almost immediately afterward the dimming light of the evening shook a thin veil between him and the two marauders, and he could not see either of them.

He set about preparing his own supper, frowning darkly. There was no impulse in Ranger that was not honest to the core, and the dishonesty of thieves who would kill a steer for the sake of cutting a few steaks out of the carcass made him hot with anger. Such men should be opposed. But he knew that he had not the skill or the power to oppose a trained man-killer like Wully. Sam, too, looked like the type of rat that fights with poisoned teeth when it is cornered.

And yet revenge might overtake both of them. The thought of the running wolf pack and of the wild young rider behind it came strongly back into the mind of Ranger.

He finished off his coffee and started to clean up the tins. It was work that he did not finish at once, for just as he put a chiming stack of things together, ready to rub them with sand and then wash them with water, he heard far away the wavering cry that for twenty-four hours never had been quite out of his ears. It was the wailing call of the wolf pack on the run, many cries joined together.

Regardless of the almost utter darkness, he caught up his glasses and, running to the verge of the hill shoulder, tried vainly to probe the dull twilight. It shifted and rolled before his eyes, and would reveal nothing to him. He could only read the voice of the pack, and that swept closer and closer to him, so that the hair began to stir on his head as the scalp prickled and contracted with horror. What was happening there on the smooth green of the Crosson fields, or in the thickets that spotted the ranch?

The yelling notes came nearer and nearer. And the notes changed. They grew shrill, and he knew that the runners were closing in on prey of some sort. Could it be Wully and Sam?

Then, up from the plain, like a voice shouting

from the deeps of a dark well, he heard human cries ringing. They seemed to start up from the ground beneath his feet, those screams. Not of agony, he repeatedly told himself, but of utter dread.

Was it Wully and Sam? Even if it were they, he pitied them mightily, and at the same time he wished himself far away.

Just at the foot of the ascent, so far as he could judge, the noises of the pack ceased suddenly, and not a murmur of it followed. Were they saving their breath as they swept up the slope? For he heard noises approaching. There were scratchings and scramblings along the sloping shale of the bank, and they seemed to come toward him at greater than human speed.

He crouched back in the shadows of the pines. He cursed the bad luck that caused the fire to find a resinous mine in the heart of one of the pieces of wood in his fire, so that the flames suddenly threw up brilliant yellow beads of light all around him. The pines were great black silhouettes, and the stars went out. And Ranger, gripping his rifle hard, prepared for whatever might come.

It came in unexpected form.

Over the brim of the hill shoulder appeared two men. They were hatless, and their coats hung from them in rags. They were running at their full speed, though it was only the staggering speed of utterly exhausted men.

Into the light of the fire they dashed, and Ranger recognized Wully and Sam, with Sam well behind in this race for life, for such it seemed to be. Ten thousand small slashes seemed to have been inflicted upon each of them, for they were crimson with their own blood, issuing through the many rents in their clothes. Either their guns and cartridge belts had been taken from them, or they had thrown the encumbrances away to lighten their flight.

Straight across the patch of firelight they fled. There was no sound of pursuit behind them, but they did not pause. The hoarse, rasping sound of their panting would be long in the ear of Ranger. But more than the sound was the sight of their faces, blank and terrible with dread. They fled as from an inescapable spirit. They would flee forever, it seemed. Never again would they be what they had been that evening when they went out with a surly and haughty insolence to rob the Crosson Ranch.

Ranger stood up and looked with a cold heart into the pit of darkness that covered the plain.

Where they had failed together he must try his hand alone, and before long.

# CHAPTER TEN

When Ranger saw the dawn rise on the next day, he was ready to face his blackest fortune. That is to say, he was sufficiently desperate to seek the thing that he feared, like a small child asking for the promised whipping to escape from the long suspense.

He had to enter the Crosson estate. And there never would be an easier time for such an approach than the present moment. Therefore he got his breakfast, put the little lean-to in order, took his rifle, and marched down across the slope of the hill and out upon the green of the Crosson spread.

His purpose was simple and obvious on the face of it. He would simply go up to the house, announce that he was now a comparatively near neighbor for the season, and introduce himself by name. If he were received in a surly manner, at least he would have made the fair and aboveboard approach, and could not be suspected of spying. On the other hand, he would have an opportunity to keep his eyes open, and, no matter how short the time for looking around, it would be very strange if he did not succeed in seeing something of interest worth reporting to Menneval at the end of the trip.

That was the simple plan of Lefty Bill Ranger, but he knew, in his heart, that it would hardly work out as smoothly as all this. There was danger down there on the Crosson land. He had seen the result of it twice. And he felt as cold and brittle as ice when he approached the central wood in the midst of which the Crosson house must be.

It was hardly a grove. It was more like a forest, the size of which he had underestimated both because it was at a distance and because he had been looking down upon it from a height. No wonder that the wild timber wolves had fled here. They might not all be the half-tamed pack that obeyed the strange lad who he had seen riding the mustang. There would be room in the avenues of this wilderness for both kinds to find refuge.

He was amazed, and could have been delighted by the scene. For the bright morning sun broke through the lofty roof of green and came pouring aslant through its columns, splashing the ground with a wild patterning of shadows and bright, shining gold. The resinous sweetness of the pines made the air fragrant. And his feet slipped quietly upon the deep beds of the pine needles.

But all the forest was not of this single pattern. In places the trees receded and dropped down from the great height of their companions. Wherever this was true, deciduous trees were growing, and hedges and masses of shining shrubbery.

He began to lose some of his fear. The place was such a delight and so ideally fitted to surround a house with shadow and coolness in the heat of the summer, and to break the force of the storm winds in winter that he began to envy the Crossons, and we hardly fear those who we envy.

He began to feel that he would like to have such a place for a home. And why not? There were still unnumbered acres in the mountain wilderness where a man needed only to take up his homestead in order to make the land his own. Why should he not prospect, not for gold, but rather for a home where he could spend the end of his days?

He paused, looking down a long avenue, partly clouded with the dark of shadow and the green of foliage, and partly glowing with rays of sunlight from above. This silent joy of the trapper's was rudely shattered. He heard behind him a sound like the whisper of the wind. But there was no wind about he knew, and, whirling about, he confronted, not three strides behind him, a huge wolf, a veritable giant of his race. It favored the man with a view of its flashing teeth and bounded from view behind the trunk of a tree.

Ranger put out his hand and leaned heavily against the nearest support. He felt sick and faint. Was he to be run and hounded as Sam and Wully had been? Or had that softly moving, gray devil been waiting to leap at him and take him by the nape of the neck? The wolf was huge enough to have delivered a death blow with a single stroke of his fangs. He was of the kind that, long before, had been able to rip and tear pounds of living flesh from the flank of the buffalo as they raced over the plains.

The grisly dread that he had felt before now swept back upon him. His heart raced. His face was icy-cold. But he decided to go straight on. What else could he do? If the inhuman Crossons actually could send out these animal spies to work for them, would they not receive a report that a man had been seen stealing through the woods and had been frightened out of them? In that case, he would expect worse treatment than Sam or Wully had known. But if he went on toward the house, his honesty of purpose would be evident.

So he marched on, but in a very different humor. Now, with every step he took, his straining, aching eyes were driving among the shadows, trying to look around the corners of the big trees, or darting to the side. Every moment he was pausing to stare behind him, and he felt like one walking a tight rope over a chasm.

The next alarm did not come from behind, however. There was a sudden outbreak from the yelling throats of wolves immediately before him. He was at that moment on the edge of one of those clearings where the great heads of the forest stepped back a little, allowing a smaller and tenderer growth of trees and shrubs, and a small meadow that flashed like a jewel in the sun. He shrank close to the side of a big tree, grasped his rifle with trembling hands, and waited.

What he saw, first of all, was not the wolves, but a thing he dreaded more than wolves—the youth who had killed the puma in the brake. He bounded from the farther side of the clearing and went across the meadow like the wind, his long, black hair driven straight out behind him by the speed of his going. He was dressed in a sleeveless, closely fitted jacket of buckskin. He wore Indian leggings of the same stuff.

As he shot past the trapper, his face tense with the effort of running, there was an additional shock for Ranger. It was the color of the eyes. He was no Indian; there was no taint of Negro blood in him, either, in spite of the darkness of his skin. Sun and hard weather had accomplished that feat of double dyeing. The eyes of the lad were a piercing, brilliant blue, reminding Ranger of a pair he had seen before. He could not tell where.

The reason for the boy's flight? It was at his very heels! Three huge timber wolves broke from the trees right behind the fugitive, and, red-eyed, slavering with eagerness, now yelling and now whining, they rushed after the youth.

The latter half turned his head. He made a

still more desperate effort to put on speed, and Ranger, at last coming to himself, pulled the rifle to his shoulder. He was in no state for accurate shooting. For his hands shook and the muzzle of the weapon wavered violently. It was as though he had seen the lions turn upon the lion tamer.

The whole universe seemed turning topsy-turvy. For right at the heels of the running wolves, gaining upon them in a tawny streak, ran the biggest mountain lion Ranger had ever seen. It looked less like a puma than a maneless African lion, and it was fairly running through the wolves, not to tear down one of them, but uniting with them to overtake the boy.

Ranger swiftly shifted his aim from the leading wolf to the puma. There was, certainly, the chief danger.

But at that moment the boy disappeared from the earth to which he had been running. He was passing under a big tree whose lowest branch was a full nine feet from the ground to the eye of the trapper. Bounding high up, the youngster caught this branch with both hands, and the impetus of his running swung him on up. With an incredible agility, he climbed higher among the branches, and the wolves, gathering about the trunk of the tree, sat down upon quivering haunches and gave utterance to the long, rolling, heartbreaking cry that tells of a quarry at bay.

They had an ally who was not checked by the

trunk of the tree. The puma, giving one upward look into the branches, sprang instantly up the trunk to the first forking, and then rushed higher through the limbs of the tree.

Lefty Ranger cuddled the rifle into the hollow of his left shoulder. He tried to take a bead, but the thing was nearly impossible. If his nerves had been steady, he could have sent a slug through that great, golden cat, but his hands were still shaking, his whole body was unnerved. And what he drew a bead on was a tawny shape that flickered upward among the branches, snarling terribly, its teeth already bared.

Still the boy was not quite lost. He swung out to the end of a long, powerful branch. It grew small. It yielded under him. The big cat crept out along the same limb, but now the boy was dangling from what seemed a mere handful of the outermost twigs. There he hung and began to swing himself back and forth with a strong oscillation. The three wolves, their yelling ended, gathered under him, waiting for the fall, crouching close to the ground and quivering with a dreadful eagerness.

What hope was there for the boy? Some hope still, it seemed. As the limb swayed back and forth and the youngster gained a greater and a greater vibration, suddenly he loosed his hold and shot outward and upward through the air. He turned as he sailed forward. Hands first, he plunged among the twinkling leaves of the nearest tree.

Down he quickly shot. He had grasped several small branches that yielded with him, and the shock of his fall carried him down. Under him raced the ravening wolves, but, as they reached the spot, the recoil of the limbs jerked the boy up as far as he had fallen. And there he was again, a twinkling shape among the upper branches.

Safe!

No, not altogether safe, as yet. For a golden form dropped out of the shadows of the first tree, flashed across the ground, and darted up the trunk of the second. Under the strain of the two heavy climbing bodies, the whole tree shook here and there, and the top of it nodded and trembled as though in the grip of a heavy storm.

The wolves were snarling, the puma whining with its frightful eagerness, and then a third sound distinctly came to the horrified ears of Ranger. It was a succession of beastly noises— snarls, whines, growls—but different from those of wolf and mountain lion. He could not believe his ears, but, as he stared, he saw the boy on an outer branch and knew that the voice was his, and that those animal sounds actually came from a human throat!

# CHAPTER ELEVEN

Was he, then, more beast than man? Was that the reason the boy had been able to hunt with the wolves? Was that the reason that he was now actually escaping from both wolf and mountain lion?

To Ranger it was not like seeing a human being chased by beasts of prey. It was like seeing one destroyer pursued by others. How could he have more sympathy for one than for the other? And what was the mysterious story that lay behind this spectacle?

Still he strove to get a bead on the climbing puma, and still he failed as the thing went flickering up among the branches. The boy was now again at the outer end of a branch, and was beginning to swing from it, evidently planning to repeat his former maneuver of leaping from tree to tree. Monkeys, Ranger had heard, could do exactly that thing. But what man, since the world began?

It was not so easy, this time, for the tree was smaller, and the branch sagged so that, in the lower part of the swing, the wolves were leaping for the legs of the boy—leaping so high, indeed, that it seemed momently possible that they would reach him.

Yet as he swung, the same beastly sounds rolled from the throat of the man. Plainly he was deriding the other creatures, for, as they heard him, they fell into a veritable frenzy. The wolves yelled a death song. And the puma, pausing an instant in its advance, uttered the long, grisly cry that ends in a human whimpering and sobbing like that of a child lost in the wilderness.

They were maddened, wolves and puma, by the challenge that was being poured at them from the human throat.

And that instant came disaster. For as the youngster swung, the branch that supported him suddenly broke off short, and down he dropped a dozen feet. Cat-like, he twisted in the air and landed well, on hands and feet, so that he was instantly up again. Up again, but only for the moment. The biggest of the wolves leaped, gave the man its shoulder, and toppled him head over heels, and all three instantly swarmed over him.

He was lost!

In five seconds those powerful jaws, those cutting fangs, would tear him to pieces. And now into the tumult dropped the golden streak of the great cat. As it landed, the wolves bounded back, as from an acknowledged master, and there lay the boy, prone on his face, and the huge mouth of the puma was opened, ready to take him by the nape of the neck.

At that last instant Ranger finally drew his

bead. Just behind the shoulder of the puma he took his aim. That bullet should cut through the heart and give the boy a fighting chance for his life. But he did not pull the trigger. For a strange thing happened then.

The prostrate lad, turning, sat up under the very face of the great cat, and with one hand grasping the lordly tuft beneath its chin, actually shook his fist in the eyes of the lion!

And the terrible puma, the man-hunting puma, merely blinked its eyes and sat down, curling its long, snaky tail around its flank.

The boy, flinging himself on his back on the bright emerald of the grass, threw his arms wide, closed his eyes, and lay still, except for the great labor of his chest, which rose and fell rapidly. The race in itself had been enough. The frantic climbing in the trees had been more than the trapper could believe of human sinews and muscle. There the boy lay, stretched out, eyes closed, regaining his breath with gasps.

The three man-hunting wolves came stealthily to him. They licked his face. They licked his hands. They would have lain down beside him, but the puma, rising suddenly, bared its great teeth and warned them away with a snarl.

A word came from the boy. Or was it a word that had no syllabification, and seemed only a prolonged mutter deep in his throat? At the sound of it the puma drew back, little by little, still sounding its grim warning. It lay down on the ground, lashing its side with its tail, its two forepaws covering the extended hand of the lad. The wolves instantly disposed themselves about him, one at each side, and one, a dark-maned giant, lay down at the boy's head, panting hard, its big red tongue lolling and its glinting eyes constantly fixed upon the lion.

It was plain that no love was lost between these beasts of various species.

Ranger, bewildered and stunned by the dream-like nature of what he was seeing, told himself that he had left the world of reality and come into a world of madness. He would have turned and fled at that instant, but something told him that he could not disappear softly enough for his footsteps to miss the hair-trigger ears of the wolves or the huge cat. And, once discovered, would they not run him down in earnest as they had run down their master in play?

So he remained still, hardly daring to breathe, and gradually silence came over the scene as the panting died down, and there was nothing heard except the secret whisperings of the wind among the upper branches and the quiet music of the brook that ran into a big, bright-faced pool not far away.

This silence seemed to Ranger, from in his place, to endure for an hour; perhaps it lasted hardly two minutes. At the end of that time the boy stood up suddenly, and the four animals rose with him. He leaned above the puma, stroked its head, and, muttering a word, he sent the creature away. It went reluctantly, flicking the long tail from side to side, and twice pausing to look back at the master before it faded away into the gloom of the woods.

The youngster went to the bank of the pool, threw off his clothes, and tried the temperature of the water with his foot as his sun-black image reflected on the still face of the water. Ranger never had seen a man like him. He was not more than middle height. Certainly he never would be called heavy. Yet, as Ranger looked at him, he felt that he was seeing the perfect type of the athlete.

From head to foot there was not a sharp angle in his body. At no point was he overweighted; nowhere was he sparsely made. He was as smoothly made, with as round and deep a chest, as one of those sublime idealizations of humanity that the Greek sculptors loved to chisel from marble or cast in bronze. When he moved, a ripple of light passed over him. There was no hint of exaggeration in him, except, perhaps, the extraordinary size of the loin muscle, where it draped across the top of the hip. No wonder that he could run like a deer and climb as easily as a monkey.

When he had tested the water, he jumped to

the top of a rock three or four feet above the level of the pool. The three wolves instantly bounded up beside him, and then he leaned into the air and sprang. His heels tossed up, pressed close together, his joined hands broke the water before his head, and into the pool he slid like a quiet image rather than a heavy, falling body. There was only a slight sound behind his feet as they disappeared; a small fish, jumping for a fly, makes a louder sound.

Ranger could see the swiftly sliding shadow beneath the surface, and, having fetched to a distance, the boy rose, shaking the long hair from before his face. He whistled, and into the water plunged the three great wolves. They swam strongly, their heads high, aiming straight for the man. But trouble was before them. They were in the middle of the pool when he dropped suddenly out of sight.

The instant he was gone they swung about and started desperately for the shore that they had just left. There was no ploy in their effort. With ears flattened, they struggled forward, each casting off a strong bow wave from its shoulders. One of them, caught from beneath, was jerked under. It bobbed up again, snorting, gasping, shaking its head. This was the central wolf. Its companions diverged to either side, swimming more furiously than ever, so that their mighty shoulders came well up from the top of the water. All its speed did not avail the right-hand monster. It, in turn, was caught from beneath and rolled under, and, as it rose, the boy rose, also, and swam like a glimmering fish after the third wolf. His reaching hand was at the tail of the latter when the wolf's feet touched bottom, and out upon the grass it scrambled, the boy after it. All three of the lobos were in the meadow now, and they went for the boy in unison.

Play? It might be called play in a world of Titans. To Ranger it looked like a very near imitation of battle. Their knife-like teeth the wolves did not use, but they wielded their solid shoulders like clubs. They strove to knock the legs from under the lad, sliding in with deft, dodging movements. And he, in turn, tried to catch them off balance and tumble them over. Again they shot into the air and tried to knock him flat with a blow delivered against his shoulder or chest. They flung themselves at him like football players; all four were often one stumbling, gasping, panting mass. But finally they had their way. The legs of the boy shot into the air. He landed with an audible thump, and the wolves jumped back from the prostrate master.

With their open mouths, their lolling red tongues, their wrinkling eyes, they appeared to be laughing silently in pleasure at their feat.

And the boy, for his part, rose slowly and shook his head to get the mist out of it. For that had been a stunning fall. He went to the edge of the pool again, rinsed off his body, and then whipped away the water with the edge of his palm.

But Ranger was still wondering. Three wolves had put him down. How many men would have been needed for the same task?

Now the youngster wrung the water from his hair. Now he stepped into his clothes. And in a moment he was fully clad. He was buckling on the knife belt and the knife when Ranger stepped from behind the tree.

Animal or man, he could stand it no longer. He had to accost the stranger. So out he came, into the blinding brightness of the meadow. The lad turned toward him without haste. And there seemed to be nothing hostile in his expression.

"Here you are," he said. "I didn't know that you were in this part of the wood."

Ranger breathed a sigh of relief. Afterward he felt like laughing at himself, but at the moment there was almost a sense of wonder that the lad, for all his human shape, could actually speak.

# CHAPTER TWELVE

Ranged before their master, the three wolves eyed the stranger with anything but tolerance. The one upon the left, the great, black-maned tyrant of the lot, shrank a little toward the ground and began a stealthy advance.

"I came down to see who was living here," explained Ranger as carelessly as he could. "I got a string of traps up there on the face of those hills, and I saw your cattle in the fields and the smoke coming up here. So I came down to see you and have a yarn. It's been a spell without much talking to folks."

"I knew that you had come down," said the other. He snapped his fingers; the black-maned wolf shrank suddenly back.

"You knew that I had come down?" echoed Ranger. "How did you know that?"

The other pointed, and as Ranger hastily turned, he saw behind him a pair of timber wolves standing at the edge of the shadows cast by the big pines. One of them was the same full-grown lobo he had seen before trailing through the woods. The other looked like a yearling.

"Hold on," said Ranger. "You mean that one of these came and told you?"

"Not in so many words," said the other, smiling a little. "But I knew that it was a man, and I guessed that the man would be you."

"Well," said Ranger, "I dunno that I follow that. The fact is that I've never been on your place before, so how could you guess that I was myself . . . if you follow my drift?"

"Certainly," said the boy. "But we've seen your camp smoke in the hills. And that youngster came back with trap marks on his hind leg."

He pointed to the yearling, and suddenly Ranger remembered the gray, pointed head of the timber wolf he had caught and turned loose. A scalp wound and swelling between the ears told where the butt stroke had fallen.

"And they came and told you that I was in the wood?" asked the trapper.

"They came and told me perfectly clearly that a man was in the wood, and the youngster was a little mean about it. So I guessed that he'd recognized the scent of the man who had clubbed him."

A chill went up the spine of Ranger. "A doggone' wonder that they didn't jump me," he declared.

"They don't jump people," said the boy.

"Don't they?" asked Ranger. "Unless they're ordered, maybe?"

The other started a little. "What makes you say that?" he asked. And his steady blue eyes grew for a moment half dangerous, so brightly were they lighted.

Ranger scratched his head. But it seemed to him better to come out with the truth as much as he dared to speak of it. So he said: "Well, I saw a pair of thugs come out of the hills to your place . . . and I saw them when they left it, and they looked as though the wolves had a taste of both of 'em."

"A pair of cattle thieves," said the boy carelessly. "We don't believe in keeping guns on our place, so we have to have some means of protecting ourselves. You haven't told me your name?"

"My name is Bill Ranger. A lot of people call me Lefty," said the trapper.

"My name is Oliver Crosson," said the boy.

They shook hands.

And as quickly as their hands parted, Oliver Crosson stepped lightly back, as a dog steps back to get a sufficient distance for attack or defense when a strange dog is near. One could not have called it fear, but rather a semi-barbarous readiness to be on guard.

Ranger had an odd feeling at the moment, for, when seen at a distance in action, Oliver Crosson had appeared big enough—powerful enough, certainly—to deserve the attention of any half dozen of his peers when it came to troublemaking. But when he stepped up close for the handshaking, he seemed shorter and slenderer than the average man.

"I'd like to ask you two things," said young Crosson.

"Fire away," said Ranger.

"Why did you turn that wolf loose once you had it safely in your trap?"

"Well," said Ranger, puzzled, "I don't exactly know."

"You know that there's a bounty on scalps?"

"Yes. I know that."

"Then what made you turn it loose?"

Ranger sighed. "Fact is," he responded, "that after I got into these here hills and on the way up to them I saw wolves do things that I wouldn't've believed. I've seen wolves that stood their ground and watched me go by them ten feet away without budging, and me with a rifle in my hands. I dunno how it was. I got a sort of a queer feeling about 'em. And I'd seen you run that puma into the brush with your wolf pack."

"Well?" said the boy coldly.

It occurred to Ranger that the best way was to stick as closely to the truth as possible. The youngster was not exactly hostile, but he impressed the trapper as cold lightning, likely to strike at any given moment. And when he struck, the blow would be remembered all the rest of a man's life.

"Well," said Ranger, "I'll tell you. I didn't know

whether there were such things as werewolves or not. You'll say that I'm a fool, I guess. But somehow I thought my scalp would be a lot safer if I turned that young wolf loose."

He looked up from his explanation and found the cold, blue eyes of the boy fixed steadily upon him.

Then Crosson nodded. "I can understand, in a sense, the way you must have felt," he said. "It seemed a bit weird to you?"

"Weird?" said Ranger with an honest outbreak of emotion. "I'll tell you something. It seemed so dog-gone' weird to me that I couldn't sleep good at night. I've been worried ever since I came up here, and that was one reason that I decided to put in half a day and come over here and have a look at you folks."

Crosson nodded again. "I can understand that," he said. "But I can't answer for the second question I want to ask you."

"Well, try me," said Ranger.

"What made you want to come to this part of the country, anyway?"

"Why, down there at Tuckerville," said Ranger, "they told me there was more game here to the square mile than any place in the mountains."

"There's a good deal of game." Crosson nodded. "Some on four feet. Some on two. Did they tell you that, also?"

"They told me that. Sure they did."

"But that didn't stop you?"

"Why, I've been around a good bit. I don't mind rough going," said the trapper. "I wanted to be out where I could fill my traps, and this is certainly the country for that."

"A long haul back to town, since you've lost your burro."

He knew that, also. Ranger began to sweat a little. It seemed that this youth had a sort of omniscient eye, and that he was playing with Ranger as with a double dealer.

"Yeah. A wolf chopped open the throat of that poor little burro. But I could likely get a horse or another burro off your ranch."

"We don't sell our horses," said the boy. "We raise them."

"Hold on. You mean that? How d'you make money?"

"We don't make much. We don't need much. Now and then my father drives a few head of cattle down to Tuckerville. That's all. But I wonder at seeing a trapper head away on such a long trail. Not for fine furs . . . just trash like red foxes and coyotes and such stuff!"

It was time for Ranger to scratch his head again. "I'll tell you," he said. "The thing of it is that I've been away from God's country for a long time. I've been away up in Alaska, where there's nothing but wind and snow." He hoped that the fair white land would forgive that slander. How greatly, at that moment, did his heart yearn to be back in the white wilderness rather than in this green pleasant meadow, talking to a wolf-man.

"And gold?" suggested Oliver Crosson.

"Yeah. You work all year for it and spend it all on one Friday night. That's the kind of gold that you get in Alaska. You do the finding and the saloonkeepers, they chip it out." Another blasphemy, he felt. Somewhere in that northern land there was a fortune waiting for him, he was sure. And one day he would go back and find it.

Crosson was smiling a little. "I don't know much about it," he admitted. "I've heard very little. However, I don't see what Alaska has to do with putting you here. Can you explain that . . . if you feel like talking that much?"

"Why, no," said Ranger. He saw that the time to lie had come, and lie he must, with unction. "You turn an eye around you. What more would a man want than a place like this?" he said.

"It's pleasant." The boy nodded.

"It's more'n that. It's a place for a man to die in."

"I suppose that men will die here one day," said the boy, and he looked about him toward the noble trees with a certain darkness in his eye. Plainly all was not well within the spirit and the mind of young Oliver Crosson. He shrugged his shoulders. "And you wanted to get out into a soft, easy country?" he asked.

"Not soft and easy," answered Ranger, dodging a trap. "But a country where I could make my own place, and not be worried about a lot of real-estate dealers coming along and opening up new farming tracts all at once. I wanted a country where there'd be green grass and big trees, and a chance to be alone. So I heard a lot about this, and I came up from Tuckerville to have a look at it."

The boy looked steadily, grimly upon him, and there was a glimmering, dubious light in his eye. Nothing could be plainer than that he doubted all that he had heard. "Well," he said at last, "suppose that you come along with me to the house? My father'd like to talk to you, I know."

"All right. Let's start along," said Ranger.

But his cheerful voice belied his spirit. He felt that he was walking into a trap from which there would be no escape.

# CHAPTER THIRTEEN

They walked on through the quiet woods briskly. Ranger would have been glad to talk on the way, but the head of the boy was turned straightforwardly, and his expression was so sternly forbidding that all subjects for talk immediately fled from the mind of the trapper.

Presently he was vaguely aware of a branch bending slowly above his head, and he looked up to find a long bough, upon which stood a great mountain lion. He leaped back with a gasp.

"That's nothing," said Oliver Crosson. "That's only one of the pets. He'll do you no harm . . . while you're with me."

The great cat looked down at the stranger with eyes as glowing as yellow lights. And the trapper took a breath. "That big devil has a bad eye," said Ranger.

"Nothing compared with his brother," answered Oliver Crosson.

They stepped on, Ranger keeping an anxious glance turned up toward the lion, which was lashing its sides with its long tail.

"You have his brother, eh?" asked Ranger.

"Yes. We got the pair of them together."

"Trapped?"

"No, out of their cave."

"You found 'em while the mother was away, eh?"

"No, she was there."

A blue jay flashed above their heads. At that a harsh sound came from the lips of Crosson and the bright bird staggered in its flight, swerved downward almost within reach of Crosson's hand, and then veered upward again, its own rasping note trailing behind it. Crosson had held up a hand to it, but more by way of greeting than to capture it.

"That mother puma was in the cave, eh?" persisted Ranger, for he sensed something worth hearing on this incident of the capture of the two cubs.

"She was there," said Crosson.

He looked upward idly. By the special sense of their own, his feet seemed to find the most level way over the floor of the wood. Then, making a quick, musical murmur, it brought down a chattering response from a pair of squirrels above him.

"You asked her for the two cubs, I suppose," said Ranger ironically, "and she just pushed them to you. Was that it?"

Crosson chuckled. "She was a mad cat I can tell you," he said. "I never saw a cat carry on worse than she did. She gave a yowl when she saw me moving into the cave and then started for me."

"And you started out?"

"How could I do that? The passage was pretty narrow. Only at the last second I'd stepped into a place where the space was a good deal bigger. It was the main part of the cave, where the water had washed away the limestone and made a good big room out of the interior. But that cat acted as though she were sure of me for supper." He paused, to laugh at the memory.

"You shot her when she was crouching?" suggested Ranger, wild with eagerness to get at the details.

"No, she had her spring, all right."

"You had to pot her in the air, then?" suggested Ranger. "That takes shooting when they jump at you like that."

"Why, you might know that guns are not allowed on the place by my father."

"Doesn't he?"

"No."

"That seems to me a strange idea."

"I suppose it is. It's his way, though."

"But do you mind telling me, Crosson, how the devil you managed to handle that puma after it had jumped you, and you hadn't so much as a revolver to defend yourself?"

"Why, you can guess," said Crosson, half turning toward his companion, so great was his apparent surprise.

"I can guess what?"

"How I got rid of the mother, of course."

"I can't imagine it."

"All right. You just put yourself in my place. You've had a cat of some sort jump at you, I suppose?"

"No. Not even a house cat."

"Haven't?" said Crosson, apparently more surprised than before. "Well, it's a stupid way that they have. When they stalk a thing and run up on it without jumping, that's a different matter. They're harder than the lightning to dodge. But when they jump out into the air, poor fools can't help spreading themselves out. They get into a beautiful position in the air and come arching at you with their teeth like flickers of white fire."

"That sounds pleasant," said the trapper dryly.

"Does it sound pleasant?" Crosson turned his head again and looked curiously at Ranger. "It's a good trick," said the boy. "It's a great deal of fun, and it isn't hard. But it's like climbing after them mountain goats. Suppose that you do make a mistake . . . suppose that your foot slips or a pebble rolls . . . that's the end of you, absolutely. You see, a cat like that would tear you up in no time."

Ranger nodded. "I'll bet it would," he agreed. Then he added: "You wound up with the big cat in the air. What happened then?"

"Oh, that's easy enough, then. Only, one has to be careful not to slip. You just side-step and let the cat have the knife as it goes by through the air. That's easy. You put the knife into it and make a jump yourself. The cat lands and whirls for the second spring, unless that first thrust has been enough."

"How about the mother of that little house pet back there on the limb of the tree, looking at me like he wanted to digest me? What about her?"

"That was a bad time," said the boy, nodding. "That time I made a bad stroke. You see, it was very dark in the cave. Like twilight, at the most."

"The deuce it was," muttered Ranger.

"Yes. It was pretty dark. It was so dark that I could see the burning eyes before I saw the rest of her."

"But you didn't back out of that place?" asked Ranger.

"Well, it's always pretty dark in a cave like that, you know. You have to expect that sort of a thing, unless you're just going to throw the fun away and simply catch your mountain lion in a trap." He made a gesture with both hands, palms up.

"I dunno that I'd bother about the game. Well, tell me what happened on this job?"

It was very difficult to keep the lad on the story, for his attitude seemed to be that the yarn was of so little importance that there was nothing that could really interest a listener. At every pretext he was ready to break off and let the story die.

"Oh," said the boy, "the fact is that I stabbed

rather blindly and put the point of the knife into one of her ribs. It broke off the point two inches from the end and nearly jerked the handle out of my hand."

"How did you get out of the cave, then?" asked Ranger. "There she was, between you and the entrance, I suppose."

"Yes, there she was, and she was in a fine tantrum. The knife point had gone right into her rib, very deep, and she was screeching and meowing at the top of her lungs. She gave me a concert for a while."

He chuckled, but Ranger kept him to the appointed task. "And then she jumped you again?"

"Yes, she jumped me again, of course, and she meant business that second time. Of course, that was what I wanted. The angrier I could make her, the easier the job would be . . . but I had that dull, pointless knife in my hand this time. I couldn't very well jab it deep into her. I could hardly do better than scratch her and irritate her a little.

"So, when she jumped the second time, I had to drop on my knees while she was in the air. It's an odd thing, Ranger. It seemed to me that I was made of feathers. I mean, I dropped to the rock a lot more slowly than I could have wished. And every chip of a second was pretty necessary just then. Anyway, I got down, and, as she sailed over me, making a futile sideswipe with her right paw as she went, I gave her the edge of the blade . . . what was left of it . . . right down the crease of the belly. That was all."

"Hold on!" cried Ranger. "You mean that that finished her?"

"Well, practically. I had just sharpened that knife, and it was so keen that its own weight would almost sink it into wood. That knife blade opened up the mountain lion. She made a few more passes at me, but she was half blind with pain and the blood poured out of her so fast that she was on her side, dying in a very short time. I took the hide off her and wrapped the cubs in it and brought the pair of them home."

Ranger rubbed his knuckles across his chin and blinked. He had a feeling that this could not be a fact, but that he was being made a fool of, and that afterward he would be mocked for the easy game that he had proved. It might be so, but the open eye and the brave, calm face of the boy decided him that there could be no lie in this. All was as it had been related to him, incredible though that might appear.

"You've practiced it before, I suppose? You've got quite a lot that way?" said Ranger.

"Let me see," answered the boy. "No, not a lot. Only five."

"Five in their own caves?"

"No, only three in their own caves. Two of 'em were out in the open. Of course, that's quite easy

. . . when you have so much foot room and plenty of light."

"And all with knives?"

"Yes. All with knives."

"What made you get up that way of hunting them?" Ranger asked eagerly.

"Well, I'll tell you. My father had heard of a man in India who used to kill tigers that same way . . . he had a short scimitar, and he cut the throat of the brute while it was on the wing, as you might say. We haven't anything to match with tigers around here. A mountain lion was the best I could get to try out the dodge. That's what it is, of course. Just a dodge. You put home the knife, and at the same time you're dodging under or outside the paws. You don't have to bother so much about the teeth. It's the claws that will do the business if the puma can have its way. Have you never tried the trick yourself?"

Making game of Ranger? On the contrary, the eyes of the lad were as open as the frank, deep blue of the sky overhead.

# CHAPTER FOURTEEN

The trees opened out before them; through the huge, pale-brown trunks Ranger could see the ranch house. And what a house it was! At the first glance it was a mere tumble of logs. It was hardly more at the second. A pack of cards, allowed to fall fluttering from shoulder height, might have stacked themselves into such shape. It consisted of a central part with a broken back, and at either end there was a shed, feebly propped up on knock-kneed poles. The very chimney, which rose above the cabin, staggered to one side, and the whole place had the air of a structure that the next puff of wind would knock flat.

It was such an absurd house that Ranger, familiar as he was with the shacks and lean-tos of the wilderness, could not help smiling a little when he saw it. Yet, with another look, he found something very pleasant about the cabin, too. For the moss had worked from the ground to the eaves here and there, and, above all, the odd shape of the cabin and its uncertain patterning of logs of all sizes made it fit back among the great trees like an odd shadow. A deep peace lay over this place, and nearby there was the voice-like murmur of a little stream of water, drifting near and far with many conversational pauses.

A very odd and amusing place, but Ranger shook his head. Where were the stacks of straw or hay, the tangles of corrals, the barns, the outbuildings, the smokehouse, and all that might have been expected at a house so far from the rest of the world, so buried in a sea of wilderness that here men had to live as castaways upon an island?

Nothing was as he expected it. He glanced at his companion and guide, half expecting to see him smile in turn.

"Well," said Ranger, "it's a funny little old house, ain't it?"

"Is it?" said the boy. "I've never seen any other."

He threw open the front door and Ranger stepped into an interior as odd as the outside of the place. It was all one room. A ladder in one corner led up to a hole in the ceiling, above which, no doubt, extended an attic. The ceiling sagged deeply under the weight of whatever was piled up there. Or was it merely time and decay that made the ceiling stoop? As for the lower room, it was paved with beaten earth alone, and it had not much more furniture than the teepee of an Indian chief. Hardly so much. There were no bows, arrows, guns, and spears.

A pair of backrests and two rolled Indian willow beds in a corner showed where the Crossons slept. There were a few axes and hatchets of an ancient, battered look in another corner, together with some fishing rods. There was a home-made table, but no sign of a stove or of a fire. It was the most barren, wretched-appearing human habitation that Ranger ever had seen. An Arctic igloo seemed a cheerful memory by comparison, and his eye rested on only one thing with interest: a single short row of books ranged across one end of the table. Books in such a barbarous habitation? They made the nakedness seem yet more naked.

"Father's not here," said the boy. "He's down the creek, fishing, I suppose. I'll find out."

"Telephone?" asked Bill Ranger, rather grimly amused as they stepped back into the open. The smile left his face. He almost had stepped against that same black monster of a wolf dog—no, it must be a wolf, in fact—that he had noticed before that day. The beast flashed its teeth an inch from his leg and leaped to the side.

The boy leaned over it with a murmur and a wave of the hand, and the wolf bounded instantly away and out among the trees.

"Is he gonna bring back your father thrown over his shoulder?" asked Ranger.

"He's going to find Father for me . . . that's all," answered Oliver Crosson.

Ranger shrugged his shoulders; he was beginning to feel that old cramping chill at work between his shoulder blades.

"You told him to, eh?" said Ranger.

The youngster flashed a quick, surprised look at him. "Of course," he said.

Ranger blinked. He would not and could not believe that a human brain and a human tongue would master the speech of beasts, even if animals truly have speech of their own. Staring thoughtfully down at the ground, he surveyed the blackened stones of the open-air fireplace where it was apparent all of the cooking of the house must be done.

Why should a man with any sort of a human habitation be content with the miseries of an open hearth on which the rain must beat freely and the wind blow, either fanning the fire from the pot or sweeping the smoke stifling thick into the face of the cook? It would not take long to cut through the cabin wall and run up a chimney properly with the stones that so readily might be brought from the bank of the creek.

But the ways of these people who spoke with animals and lived like wild Indians were beyond him. No, even an Indian will burn a fire at the center of the lodge.

He looked up suddenly and stared about him. He had a feeling that he had come to the end of the world, or that he was standing in the center of an unearthly dream. And then, turning a little toward the boy, he saw a gray squirrel sitting upon his shoulder, holding between its almost human paws a bit of bread at which it nibbled busily. Some of the crumbs fell, disregarded, upon the shoulder of the boy.

Ranger shook his head, but the vision persisted.

Why did young Crosson fail to speak? It was not the sullen taciturnity of one ill at ease with a stranger. No, he stood at ease, as indifferent to Ranger as though the trapper were no more than one of the great brown tree trunks that arose about them. Indeed, it seemed to Ranger that human beings had little more significance to this lad than the animate and inanimate objects of Nature that were around him every day of his life.

Presently he heard the soft pad of galloping feet, and the black wolf came in view at a little distance.

"Tell me, partner," said Ranger in an outburst of curiosity. "Is that an honest dog or a dog-gone' wolf?"

The youngster turned to him again with the same expression of half-incredulous surprise in his eyes. "That's an honest wolf," he said. He added, still looking straight into the face of Ranger: "Why, he'd die for me."

The big lobo came up to them, and, swinging about, looked over its shoulder at its master and started to trot swiftly away, quickly breaking into the long wolf lope. Young Crosson followed, and Ranger followed the boy.

The black wolf, since it seemed so thoroughly under the thumb of its master, might have been called back to a milder pace, but this rapid gait did not seem to trouble Oliver Crosson in the least. He did not run as most men do, even the best athletes, with a decided forward angle of the body above the hips, or with any sense of strain in the bent position of the head. Instead, he ran as though running were a pace more natural to him than walking.

While Ranger, magnificent Arctic traveler that he was, was slipping and sliding among the pine needles, or dodging among the rocks along the bank of the creek, sweating and straining until his face was hot as a stove, Crosson, at his careless ease, let his noiseless feet take care of themselves, as it seemed, and looked from side to side among the branches of the trees, or actually upward toward their sun-brightened tops and the brilliant sky above. He ran as a deer runs.

It occurred to Ranger that to attempt to chase this lad one would need a horse—and a very good horse, at that, if the way led through broken country. And as for escaping, if he were the hunter, why, that would be a matter that would require a horse still better.

They went like the wind for a good half mile. Then, breaking out of a clump of brush on the edge of the creek, they saw where the waters turned a sharp corner, the stream narrowing to shadowy, swift-flowing ripples, and on the bank of this angle of the stream sat one of the strangest figures Ranger ever had seen in all his days.

A bent back and bony shoulders, a tattered, battered old hat, a white flow of beard down his breast, a book in one hand and a fishing rod in the other, that was the first impression. But as the boy stopped running, and Ranger, panting heavily, stopped in turn and walked slowly on behind him, he could see further details.

This oldster, like young Crosson, was dressed in deerskin, but what a suit! No Indian ever was so beggarly, after the winter famines, as to appear so dressed. A great patch of an alien hide appeared in the center of the shirt back; the elbows were worn to rags, and the skinny elbows stuck out. The trousers fitted hardly more closely than a woman's pantaloons, and upon the feet were what hardly could be called moccasins. They were, rather, shapeless wrappings of leather rags.

And that was Peter Crosson?

Upon some clean bark beside him, half packed in damp, cool moss, were seven or eight good-size trout, and at that very moment he laid his book aside, face down, and jerked another trout from the stream. The twisting body flashed through the air in a wide semicircle and dropped beside the old man, who calmly killed the take.

Now Ranger and Oliver Crosson were beside him, but he did not look up. He might be deaf, perhaps.

"Father, this is a man named Ranger . . . he's the trapper up on the hills. He came to see us."

So said the boy by way of introduction. Then he sat down on the end of a fallen log with the great black wolf beside him and began to run his fingers through the thick mane of the brute, looking up the sparkling waters of the creek as though he had lost all interest in the scene that was to follow.

Peter Crosson calmly baited his hook and dropped it again into the stream, after which he picked up his book, seemed to find his place with a frown of annoyance at the interruption, and finally looked up at Ranger.

It was a memorable face that Ranger saw— long and thin, and brown as a half-withered leaf in the autumn of the year. The beard was brighter than the gleaming water below. And under the great dark arches the eyes looked out upon Ranger with unfathomable meaning. They were dull eyes. Time or thought had dimmed them, and they were lost in the shadows of the brows.

First he stretched out the hand that held the book and pointed. Then he nodded. He looked back to the creek and laid his book on his knees.

"It's the beginning of the end, Oliver," he said in a deep, husky voice. "You've let the first rifle come into the grove . . . and, now, when will the first bullet strike us?"

# CHAPTER FIFTEEN

Ranger, at this strange speech, turned a hasty glance toward young Crosson, and he was surprised to see that the youngster seemed to contemplate no answer whatever. It was as though the voice of the older man were no more to him than the sound of the wind in the trees. He continued to stroke the contented wolf, and the latter turned up toward his young master those keen, red-shot eyes, with the wise wrinkles framing them. No sign of emotion or of interest appeared in the face of Oliver Crosson as he heard the speech of the other. It threw the difficulty of the answer entirely upon Ranger.

Oliver Crosson was not even breathing hard. Ranger panted and steamed like one who had just finished a race. And through his panting he exclaimed: "Why, look here, Mister Crosson, I just happened down here to see my next-door neighbors, like you might say! That's all that I come for."

The old man did not look at him. "Nobody just happens down here," he answered. "Fact is . . ." There he paused.

It appeared that something on the edge of the sky, a cloud or the flight of a bird, interested him.

"Oliver?" he said.

"Yes, Father," said the boy.

"What's that yonder?"

"Where?"

"There on the rim of the horizon. Pair of eagles?"

"No, hawks," said the boy, unhesitant.

Ranger stared in the indicated direction. He could see no more than two obscure specks that drifted against the sky.

"No," said the father. "Eagles, I'd say. Or else, maybe they're buzzards?"

"Hawks," said the boy. That reply of one word was not uttered with impertinence, but the curtness of absolute assurance.

"I don't see how you make that out," said Ranger. "Might be eagles, hawks, or buzzards."

"They don't float like buzzards," said Crosson. "And they're climbing too fast for eagles. Eagles are all fat and beef. Those fellows are all muscle and wind."

In fact, as the trapper looked again, it seemed to him that the two specks were lifting rapidly in the air and drawing nearer them.

"You can see a bird," said the fisherman. The boy shrugged his shoulders. "But you can't see trouble," went on Peter Crosson.

"What sort of trouble is ahead now?" asked Oliver.

"A man and a gun."

"What harm can he do us?" asked Oliver.

"He could kill both you and me with two touches of his forefinger."

"Could he?" echoed the boy. He turned the bright blue of his eye upon the trapper. An intolerable brightness was in that eye.

And Ranger was troubled more than before. It was true that he had a rifle in his hands and that he was a fair master of the weapon. Nevertheless, he did not feel that he was endowed with a power that would win in a battle against this uncanny youth who spoke, or seemed to speak, the language of birds and beasts.

"Why, sir," said Ranger to the older man, "you take me for a gunman, I think."

"You're a man, and you've got a gun," said old Crosson.

"He's just up here to trap," suggested the boy. But there was no real kindness in the glance that he turned upon the stranger.

"That's a lie," said Peter Crosson. "He's up here for more than that."

Ranger endured the insult and said not a word for a moment. He waited to hear the idea developed by either of the two, but, after the man with the rod had spoken, he would not enlarge upon his idea. He merely stared at the water, as though he had said enough.

"Well," said Ranger, "if that's the kind of neighborly folks you are, I suppose that I've found out what I came to know." He waved his hand to them. "So long," he said, and turned upon his heel.

He had taken a step or two, with a gloomy feeling that all his mission was a failure, and that he would be able to report little or nothing to the man who had hired him for this extraordinary mission, when the voice of the boy called out sharply behind him. He turned about with a feigned reluctance.

"Well?" he said.

"I don't think you're entirely fair, Father," said the boy.

"If you know better than I do," said the other with his usual air of almost sleepy indifference, "make up your mind to please yourself."

"This is the man," said Oliver Crosson slowly, "who turned loose Birdcatcher after he was caught in the trap."

"If a trapper turned a wolf loose," said the old man, "it shows that he's aiming to catch something bigger than wolves . . . men, likely."

"Are you?" asked the boy pointblank.

He was naïve, but he was most decidedly dangerous. There seemed just enough humanity in him to temper a natural ferocity.

"I'd like to know," said Ranger, "what I have to gain out of you . . . either of you or both of you? Have you got a private gold mine? Can you make rain? What's in the pair of you that anybody should want to be stealing?"

"Do you hear that?" asked old Peter Crosson.

"I hear," said the boy.

"Does it sound all right to you?"

"Yes, it sounds all right."

"Well, it's not all right, and don't you forget it!"

"Tell me why," said the youth. "You just say so. You don't give me any proof."

"The fish doesn't have any proof that the worm's unnatural," said the old man. "Not till the hook is through his jaw. He finds out the truth, and he fries for it later on."

*"Humph!"* said the boy.

He sat with his chin in his hand, staring fixedly at Ranger. It was the stare of a wild animal, unashamed, curious, bold, terrible. Ranger, to save himself, could not answer the glance, for it seemed to him as though his very soul must be revealed if he allowed the inquiry of the boy to pierce the open windows of his mind.

"Well," said Oliver Crosson, "I think that you're wrong. Hello! There goes the Chief!"

The big wolf, as though his ears had caught some sound of the wind, leaped up and vanished among the trees with a scratching sound as his nails tore at the ground.

"One of those fool deer have got inside the grove again," said the old man.

"No," answered the boy. "It's not that."

"What is it, then?"

"Well, it's a mountain lion, at least. Perhaps it's a man." As he said this he began a laugh, a merry, ringing, mischievous laugh.

"Oliver!" exclaimed the father abruptly.

"Yes, sir?"

"Stop that laughing. You give me chills and fever."

"Yes, sir." He was obediently silent.

"I suppose that you'd enjoy plaguing another robber out of the wood?"

"Well, perhaps I would," said Oliver frankly. "The last two . . ." He laughed again, but subdued the laughter suddenly.

"One of them will come back," said Peter Crosson. "One of them will come back. Perhaps both of them. And they'll bring friends with them."

"And perhaps their friends will be handled in the same way," said the boy. His teeth clicked as he spoke.

"Aye, perhaps, perhaps," answered the other, nodding at the water. "But the day will come when there'll be more than two or three. There'll be five or six. All of them armed men. All of them good with rifles. What will happen to you then?"

"I don't know."

"And you won't know when the time of that visit comes, either. Because there'll be a whang and a flash of fire, and that'll be the end of your young life, Oliver!"

Oliver lifted his head and frowned at the distant sky, out of which the two birds were sweeping rapidly toward them. He nodded, as though he agreed with his father. "Why shouldn't I have a rifle of my own, then?" he cried out suddenly. "Why not, after all?"

Peter Crosson jerked his head around from his fishing. His jaws were set hard for a moment, and then his lips parted to let out words that rang long in the brain of the trapper.

"Because there's a curse on powder and lead, and on all who use 'em!" he exclaimed.

# CHAPTER SIXTEEN

On the very heels of his speech there was the report of a rifle out of the more distant woods. Old Crosson lifted his head a little, listening with an apparent placidity. The boy, however, had thrown himself flat upon the ground, very much as though he had heard the bullet whistling past his ears and instinctively had flinched.

It was not mere fear, however, as the trapper could tell in another moment. The boy had his ear to the ground, listening, tense with concentration.

"A curse on powder and lead," said the older Crosson slowly, and pulled another trout, a great flaming fellow, out of the waters of the creek.

Ranger stood by, saying nothing. After all, without words on his part, he was learning more than mere questions could probably have drawn from this strange pair.

Oliver Crosson sprang up to his feet from the earth, light as a feather. "You see?" he said. And he pointed toward the south. Out of it flew two wide-winged birds, and now it was plain that they were hawks.

"And what about the hawks in the grove?" asked the father calmly. "Is there only a pair of 'em, or more?"

"Oh, four or five . . . on horses," said the boy. "We'd better start toward the house. You start on toward the house, and I'll go to meet 'em."

He was off with a leap into the brush, but his father called him back as, with perfect calm and slowness, he rose from his cross-legged position beside the creek. "You'll stay here with me," he said.

"They're shooting at our wolves!" exclaimed the boy impatiently,

"Let 'em shoot at the wolves, before a strange wolf shoots at one of us. I'm not ready to have my bones gnawed white." He looked grimly at Ranger as he spoke.

And the trapper said suddenly: "I'll tell you what. In a pinch, I'll promise to stand with you, if that's any good."

"In a pinch he'll stand with us," said the old man sardonically. "That's a mighty lot of help. One rifle . . . against four or five."

"I believe him," said the boy. "Go on with him to the house. I'll cut down the draw and head them off."

"Stop!" cried out his father loudly. "You've met one and you've met two. You've never met four or five."

"They'll only be twice as hard, and that's not too hard," said the boy. His face was aflame with excitement and eagerness. Plainly he wanted nothing more than to join whatever excitement was in the air, yonder where the rifle had been fired.

"Twice as hard?" echoed the old man. "I tell you, one man is one, and two men are two, but four men are an army. One Indian could kill one white . . . one Indian could kill two whites . . . but four whites could run forty Indians ragged. Back to back, shoulder to shoulder, and the courage of companionship." He paused and made a sweeping gesture. "Pick up the fish and come with me," he concluded abruptly.

The youngster hesitated. Then he looked to Ranger like a hunting dog, but an invisible leash held him fast. Sullenly he scooped up the fish in their moss, and the three went on together. Out of the distance the long, wailing howl of a wolf came up through the trees and rang weirdly in their ears. Another, another, and another answered, until there was a chorus.

"Which are they?" asked the elder Crosson.

The boy, head high and eyes raised as he walked lightly along, seemed to be separating the sounds one from another.

"The yellow female and her son," he said, "and Birdcatcher, of course, and Whitefoot and Skinny and Old Tom and . . ."

"If Old Tom is there," said the senior Crosson, "he'll keep the rest in proper cover. He'll keep the rest in proper cover . . ."

Half a dozen shots fired in rapid succession now boomed through the woods.

In answer came the thin, high-drawn yell of a wolf.

"They've got one of them," said the boy almost under his breath. He halted in mid-stride. His face was pale and set with anger. "I'm going after them!" he exclaimed.

"You'll stay with me," said Peter Crosson. He reached out and caught the boy by the arm. "You'll stay with me," he repeated.

Ranger suddenly, for the first time, stopped watching the boy and stared at the father. And there, plainly, he saw a mortal terror. Was it terror of the strangers? Perhaps—but even more probably, as it appeared to Ranger, there was terror for fear he should not be able to control the youngster. It startled the trapper, so completely had Peter Crosson seemed the master of the boy's actions up to this moment.

In spite of the extended arm and the gripping hand of his father, Oliver Crosson did not stir to go on with them. His eyes were fixed upon his father's face, but plainly his thoughts were leaping away toward the sound of the shooting and toward that wolf's howl.

It came again now, high-pitched and wailing.

"No, not dead . . . not mortally hurt," said Oliver Crosson, "but badly stung. They've put a bullet into him, but he'll live. I'm going to meet them. I'm going to stop them. I'm going to hunt them as surely as they ever hunted dumb beasts."

Suddenly Peter Crosson released his grasp and flung out an arm before him. "Run on to the house," he said. "Run on. Get the axes ready. We have those, at least, if the pinch comes. Run on to the house and get everything ready. It must mean a fight."

Oliver nodded, and away he went. There was only a flash of him in the eye of Ranger, and then he was gone, with long, bounding, noiseless strides.

Old Crosson immediately went forward with a shuffling run. His age showed there. He could not make fast progress with his stiff muscles and his brittle joints. Presently he fell to a walk. And Ranger remained beside him. He could not tell why he had chosen to keep with the old fellow instead of the young greyhound.

With head thrust forward and with set jaws, Crosson strode along, not speaking at first. But suddenly a muttering came from him: "This is the day. This is the day."

"What day?" asked Ranger.

"Dead man's day!" exclaimed the other. "Didn't you hear it? Didn't you hear the song of it in the air?"

"You mean the guns?" asked Ranger. "You know, wolves don't make dead men even with bullets through 'em."

Old Crosson turned an impatient eye toward him. "You're like the rest," he said. "You won't understand . . . you won't understand. They'll rub him the wrong way. They'll laugh at him . . . they'll treat him like a fool, and then . . ." He paused and began a coughing fit so violent that it stopped his walking for an instant. Then he went hurrying forward.

Who was it that he feared they would laugh at? It could only be his son that he had in mind.

"I tell you," said Ranger seriously, "I'll stand by you to the end. I'll help to keep him out of danger, if I can."

"Keep him out of danger?" cried out old Crosson. "What does he live on? What does he breathe? Nothing but danger! Nothing but the air of it. Keep him out of danger? There's no danger to him. There's no particle of danger to him. Only to the others . . . to the fools! That's just where the danger will strike." He threw up both his hands. His long white beard, suddenly divided by a gust of wind, blew half over either shoulder, and he leaned to make better progress.

There was tragedy and mystery in the air, greater than appeared to the naked eye of Ranger. To be sure, he could guess that the gunshots in the wood came from armed riders who were invading the place on an errand of no good to the Crossons. It might very well be that Wully and Sam had returned with friends, as old Crosson had prophesied they would. That would seem to make the picture black enough, but something greater undoubtedly was in the mind of Peter Crosson.

"By heavens!" cried out Ranger. "It sounds like you were more afraid for the gents who are riding in here than for your boy!"

"Afraid for him? Why should I be afraid for him? They can't harm him. Not with bullets . . . not with bullets."

He groaned as he spoke, and a prickly sensation ran over the scalp of Ranger. Did this old fellow believe in spells of witchcraft, perhaps, that could turn leaden bullets, or steel-jacketed ones, for that matter?

"Then nothing can happen," suggested Ranger.

"*Ha!* Nothing happen? They can lay the powder trail. No, it was laid before. The powder trail was laid long ago. Only the match hasn't been touched to it. And they'll touch the match today. They'll set him on fire."

He finished with another groan, and began to run again, panting heavily, his eyes rolling in his head. He looked as though he had drunk too much. Plainly he was in the grip of a great mental misery.

"Mind me," said Ranger. "It'll come out all right. They won't use guns on men that haven't any. Don't worry about him."

"*Bah!*" cried the old man. "What do I care

for them, whoever they are? And the fools don't know. They don't understand."

"They don't understand what?"

"That if they set him on fire, he'll explode. He'll blow them to bits. The idiots are riding over a mine . . . over a mine. The trampling of their horses may be enough to blow them to smithereens . . . to blow them up into the sky. And they don't know. They come right on."

Ranger could say nothing for a moment. He could only decide that age had taken too great a hold upon the mind of his companion. At last he said: "Why did you send him on alone?"

"Because I had to give him something to do. That's why. Couldn't you see? He was bursting. He was going mad. The red was in his eyes. I had to give him something to do. I've had to do it before. I've had to keep his hands filled, his mind filled, or else . . ." He stopped once more. He was panting from his hurry, from his mental distress, and every pant was a groan. "They don't know," he said again breathlessly. "They'll never dream. They can't imagine what he is. No one can . . . not even his father."

*Mad,* thought Ranger to himself. *Utterly mad. The old man's brain has turned. Turned long ago, and that's why he's kept the boy out here in the wilderness and given him a kennel for a home to live in. That's the only real reason.*

They were nearing the house now, and a fresh,

strong chorus of howling broke from the throats of many wolves. A crashing of rifle fire answered the outbreak, but there was no yell of a dying wolf to echo the rifle fire.

"They've missed. The cunning devils are under cover. He would teach them that. He has taught them. He's given them the brains of men and women. Oh, God help the people who teach him his strength."

"Do you mean your own boy?" cried out the trapper, amazed and horrified.

"What else would I mean? Oh, the fools, the fools. But they don't know him. They don't know how he was born."

Ranger stared wildly around him. He felt as though he were losing his own brains as he listened to the excited ravings of this old dweller in the wilderness.

"But how was he born?" he asked.

"You've seen him, and you ought to know," came the unexpected answer.

"I don't know what you mean."

"You've seen him. It's in his eyes."

"He's a little wild."

"Wild? Oh, man, man . . . he was born with blood on his hands . . . blood enough to stain half the world."

# CHAPTER SEVENTEEN

They came in view of the shack presently. And as they came up, out from the woods there burst a cavalcade of half a dozen riders. The very first face upon which the eyes of Ranger fell was that of Wully, the renegade, the outlaw, the yegg—a Wully very changed from that evening when he had snarled at the camp of Ranger. Now his face was swathed with bandages, and his clothes were rags, loosely sewed together. It was the forward thrust of his head that identified him, and, in addition to this, something vaguely brutal that distinguished him from other men.

He was enough to give Ranger concern, but he was not alone.

There were three other men along with him with the look of cavaliers of the wilderness about them. Unshaven, red-brown from the fierceness of the sun and the cut of the wind, erect in the saddle, wild of eye, they looked like beasts of prey to Ranger. He knew the type. He had seen it from Arizona in the south to Circle City in the north. And beasts of prey, they were, making of other men their game and their profit.

The fifth rider, however, was apparently the leader of the crew. He was a man of middle age, at least. His pale mustaches, short-cropped as they were, had been sunburned so white that one could hardly tell whether they were gray from age or weather. He was very straight in the saddle. His cheeks were so sunken that his cheek bones thrust out and the corners of his mouth were drawn in a faint smile that seemed rather mockery than mirth.

He was as neat in his appearance as his companions were wildly ragged. Boots, long-tailed coat like a gambler, a neck scarf neatly wound and fastened with a jeweled pin, a wide-brimmed hat that kept his face continually in shadow—Ranger noticed these details, but most of all he paid heed to the hands. One was clad in a long-gauntleted glove of the thinnest doeskin, but the right hand, brown as a berry, was significantly bare. The left hand reined the horse. The right hand rested lightly upon the thigh of the rider, and close to that hand was the butt of a revolver, holstered at the side of the saddle.

Here was a man to command; here was a man of action. And here, in addition, was one man in a thousand, even where the roughest of the rough were concerned. Even this commander, however, engaged his attention less than the last of those who issued from the wood.

This was a girl, dressed almost exactly like the leader. Divided skirts of none too widely flowing pattern made the only distinction. She had the same pale-golden hair, the same cravat, the same pattern of boots, of coat. She was not twenty, but even youth and beauty could not cloud her obvious relationship to the man. He was older brother, or some relative; there could be no doubt. Her smile was not a mockery; her eye was a deeper and a brighter blue, but the likeness was very marked. Like him, she had one gloved hand. Like him, her bare, brown right hand was kept significantly close to the handle of the revolver.

They came out from among the trees with a rush and a sweep, the leader and obvious commander well in advance. He went straight up to the door of the house, but Wully, seeing the two who were approaching on foot, shouted out, and the other turned the head of his horse toward Ranger and the old man.

"It's Lyons," said old Crosson. "It's Chester Lyons of the Timberline. God forgive our sins. It's Chester Lyons."

The mind of Ranger leaped backward. He had heard the name before, many times. He tried to remember where—in a newspaper, somewhere, connected with a story of killing, or robbery, or of some such thing. And then there was a campfire in the Montana brush, and a sourdough was telling him a long and grim story of battle, hard riding, and revenge. That had been about Chester Lyons of the Timberline, who lived on the heights and dropped down on other men like an eagle out of the heavens. Yes, that was Chester Lyons.

Once, at the end of a hard day's mushing through the Alaska snows, a bunkie had told him another tale more dreadful than the others. That had been about Chester Lyons, also. He could remember few details. He chiefly knew that the name of Chester Lyons rang in his ear, awaking grim echoes and sensations of dread.

When he looked again at this lean, hard-faced rider, the echoes turned into reality. The man looked resistless—resistless in wisdom and in cunning and in steel-tempered hardness of resolve.

They were close to the troop of riders. Wully, his one visible eye contracted to a spark of light, swung his horse behind them to cut off any retreat and unshipped a revolver as he did so.

"We'll go on slowly, Wully," said the leader.

His voice was low and hushed by hoarseness, like one who has been out in a duststorm, or who has been suffering from a bronchial trouble. It seemed painful to him to speak. He never coughed. One wished that he would. His throat seemed strangling as he talked.

*We'll go on slowly, Wully.* That was what he had said, but to Ranger the implication was that they would relentlessly cling to their course until the end.

"Here's a desert rat that is crooked . . . that's

against us," said Wully. "I've seen him. I know him. And this here is the old ferret. If you got rid of the two of 'em, it wouldn't do us any harm."

*What did the man mean?* The mind of Ranger whirled. *Murder was what he meant. The fellow was mad—mad with shame and with hate for what he had endured.*

"We'll see about that," answered Chester Lyons. "You're Peter Crosson, I take it?"

"I'm Peter Crosson," answered the old man.

"You have a boy living with you here?"

"Yes."

"You've been deviling some of my men," said Lyons. "I've sent you a warning before. I've told you what I'll do. And now I'm down here to do it. I've warned you not to devil my men, haven't I?"

"I've deviled nobody," said Peter Crosson.

Never increasing the soft volume of his tone, the husky-voiced leader spoke. "You lie. You've refused to put up my men when they're traveling through this cut. You've been offered good money for everything you furnished to them. And you've refused the money. You preferred to shut 'em out and let 'em starve, if they had to."

"No . . . ," began Crosson.

The leader raised one hand.

"Harley Morris came through here after I'd talked to you, or, rather, sent you word of what I wanted. Harley was sick. He could hardly sit on his horse. He was sick all through, and he reeled in the saddle. He stopped here and asked you to take him in."

Crosson said nothing.

"Is that true, Crosson?"

"I was afraid to take him in."

"He had to ride on, and he died of it."

"He was already dying when he came here," said the old man. "He was dying of the bullets that were in him."

"Take it one way or the other. You turned away a dying man."

"I was afraid to take him in," repeated Crosson.

"How could he have hurt you? He was weak as a cat."

"His friends that were sure to come down for him, they wouldn't be weak as a cat."

"Crosson," said the leader, "one of my men has died, and I think you've had a hand in killing him. Others of my men you've badgered away with your wolf dogs. There's one of them right now." He pointed to Wully.

"Aye," said Wully, "and he'll sweat blood for it."

"He was no friend of yours when he came here," said Crosson. "He never had had anything to do with you when he came here."

"What makes you think so?"

"Your men don't come like thieves. They come up to the door and rap. They'll pay for what they get. This fellow, he came like a thief in the dusk. We hounded him away. It's as good as he deserves."

"I'll be a judge of that," replied Lyons.

And Ranger wondered at the nerve of old Crosson in speaking back to the outlaw so briskly.

"Crosson," said the other, "I'm a patient man, though I'm not famous for patience. But my patience has run out today. Harley Morris died, and his hand was in mine when he begged me to come down here and put things right between him and you. I'm here for that purpose. So keep your wits about you. I'm going to ask some more questions."

"Go on," said the old man.

The rider waved to the girl. "You know better than I do," said Chester Lyons. "You ask him the questions that I want to know."

The girl brought her horse closer. It was a little gelding made of watch springs and leaping flame. It came with a bound that failed to disturb her in the least, so perfectly was she balanced in the saddle. Calmly and sternly she looked upon Crosson.

"You're a stool pigeon and a spy," she announced. "That's the only thing that keeps you out here on the edge of the falling-off place."

Crosson looked grimly back at her. "You can think what you want," he said.

"I think what I want, and I know what I think," she told him. "The fact is, you've no business here on the farm. You're making no money here. Why do you stay, then?"

"I'm making a living," asserted Crosson. He began to frown at her.

"You don't make a living. You live like a wolf in a cave," said the girl. "No other two men would live on what keeps you and your boy."

"I drive in a herd every few years," said Crosson with an apparently rising impatience.

"You drive in a few, a handful," said the girl. "You drive in enough to pay taxes, and that's about all. You buy salt and sugar, and that's about all that you do buy. Well, Peter Crosson, we want to know what keeps you out here?"

"It's the quiet life," he answered.

*"Bah!"* said the girl. "You're here because you don't want your face seen too far away. Isn't that right? How glad would the right sheriff be to put his hands on you?"

Old Crosson merely smiled.

At this the girl leaned a little from her saddle, as it seemed to Ranger, as though she wanted a closer view of the face of the old fellow. "Well," she said, "I'll tell you what we want. We want the crazy man you call your son, and we want him quick. Where is he?"

# CHAPTER EIGHTEEN

The others of the party—even Wully after his first savage outbreak—had remained quietly attentive to the central conversation, never removing their fierce, bright eyes from the faces of the speakers. But now a stir went through them.

"Now you're talking for us, Nan," said one of them. "Don't let the old ferret wriggle out of that. We want the boy. We want him *pronto!*"

"He's gone," said Crosson.

The trapper looked at the ground, thinking: *Do they intend to lynch the lad?*

"He's gone, eh?" said the girl.

"Aye, he's gone."

"Where did he go?"

"Over the hills." Crosson waved his hand toward the north.

"What for?"

"He's looking up the sign of a puma that came down here and tried to kill a calf or two for itself the other day."

"How long ago?"

"Three days."

"There's been a rain to wash out the sign since then," said the girl.

"Rain don't wash out the sign that he reads," said Crosson.

"Bunk," said the girl.

Crosson looked at her with an odd, small smile. "If you've ever watched him trailing," he said, "you wouldn't doubt."

"I've heard a lot of stuff about what he can do," said the girl. "You think that we'll believe such rot?"

"I don't care what you believe," said the old man angrily. "I don't care a bit. Ask this man." He turned and pointed toward Wully. Wully was furious.

"He never could've done it without mind-reading . . . he's a wizard. That young crook is a wizard, and oughta be skinned alive. And I'm gonna do it," said Wully.

"You'll do what you're told," said the haughty girl they called Nan. "You're not your own boss now, Wully. You belong to us, to all of us."

"Then let me see you do something for me!" exclaimed Wully. "I've joined you. Now let me see if you live up to your promises. Or is it all yarning and talk?"

"You'll see what part of it is yarning and talk," said the girl. She turned back upon Crosson. "You say that the boy's gone?"

"Yes."

"Which way?"

"Over yonder."

"Search the house, a couple of you," said the girl briskly.

Her father sat by, apparently glad to escape from the necessity of talking and giving commands, or of listening to explanations. Two of the men leaped down from their horses and hurried into the cabin, while Ranger held his breath. What would happen when they encountered the lad inside the house? What battle would break out between them?

The door was jerked open. They stepped into the dimness of the interior, but there was no sound of an encounter. Ranger began to breathe more easily again.

"Now, then," said the girl in her sharp, quick manner, turning upon Ranger. "Who are you?"

"Lefty Bill. Ranger is my last name. Who are you?"

"I'm Nan Lyons. What's brought you here?"

"Alaska."

She looked fixedly at him. "What you mean by that?"

"I come to California to get thawed out."

She looked him up and down. "You trap for a living?"

"Yes."

"Are you going to make a living around here?"

"No," said Ranger.

"Not enough animals?"

"Too many crooks," said Ranger.

The girl smiled a little. The faces of the

listening men darkened. "But you're staying on?" asked Nan Lyons.

"I'm staying on."

"Why?"

"Because I'm interested, and because things may settle down later."

She tapped her ungloved fingers on the pommel of the saddle and looked fixedly at Ranger. "Cousin Chet!" she called.

Ranger drew a quick little breath. He was strangely relieved to learn that the relationship between the two was so distant.

"Cousin Chet, he beats me. Is he telling it straight?" she asked.

Cousin Chester Lyons had been looking on and listening with the faintest of smiles.

"He's lying like a clock," said Lyons.

"I don't think so," said the girl.

"You can't tell this kind. It's mostly honest, with a little lie in it for salt and seasoning."

"You question him, then," said the girl.

"No. Go ahead for yourself. It'll do you good. Get the truth out of him."

The girl turned on the trapper. "You didn't come for trapping. You didn't come to prospect."

"How do you know?" asked Ranger.

"We've followed your back trail, and you never chipped a rock. No old sourdough can keep from clicking out a bit of stone here and there."

"I came to trap," said Ranger.

150

She pointed to Crosson. "You came on account of these people," said the girl.

Ranger would have sworn that his nerves were well-set and steady. But this sudden touch made him start. It was only a momentary contraction of the muscles, and he hoped that it would not be noticed. But he was wrong. He could see the girl's faint smile of triumph, and her cousin said quietly: "Well done, Nan. I wouldn't have thought of that."

Peter Crosson looked abruptly toward the trapper. He seemed bewildered and a little angered. Under his breath Ranger heard him muttering: "The first rifle in the woods . . . there had to be trouble out of that."

"You came on account of the Crossons," repeated the girl.

"I didn't say that I did."

"Your face said it for you. Now, what's your game?"

"I've told you my game. Why should I answer to you?"

"There's a good reason. My cousin is the top rider on this place."

"What place? The ranch?"

"From here to Jeremy Peak. And both sides." She waved her bare hand. Then she added: "Will you talk?"

"I've finished my talking," said Ranger, and he freshened his grip upon his rifle.

"Hold on," said Chester Lyons grimly. "I'll make him talk fast enough."

"Be easy with him, Chet," urged the girl, suddenly anxious.

"Never mind that. You take a ride through the trees yonder, and, when you come back, I'll know the whole inside lining of his mind."

"I won't go," said the girl. She changed color. "I didn't bargain for that sort of thing."

Suddenly Chester Lyons pointed toward the woods. "Get out of here, Nan!" he ordered abruptly.

She hesitated, but it was the hesitation, Ranger saw, that goes before surrender.

Here Wully broke in, in spite of the tenseness of the moment: "What's happened to the boys? What've they found in there? I don't hear a word out of 'em."

He jumped off his horse as the leader said: "Take a look inside. Nan, you can start moving."

But Wully, reaching the door and throwing it wide open, exclaimed: "Why, there ain't a soul in here!"

For the instant Ranger was almost forgotten. Lyons merely snapped to his last man: "Keep a bead on that fellow, and on the old dodger, too. There's something queer in the air around here, and we'll find out what it is." So saying, in his turn he jumped to the ground and entered the shack at the heels of Wully.

The two were not gone long. They returned with grave faces, carrying a slip of paper.

"What's become of them?" asked Nan.

"They've faded out, and left this behind 'em," said her cousin. He read it aloud: " 'I'll hold the pair of them till you clear out. If you don't clear out, I'll put you all in a place where you will keep.' "

"What?" cried the girl.

"He'll put us all in a place where we'll keep," said Lyons, his face suddenly crimson and then pale with anger. "Wully and Tom, scatter for sign, and look sharp. They can't be far. Pick up the trail, and then sound on it. Quick, now, and look sharp. You have your guns. Use 'em first and ask questions afterward, if it comes to a pinch."

Wully and the other hastily departed around the corner of the house. The leader remained with an eye upon Ranger and Crosson, but his forehead was darkened.

"But what could have happened?" asked Nan. "What could have happened in there?"

"I don't know," said her cousin briefly.

"A trap door or something like that?"

"Don't be romantic, Nan. The floor of that den is mere beaten ground."

"I didn't hear a sound," she said.

"Confound it," replied the other. "Neither did I. Don't speak. I have to think. And keep your eye on the woods around us, Nan. The devil is in the shadows of these trees, I have an idea. Crosson, what could have happened to these men of mine?"

The smile of Crosson seemed to Ranger both sad and sardonic.

"You'll find out better than I could tell," he said.

# CHAPTER NINETEEN

This singular and indifferent reply from old Crosson made the outlaw look sharply at him, and yet he did not break out into anger at once. He simply said: "You think that you have me in the hollow of your hand, Crosson?"

"I think nothing," said the other. "But if I was you, I certainly would get out of here. Out of the woods, I mean . . . out of the whole countryside, maybe."

"For fear of your boy?" asked the outlaw, rather in curiosity than in scorn.

"Aye, aye," said Crosson steadily. "For fear of that boy. Man, man, I'd lose no time in going."

"You expect me to do that, Crosson?"

"No," said the other. "I don't expect you to. I expect you to stay on here until your blood and brains are spattered on the trees around the shack. That's what I expect. That's what will likely happen. Look at your girl if you doubt it. She has an idea by this time."

Lyons turned his head with a jerk toward Nan. She was pale and biting her lip. "Now, Nan, what is it?" he asked.

"I don't know," she said hurriedly. She rode her horse close to him and strove to speak for his ear alone, but her emotion made her words louder than she realized.

Ranger distinctly heard her say: "Do you put any trust in a woman's instinct, Chet?"

"I put trust in your brains, Nan," he said at once.

"Then let's get out of here."

"Do you mean that?"

"I mean it."

"And make myself a laughingstock?"

"Let the people who laugh come and try their own luck here, and I think that they'll stop laughing."

"It would turn me into a joke forever, Nan. Think what you're saying."

Instead of answering with words, she pointed suddenly. And when they all turned in the indicated direction, they saw a great timber wolf glide across the margin of the shadows beneath the trees. He gave them a flash of his teeth in a wide grin of hate and started away. Lyons had whipped out a revolver on the instant, but the girl caught his hand.

The wolf disappeared.

"What made you do that?" he asked her.

She began to laugh, and the sound was wild, half hysterical. "I don't know," she said. "After what I've heard about this infernal place, and after what's happened here under our eyes, I was half afraid that that wolf would turn into a man if you shot it."

"A dead wolf . . . or a dead man!" he exclaimed. "What do I care which it might be? I don't care a hang, my dear. You spoiled a good snap shot for me, that's all."

"It isn't all," she said.

He faced her, curious, irritated for the first time. "You don't seriously think that I ought to get out of here?" he asked.

"Yes, that's what I think."

"And leave two of my men behind me?"

"You won't be leaving anyone behind you," broke in old Crosson with a touch of surprise and hope. "He's only keeping them as hostages, man."

"And he'll turn them over to me, will he?"

"He'll turn them over."

"What proof of that have I?"

"Proof?" exclaimed Crosson, as though bewildered that the question should have been asked. Then he added: "The boy never lies. He doesn't know how to lie. His promise is harder to budge, Lyons, than one of those mountains yonder."

Ranger listened with profoundest interest. For his own part, he had decided that the instant he was free from this complication—if free he could get—he would start back for Alaska. Wild winds and bitter frosts would be nothing to him after this touch of California spring. It would be a thousand times better for him to face a year of blizzards than another day in this mysterious forest. No, he would return, give back to Menneval everything except the sheer traveling expenses, and tell him to come south in person if he wanted more accurate news.

Menneval? Aye, even Menneval might not be sufficient here.

Here came Wully and the other from the exploration of the farther side of the house.

"There ain't a sign," he said. "There ain't a single sign."

"Except wolf tracks," said the other.

There was a short, gasping cry from Nan. "Do you hear, Chet?" she whispered to him, but Ranger heard the words distinctly.

"I hear," said the other impatiently. He glared at the two men. "What sort of tracks?" he demanded.

"Timber wolves. Half a dozen of 'em, I should say."

"Looked as if they had been dragging something," said the other.

"Confounded nonsense and rot!" declared the leader, angered. Then he snapped his fingers. "Nan!"

"Yes, Chet?"

There was pleading in her voice, and he nodded at her. "I'm going to take your advice."

"You're going to get out of here?"

"Yes, I am. I'm two men down. It would be no particular satisfaction to me to break the necks of these two old dodgers. I'm going to pull out of here . . . and see if we get our two men back."

He stared at Wully and at the other to see how their faces changed. They showed no emotion whatever.

"Well, Wully," he said aloud, "what would you do if you were in my boots?"

The gentle Wully said without hesitation: "I'd tap this pair over the head . . . and then I'd ride like the wind until I got back to daylight. It's sort of like a green night in here. It gives me the jim-jams."

"We'll get out of here, but we won't tap the pair of 'em on the head," decided the leader. "Crosson," he added, "I've been turned into a fool. This time I'm beaten. But when I get my two men back, I'm going to return. Do you hear me?"

Crosson started violently. He was so excited that he even made a few rapid steps toward Lyons, almost in the manner of one about to deliver an attack. "If you return, man," he said, "you'll wish that you'd sooner gone into a sea of fire than into this forest. You're a marked man . . . a marked man. Not you or anyone of the rest of you ever could come into this forest again and go back alive to tell about it."

"I'm marked, am I?" replied the leader.

"You're marked all right. Yes, you're marked down for life here."

"By what, will you tell me? The eyes in the trees?"

"There are eyes in the trees," was the old man's mysterious and solemn reply. "Other eyes, too."

"And tongues to tell you about us, eh?"

"Yes," said old Crosson. "Listen."

Not very far away, thrillingly clear, there sounded a chorus of several wolves coming to them through the wood. The sound broke off short in the middle of a yell.

Nan Lyons gripped the pommel of her saddle with both hands, with the air of one who might fall unless supported. "Will you go? Will you go, Chet?" she begged.

"I know how you feel," he said. "It's like midnight, and a nightmare midnight, at that. Yes, I'm going to get out of here. Boys," he said to the two men, "this is a thing that won't make good talk until we've come back and put it right."

Wully's companion had one of those dark faces and yellow eyes that always suggested mixed blood. His lip twisted like the snarling mouth of a dog as he answered: "I'm willing never to come back. I've had enough. Guns are all right. But this here air . . ." He waved about him.

"We're off," said Lyons abruptly.

They mounted.

"Where shall I find the two of them?" said Lyons to Crosson.

"Whichever way you go, you'll find 'em on the way," he responded.

Lyons stared at the speaker for a gloomy moment, and then he nodded. "We're leaving you behind us, Crosson," he said, "but if there's any crooked play, and, if my two men are not given back, I'll burn this wood to a crisp and hunt down the game that the fire doesn't kill."

Then, turning the head of his horse, he rode off at a good clip down the huge, winding avenues.

He did not speak on the way. Neither did the girl nor either of the men who brought up the rear of the procession. Each of these rode with a naked weapon in his hand, and many a glance they threw over their shoulders, and many a sidelong look with which to probe the ranks of the trees near them.

They saw before them, presently, a broader and stronger glare of light that announced that they were almost out of the grove, and the girl muttered: "Will we find the men? Will we find them, Chet?"

"We won't!" he exclaimed. "I've been tricked and gulled again. By heaven, Nan, I think that the scoundrels take me for a baby that they can make free with and . . ."

Here they swung around a cluster of mighty tree trunks grouped close together, and just before them, stretched upon the pine needles, they saw their two men. But in what condition!

Their clothes were torn to shreds; blood oozed from many cuts. Their hands and their feet were bound fast together, and each man was lashed to the other. Each was securely gagged.

"I'm going to have blood for this!" exclaimed Lyons. "I'm going to have a city full of blood for this!"

He cut the gags away, cruel, cutting gags made of green withes and choking bark. But the rescued men did not leap to their feet. Instead, one of them pushed himself up on one elbow and stared at his friends with the empty eyes of an idiot, and the other, turning over on his face, buried it in his arms and began to sob heavily, like a child.

# CHAPTER TWENTY

They got the two men to their feet. There was no serious wound upon either, but one of them seemed stunned, as though he had been heavily drugged, while the other continued as hysterical as a girl after a great fright. The presence of his comrades could not prevent him from weeping and rolling his head wildly about on his shoulders, as though in overwhelming agony of mind and body.

The girl looked on him and his companion with more horror than compassion. She had been raised to feel that men will sooner die than be shamed.

"What can have happened to them?" she asked of her cousin. "It hasn't been long, whatever that fellow you call Oliver Crosson may have had time to do . . . but *how* did he steal them away?"

Chester Lyons abandoned the hysterical man. He turned his attention to the mute.

"What happened, Harry?" he demanded. "What happened to you when you got inside the house?"

Harry looked up at him with a face hideously blank. "I dunno," he said. "I dunno."

"You know something. You're all right now. You're safe, Harry. We're with you. You're safe."

"I'm safe?" muttered Harry, looking vaguely

around him. "I was safe before. I had a partner with me. But he . . . he . . ." He closed his eyes. He swayed from side to side, muttering softly under his breath.

"Out with it!" exclaimed Lyons. "Tell me, Harry. You're safe here, and we have to know!"

The eyes of Harry did not open. "I heard him drop," he said slowly. "I turned, and he had me by the throat, and lifted me into the air. I kicked . . . I hit at him. He held me up there like he'd been a giant. He choked me while I was hanging from his hands like from a noose of rope. I couldn't make a sound. My partner was lying on the floor, looking like he had a broken neck . . ." He fumbled at his throat, and his eyes, opening, stared blankly before him.

"That's it," said Lyons briskly, looking at Chet and Nan. "Slugged with a sandbag or some such thing. When Harry turns, he's caught by the throat."

"Hold on!" said Wully. "How much man would it take to throttle Harry and muscle him out into the air at the same time? Harry is man-size, I guess."

Chet Lyons shrugged. "We've promised to get on out of these woods today. I'm coming back another time, however, and I'm going to . . ."

"Chet!" cried the girl.

"Well?" he snapped, angry at the interruption in the flow of his rage.

"Don't say anything more!" she exclaimed. "Don't make any rash promises. There's something spooky about this. I'm going to have nightmares for half a year on account of it."

At any rate, Lyons was not the man to expend himself in vain threats. He said: "We'll get on out of this. What we do afterward can be seen when the time comes."

They mounted the two men on the led horses, and more slowly they crossed the remaining distance to the edge of the forest. But as they passed into the clear light of the day, there was a sigh of relief from every man. They were never gladder to leave any place behind them.

As they turned to glance back at the huge, gloomy trees, Wully cried out sharply: "There's one of the devils now!" And he snatched out a revolver as he spoke. Not till he fired did the others see his target. Then the yelp of a wolf showed them a great lobo springing away through the shadows at the margin of the trees.

"Wully!" declared the girl in strange excitement. "I think that you're a fool to have done that!"

"I suppose that I should've let the murdering, four-footed throat cutter get away?" said Wully. "Not me. And right from this day on, every time I see one, I'm going to snag it."

"Perhaps it wasn't badly hurt?" said Nan Lyons hopefully.

"Maybe not," replied Wully. "But if I ain't a fool and a liar, I sank that one right behind his right shoulder. He's a dead wolf before he's run far."

"Then . . . we'll all pay for it," said the girl.

"What's the matter with you, Nan?" asked her cousin briskly. "One might think that you're afraid there are ghosts in there. What's the matter with you today?"

"What's the matter with all of us?" the girl answered. "Chet Lyons and four of his best men rode into those woods today and rounded up one of the Crossons and a harmless old trapper along with him. Chet Lyons wants to find out all about the Crossons. He had half a mind that he would run them out of the country. But what's happened? Why, Chet Lyons had to run for his life. Isn't that strange enough? Strange enough to send the chills down my back. If I were you boys, I'd get out of here and stay away. I wouldn't come within rifle shot of young Oliver Crosson so long as I lived."

They felt better, however, now that they were beyond the shadows of the trees, and with the familiar keenness of the sunshine cutting through their coats and scalding their bodies. They shrugged their shoulders at the thought of young Oliver Crosson.

That youth, not long before, having left the two prisoners on the most probable course that

166

the strangers might follow in leaving the wood, went off among the trees with a step as light and bounding as the stride of a deer. As he went, he whirled something that glittered in his hand and twinkled above his head. It gleamed even in the shadows, and it sparkled brightly when a ray of sun dripped down upon it through the lofty branches of the forest. It was a new Colt revolver, heavy, blue-barreled, with all the smugness of a hand-fitted tool and all the beauty of efficient strength. That was his prize.

It mattered very little that he had freed his father and the stranger from the hands of the outlaws. But he now held in his hands the forbidden fruit, the knowledge that had been forbidden to him all the days of his life.

He had a guilty joy as he danced along with the gun. He knew perfectly well how the thing was put together, how it was cleaned, how it was assembled, exactly how it worked. More than once, prowling like a beast of prey through the hills, he had worked up close to the camp of a trapper or a hunter and seen them by firelight, busy at their guns. More than once the weapons had been in his hands, but he had thrown them away. His father's command had been enough to banish the guns from his touch. Yet a thing banished is not a thing forgotten. And the very prohibition that was put upon firearms on the Crosson Ranch was enough to make him desire the forbidden thing. It was like Bluebeard's forbidden chamber; it was in his mind more than all else.

Now he had a gun. He was acquainted with the method of using it. Had he not, for long hours, played with a rusted, useless relic, whipping it out from his clothes to make the sudden and perfect draw that, as he knew, was half the thing in handling guns? Had he not spent a thousand hours weighing and hefting the thing, taking its balance and learning its touch so that it responded to him as a pen to a penman? Had he not sighted it ten thousands of times, drawing the quick bead and then stooping his head, while his hand remained steady as stone, to make sure that the bead was perfect?

He had done all this. For many a year he had dreamed of guns with the passion of a child for fairyland. He had gone through the woods with that rusted, worthless, heavy old toy of his, and, taking sudden sight at the squirrels on the boughs of the trees, he had made sure along the barrel that this one would have fallen without hindquarters and the head of the other would be missing when it tumbled to the ground.

But what was that toy, that clumsy, outdated thing, compared with this living marvel? It fitted against the palm of his hand with a wonderful security. It answered his touch. After the rust that his fingers had rubbed from the ancient gun, the touch of this one was all velvet and the polish silken. It was not light, but it seemed light to him. The balance of it answered him like a familiar mind. And in its chambers were locked up six deaths! That was the chief marvel of the thing.

Sixfold death was inside the little gun, and, with the pressure of his forefinger, the doors could be opened one by one. Why, he was like a king; he was more than a king—he was a god. No wonder that he danced and leaped as he ran through the woods. He had taken the thing from enemies by the force of his hand and by the strength of his cunning, and when should he use it?

To give a perfect flavor to his happiness, there was a sense of guilt attaching to it, for he well understood that he should not have the thing. What would his father say? The wrath of the stern old man hung like a cloud in the back of his mind, like a storm cloud rolling high and higher above the horizon. It oppressed and chilled his ardor—for he knew that it would not be long before he challenged that wrath by using the weapon.

He did not go straight back to the house to see how his father did, and the trapper stranger who was with him. Instead, he made a detour, leading toward a distant side of the woods. And as he sped along, he chirped to the squirrels above him, and they, fearless at the familiar voice, stood up on their branches and looked fearlessly down at him. They had no fear, but they winced and dodged at the sight of the glimmering steel that he leveled at them. No, he could not press the trigger against such harmless creatures.

Then a gray female wolf rose out of the shadows and bounded beside him. She panted with lolling tongue as she galloped easily beside him. There was a stain of red in her fierce eyes, and, coming closer, she whined and looked eagerly in his face.

He knew that look well. He had seen it before. Either there was a stray maverick come from the upper hills, or else there was a deer near at hand.

The timber wolf, running before him, began to skim low, head close to the ground, and the boy instantly changed his running. He went more slowly. He picked the places upon which his feet fell; he went as softly as a gentle evening breeze through the shadows beneath the trees, and, coming to the place where the wolf was couched in covert behind some brush at the edge of the wood, he halted in turn.

Beyond, enjoying the coolness of the shade, was a tall buck, switching his tail at the flies and stamping now and then—a sleek, fat-ribbed buck.

No prohibitions from a father could hold back Oliver Crosson then. The deer must be his!

# CHAPTER TWENTY-ONE

He crouched near the female wolf, one hand upon her trembling withers. She turned her head to the right and then to the left. He saw them now. Except for his excitement, he would have noted them before—two couchant wolves of his own band, sure in the hunt and deadly for the kill. He had stolen them from their mothers; he had fostered and reared them; he knew, almost, their speech. They waited, their jaws locked, their eyes as bright as fire, until the master should give the word. Then out they would bound. But what would they gain?

The tree under which the deer stood was a little apart from the main border of the forest, and to get at it the lobos would have to slip across a short open space. However adroitly they slid forward, there was little chance that they could come in striking distance of the buck. Was it not for that very reason that they had waited for the master to come up with them, that the force of his mind might assist them, as it had often assisted them in other times? If the deer lay down, that would be another matter, and a single strong burst might bring the fleetest of the three close enough for a stroke at the throat or at the hamstring. But give that deer a ten-foot start and it would leave the pack behind as surely as a freshly launched thunderbolt.

Oliver Crosson measured the distances with his eye, the while patting the shoulders of the female wolf gently.

The thing might be done, of course. He might, for instance, send out that young yellow lobo to the rear of the stag. There was a certain amount of cover to which that cunning stalker could take advantage until, worming close, it sprang up on the farther side of the deer—on the side that would turn the buck in toward the trees. Once among them, two gray devils would rise in its path and finish it.

But he carried in his hand a quicker solution of the task. The gun. Would his skill be sufficient? Would his hand be steady and the bead be drawn surely? Oh, if rusty sights would do, surely these bright steel ones could not fail him!

At that moment the deer bounded from the tree's shadow and landed twenty feet away. There it stood for a quivering instant, flight already shining in its eyes, while the sound that had startled it rang faintly in the ears of the boy.

From far away, from the other side of the wood, came the ringing noise of a rifle report. The very direction, in fact, in which the strangers must have departed, and along the course of which he had left the two captured hostages. And what was that sound that followed on the heels of the report? Was it not the yelp of a wolf, dim in the distance?

Anger made him set his jaws hard for an instant. Then he forgot what might be happening in another part of the forest. He centered his attention on the deer. For the gray female wolf was rising stealthily to her feet. He could feel the tremor as her leaping muscles gathered for a supreme effort. She raised her head a trifle and rolled back her red-stained eye to ask for his permission before she bolted out into the open.

The stag, uneasy, turned its head quickly from side to side, the big ears fanning forward in the intensity of its effort to listen. It made one or two quick steps. Its hindquarters were sinking a little, and the sunlight flashed upon the gathering muscles. In another instant it would be shooting away across the green of the rolling ground, half in fear, half in the same careless joy that makes a songbird soar against the sun.

Crosson raised the revolver and leveled it. He had a mere glimpse of the bared teeth of the wolf as it snarled in silent fear of the unaccustomed tool. She knew that scent, but never in these hands. Where would he aim? There where the heart beat, behind the shoulder, under the sleek, fat side. But could a mere pressure of the forefinger turn the trick? Would the gun thunder from his hand as it had thundered from the hands of others that he had heard?

His heart raced—his face burned—his hand trembled wonderfully until, as the sights rose, he glimpsed the desired target. At the very instant that the stag sprang he pressed the trigger.

There was a report that sounded in his sensitive ears like the breaking of the assembled thunders of the world. The heel of the weapon kicked strongly back against his palm. The muzzle jerked spitefully upward and seemed to say to him—a miss!

Was it a miss? The stag bounded wildly forward, stretched out straight and true. He had only alarmed it. No, the second bound was not forward, but high aloft, and, landing from it, the buck fell loosely, heavily upon the ground. His head bounced up a little from the shock. His pink tongue lolled upon the grass. His eyes were as wide as ever, but the boy knew that there was no sight in them. The deer was dead.

Out from the brush sprang the three big wolves. And Crosson slowly followed them out from the shadow, from the cool of the woods into the burning of the sunshine, hotter than a bath of blood. He felt no heat. He had done this. The crooking of his forefinger had beckoned the life out of that strong and beautiful body, so made for speed. He had not missed in this first shot. Would he ever miss again in all the days of his life?

A small, cold, stern smile formed upon his lips. His nostrils expanded. He was tasting the most supreme joy that the world can offer, except one. To give life is greatest of all, to take life is only second. And he had taken it.

What? To sweat and strain and invite danger, knife in hand, muscle to muscle, nerve to nerve? No, that was nothing. That was to live as a beast among beasts. But to stand aloof, unharmed, unthreatened, and snuff out an existence like a flickering candle's flame—that was indeed glorious, that was indeed to be a god! No wonder that his father had forbidden him to touch weapons. It was a gate that, once opened, laid at his feet all the world. He was no longer a child. He was a man.

The three great wolves stood over the kill, drooling with eagerness, but afraid to lay tooth in the booty until the master permitted. Not until he had begun the skinning and furled back the pelt and sliced out for them their portion dared they taste of the prize. But he did not move.

What was this thing, to occupy his hands? If he chose, could he not lay whole herds dead at his feet? The puma, the grizzly bear, hitherto unapproachable, the wolves of hostile tribes, the great elk, the deer, all the beasts of the wilderness were his slaves, were almost beneath his contempt, because he bore in his hand this little glittering toy of steel, its breath of fire, its word of lead.

He made a short gesture. The wolves shrank

lower, looking at him in surprise that was almost fear. Then, waiting no longer, they took the permission and their fangs were instantly in the kill.

The boy stood by. He watched them slashing and rending. He heard the snapping of the tendons, the rip of skin like the tearing of strong cloth, the grinding snap as a bone was crunched by the power of the great jaws. They fed. His heart gloried in them, in their appetites, in his fatherhood, and their dependence. They hungered, and he supplied them. He loved them all the more because the meat was freely theirs, beneath his attention. It mattered not that they had no fresh venison in the house. Tomorrow, and tomorrow, there would be hunting days. Did he not know every water hole loved by the deer among the hills? Did he not know where to ring the favored places with his wolves and lie in wait? There would be no such rings now, no such chances of escape, if the bounding stag or doe broke through or over the reaching teeth of the lobos. He, with his gun, would be there. He would snuff out the life with a beckoning movement of a single finger, and after that he would apportion the spoils—a little for himself and for his father; the most of it for these four-footed friends. He watched them eat.

A message, mysteriously sliding through the resin-scented air of the woods, reached other nostrils. Two more wolves bounded out to the feast, another and another, until the muzzles of seven were red in the blood of it.

So the boy watched them and felt rich, like a king at the head of his long boards, watching his peers, his retainers, his doughty men at arms, eating the food that of his providence and wealth he had given to them. He felt like a patriarch, these were the younglings of the clan who would owe him allegiance, respect, and obedience because of his bounty.

A buzzard flew nearer in the upper air. It dropped close down toward them, swinging in a circle breathlessly fast, and then perching on the bending top of a tree. Others of its kindred had watched the descent of that vulture. They began to appear, a speck in the west, in the south, in the east. Still others would come, having surely marked how the hungry brothers and sisters had dropped out of their seats in the sky toward at least the hope of a feast.

Crosson smiled grimly up at them. They were detestable, but it was the law of their kind. Were not all living things subject to some such law? Did not some browse on the grass of the field, and others feed on the pastures, and still others, birds and beasts, accept the foul leavings of the feast?

So it must be among men, also. Some drew from the soil by the labor of their hands; others drank up their profits by cunning and adroitness, but still others took by the sheer right of strength. His mind was full of romance. He could understand, in a stroke, why the knights-errant had ridden forth—not to plow, or to kill, but to take with their right hands.

They righted wrongs. Well, he would right wrongs, also. They helped the weak and the oppressed. Such would be his glorious duty, also. His fancy carried him into a bright, happy dream.

He was awakened from it by the noise of the snarling as the wolves, gorged and swollen with their fine fare, now lay down to maul the white bones of the dead with their bloody jaws.

Returning from his dream, he turned back into the wood. At the very edge of it he looked back, but not a single one of the feasters had risen to follow him. He spoke a soft word. All looked up, but only the female wolf arose, sullenly, and went after him. The others dropped their ears, like creatures that know that they are doing wrong, but they waited for the second command.

Crosson disdained to give it. He went on, but a new thought was in his mind.

# CHAPTER TWENTY-TWO

Bill Ranger felt that he had learned enough and more than enough. He had no desire to enter into the narrative events of the lives of the two Crossons. He had decided before this that his best policy would be to get out of the environment immediately and to report to Menneval exactly what he had seen, Menneval to act as he thought fit and use his imagination as he saw fit, for Ranger felt like a child confronted with difficult problems in arithmetic, problems as yet untaught and unsolved.

At the edge of the creek, he watched old Crosson skillfully and swiftly clean the fish, chop off their heads, and throw them away.

"You oughta leave the heads on," suggested Ranger. "Some of the juice leaks out, that way."

"Let the juice leak," said old Crosson. "It's better than to have dead fish in front of you."

There was a delicacy in this distinction of fish cooked with and without the head that Ranger only vaguely understood. "Well," he said, "I'll be getting along."

The old man looked up at him as though amazed, and blinked his bewilderment. "But you haven't eaten with us," he said.

"I'd better be getting along," said the trapper. "It'll be late pretty soon and I'd better get started on my way."

Old Crosson continued staring. "Suppose I were to visit your camp, would you let us go without eating?" he asked.

Ranger hesitated. It was a point well taken. "Well, I'll stay," he said suddenly.

Old Crosson gathered up the fish and they started back for the cabin.

A fire was kindled in the open fireplace. Ranger helped gather the wood, while Crosson wrapped the fish in broad leaves, as if to protect them from the singeing force of the flames.

"Tell me something," Ranger said to break the silence. He was watching the fire blaze up, while Peter Crosson sat on his haunches like an Indian, considering the fire.

"Aye, I'll tell you something," said Crosson, without lifting his glance from the blaze.

"Tell me why you want me to stop here."

Crosson smiled at the fire, or was it at his own thoughts? "Because I need you, son," said Crosson.

It startled Ranger. It startled him that this Robinson Crusoe should need any man. It startled him that anyone should call him "son"— Bill Ranger, with his grizzled head.

"You need me?" echoed Ranger.

"I need you," said Crosson, and nodded at

the flames, as if to get confirmation from their jumping heads.

"Why, man," said Ranger, "I certainly ain't much to help anybody. I'm only a kind of ordinary trapper."

"You're honest!" snapped Crosson.

Again Ranger was startled. Was it not by this very formula that that man in the Far North, that robber and slayer and deceiver, that Menneval— was it not by the same formula that Menneval had addressed him, those lifetimes ago in Spooner's saloon? Menneval had said that he was honest. Therefore, Menneval had committed to his hands a weight of gold dust and this odd mission. Honesty was a strange thing, it appeared. It opened the most unexpected doors.

"Will honesty help you?" asked Ranger. "Besides, I dunno that I'm extra honest. I've slipped a card . . ." He flushed; a gentle perspiration broke out on his forehead at the thought.

The other did not favor him with so much as a glance. "Yes, you're honest," he said. "And that's the kind of a man I have to have now. He's about to jump the brink. He's about to spread his wings." He paused.

"Who is?" asked Ranger.

There was no answer.

"You mean your son?"

"I mean the boy," Crosson said almost fiercely. He took two sticks, and with them he lifted the fiery coals at the base of the fire. Under the coals he laid the limp fish in their wrappings of leaves. The wet oozed through the leaves and tiny drops appeared, like fresh dew.

"I dunno," said Ranger cautiously. "I dunno how I could be any good to him. I'd need," he added, "a leash of lightning and a hand like a thunderbolt."

Crosson chuckled. "They wouldn't be any good. Lightning wouldn't scar his neck, and he'd jerk the thunderbolt away and throw it back at you. But with a silk thread, a spider's thread, you could hold him forever."

"Hold on," said the trapper.

"You'll understand me one day," said Crosson. "I'm sorry for you, friend, but you'll understand one day. You'll never get away from him."

Ranger gasped. "Why won't I? Look here, Crosson, I ain't picked myself to be a friend of his. He . . . he's too quick for me."

"Men go where they're needed," said old Crosson. "That's the tragic thing about life. We don't do what we want. We do what other people need us to do. We're slaves. I've tried to make him free. I can't. I've tried to make him so that other people wouldn't mean anything to him. But it looks like I've failed pretty badly." He nodded soberly at the fire and beat down the crinkling, fire-twisted sticks with the end of a branch.

"Tell me what you mean," Ranger said.

The old man lifted a long, gaunt forefinger. "Am I a keeper for him any longer?" he said.

"For your son? Why, I dunno."

"Look at me again. I look like a skull. I look as though I were already dead. Am I a keeper for him? No, I'm not. And some other man will have to be the keeper. I thought it would be five years from now, but the troubles are coming on us too fast. He's tasting his strength . . . on men. Soon, he'll taste blood. And then he'll need another keeper. I'm not strong enough to keep up with him. But you're strong. And you're honest. And you'll go with him."

"Go with him where?" asked Ranger.

"How should I know?" said the other. "Go where he goes, when he's on the trail of perdition. When he starts to kill, you'll try to hold his hand."

"I don't follow your drift."

"You will, though. You'll follow it pretty well. Right now, you never saw a man in your life that interested you as much as he does. Tell me, ain't that the truth?"

Ranger looked back into his mind, into his life. It was a crowded page that he surveyed there in that moment. At length he said, reluctantly: "Yes, that's true. I never saw another man who interested me as much. What of it?"

"Then you'll try to keep him straight. That's all. You'll try to keep him . . ."

Here, out of the distance, the report of a gun came to them.

Old Crosson stood up and listened. "That was a rifle . . . from the way that Chester Lyons was riding, with his girl."

"Did you hear the wolf yell, afterward?" asked Ranger.

"No. My ears are growing dull. I heard no wolf yell. Was there a wolf's yell, afterward?"

"Aye, there was."

Crosson stood for a long moment, silent, thoughtful, with something of great emotion unexpressed in his face.

Before he spoke or stirred, a smaller sound came to them from the opposite side of the wood.

"That was a revolver," said Ranger.

Crosson looked at him with vague, horrified eyes. "Then . . . it's happened," he said.

"What's happened?"

"I've kept him away from them all the days of his life. But now he's got one."

"What? You've kept who? What do you mean?"

"I've kept him . . . the boy. I've kept him from guns. But there can't be two gangs in the woods at once. There can't be."

"I don't follow that," said Ranger.

But Crosson, lost in gloomy thought, refused to speak again on the subject. The moments went on.

Presently a gray she-wolf leaped out from the

184

shadows of the trees and stood before them, flattening herself a little toward the ground.

Crosson looked earnestly at her. "He's coming back," he said.

"Who?"

"Oliver. He's sent her on before. Look at her belly line. She's been gorging."

"Aye, it looks that way."

For Ranger knew dogs from his Arctic trekkings, and he was a judge of a heavy meal. "What's she been eating?" he asked.

"The gun shot that we last heard!" snapped Crosson. He sat down, cross-legged, heedless of his nearness to the fire, and rested his forehead on his hand.

And then, without a sound, another presence materialized beneath the brown shadows of the big trees. It was the boy, coming back with a light step and a cheerful face. For he was smiling, and his look was fastened upon the treetops. He came straight up to the fire, and sniffed the air. "You've got the fish roasting, Father?" he asked.

"Aye." The old man nodded.

"I'm hungry as a wolf," said the boy.

The old man looked suddenly up to him. "Then why didn't you eat . . . with the rest of the wolves, the rest of your pack?" said Crosson.

The boy stared at him. "Raw meat?" he asked, incredulous.

"Aye, you've had the taste of blood," said old Crosson sternly.

Oliver Crosson looked down at his clothes, at his hands.

"Not on your hands, but in your heart," said Peter Crosson.

# CHAPTER TWENTY-THREE

The nerves of Ranger had been growing more and more tense, and now the weight upon them had increased almost to the breaking point, but there was not a word said to follow up the subject for some time. The fish were duly roasted. They were drawn forth from the coals, and they were eaten as they were.

There was no fork, no knife. There was a little cold pone, badly baked, soggy, and stale, to eat with it. There was, otherwise, not even salt. For drink, they had water from the brook, which the boy brought in a leather water bag and poured out into bark cups, which leaked in little streams upon their hands, upon their knees. It was primitive living—far surpassing what Ranger had seen among the Indians, and even the rigors of the Arctic trail, where a man makes his flapjack with baking powder, grease, and flour, fries it, and washes it down with bitter black coffee or blacker tea. The fish seemed tasteless to him at first.

But, afterward, he began to enjoy a delicate flavor that even salt would have rendered imperceptible, rather than to underline and increase. There was the gamy taste of the fish itself, the freshness, the juice of life. And into this was baked the flavor of the cress and leaves in which the fish had been wrapped. The charred coverings fell away, but they imparted some of their aroma and pungency to the flesh. Yes, such a meal was not bad, aside from the bread. And the sauce of the open air, of a keen appetite, brought a relish for simple fare.

"This is the way you eat, mostly?" he asked.

"Well, when the berries are in season . . . ," said the boy in a matter-of-fact tone.

He lay back upon the pine needles suddenly, and stretched out his arms, crosswise. He was looking at the sky with steady, unwinking eyes.

And Ranger, glad of the chance, looked freely, steadily upon the lad. It was true. He never before had seen a human being who interested him so much, nor one from whom he had learned so much, either. What was in the lesson he could not exactly say, except that it had something to do with the virtue of living close to the ground, of the ground, of being one with the beasts of prey and the beasts of the field. That was the lesson—a lesson of communion with Nature, of the savagery and strength and mystery of Nature. He only guessed at these things. He could not really comprehend them.

Looking around, he had found the eyes of old Crosson fixed steadily upon him, and the dweller in the wilderness did not avoid the answering glance of question. Instead, he leaned a little forward and probed deeply into the eyes of Lefty Ranger.

The latter grew uneasy. He felt his lids parting wider. He grew nervous.

Then old Crosson sighed and suddenly averted his glance. "Oliver," he said.

"Aye, Father?" said the boy, still looking at the sky.

"What have you done?"

There was no answer for a moment.

"Well," said Oliver. "I waited inside the house until the two of them got off their horses and said that they were coming inside to hunt for me. Then I stepped beside the door. As they came in, and stood staring around, blinking like birds at the darkness of a cave, I hit one of them with my fist, there at the base of the neck, where an animal is easily stunned, there where the big tendons join to the base of the skull, and the brain is close. I struck him there, and he dropped on his face. The other one turned around. I lifted him up and choked him until his tongue stuck out and his face turned purple-black.

"Then I went out behind the house, because I thought they would soon be looked for, and it would be better not to have them found on the floor of the house. I thought of taking them to the creek and throwing them into the water. The current, tumbling them on the rocks, would soon have battered and killed them, as it sometimes batters and kills the fish at the cascades, during the spring freshets. But then I remembered that there should be no dead men on the trail. You often have said that, eh?"

Old Crosson looked not at the boy, but at Ranger, as though there was a meaning in those words worth some contemplation. "Well?" he coaxed.

"So I did not throw them into the creek. Instead, I took them out behind the house, one at a time. There were several of the pack there."

"What did you do then?"

"You know how I've taught them to walk close together and carry the weight of a good log out of the woods and back to the house?"

"Yes, I've seen them do it for you."

"I made them stand together. Then, I laid one body on their backs. You would have laughed."

"At what?"

"Why, at the way they turned their heads and showed their teeth. I could see their throats swelling, too, but I made them keep from snarling, for fear the people back here in front of the house would hear. They went on with him lying on their backs, his body wriggling a little from side to side, but lying safely behind their big shoulders. I laughed. I nearly choked, seeing how they hated to carry him. And he lay like a dead man."

"Do you know how a dead man looks?" asked Peter Crosson.

"I mean, his mouth was open, and his face was still swollen, and on his throat I could see the finger marks. But I knew that he would live. I had not driven home the thumbs, quite, into the hollow of the throat. He had frightened himself more than I'd hurt him.

"I took the other man over my back and walked after the wolves, taking care that I made no trail to follow for such eyes as those people would have. They would have had to lift the needles to find the weight where I had stepped. Then I got to a little distance. I tied them. I stopped their mouths with bark and withes. And I laid them in the avenue that points north, the easiest way back through the woods. I guessed that you would make a bargain, when the time came. That's all."

Old Crosson looked at Ranger, and Ranger, his eyes popping out, stared at the boy and at the half-smiling, half-grim face of the father. For Ranger had seen those two men. With neither of them would he have liked to fight out any battle. And here was a youngster who had handled them both, idly, easily. With a single blow he had stunned one of them. And the other? What was that about lifting the bulk of a weighty man from the ground and strangling him in the air? Ranger's face became damp with sweat at the thought. He shrugged his shoulders and shook his head, but the shudder would not leave him.

"And then?" queried Peter Crosson.

"Well," said the boy slowly, "this will make you angry."

"Tell me."

"As the wolves were carrying that man along, a revolver fell out of his clothes. I picked it up and was about to throw it into the brush, but somehow it stuck to my hand." He stopped his narrative and whistled. A blue jay stooped from the nearby treetops and flashed close overhead.

"Throw it a bit of fish," said the boy.

The father paid no heed to the request. "Go on," he said.

"You told me never to take a gun," said Oliver Crosson. "But that one stuck to my hand. It would not leave me. So I kept it. And afterward I went back to the edge of the woods, and there I found the gray wolf, watching a deer. She had run back to fetch me along. She had helped to carry the man for me." He paused.

"You shot the deer?" said old Crosson suddenly.

The boy sighed. "Yes," he said softly, "I shot the deer."

"And you let the wolves eat it?"

"How did you guess that?" asked the boy, frowning at the sky.

"Because men don't eat their own murders," Peter Crosson said gloomily.

"Murder?" said the boy.

Peter Crosson in turn looked up to the sky. "Oh,

God," he whispered, "teach me what to do with him."

"A deer by the knife, a deer by the bullet, what difference does it make?" asked Oliver.

"This difference," said Peter Crosson, "as I've told you before. The man with the knife is risking his own life. He needs courage. He needs skill. He kills only to eat. But the man with the gun bends his finger and beckons the life away. He imitates God Almighty, for only God should have such power. He makes life cheap. And life should not be cheap . . . it should be sacred. You . . . today . . . the instant that a gun was in your hand, you took a life not for the sake of food, but for your own pleasure." He raised a hand and added solemnly: "May God forgive you for it."

The boy did not stir where he lay upon the ground. Only his forehead contracted, gradually, into a frown. And he said not a word; it was plain that he was thinking deep thoughts.

As for the lesson contained in this homily, it was far above the head of Ranger. Vaguely, dimly he reached for the truth, only to find it elusive.

Suddenly the boy sat up, his ear strained for a sound. "What was that?" he asked, half under his breath.

"What? I heard nothing," said the father.

"Something gasping, something dying," said the boy. He leaped to his feet.

Never had Ranger seen a man rise so lightly, so suddenly.

Then he pointed, and, as if the gesture conjured the form out of nothingness, into the clearing came the dragging form of the great black wolf that Ranger had seen before, and well noted. It was the king of the wolf pack, the master of them all, and now its life was plainly near an end.

The old man, unnoticing, his eyes half closed, went on speaking: "You have taken a life for pleasure. Blood calls for blood, in this bitter world." Then he saw the wolf and paused.

Straight up to the feet of young Oliver Crosson came the big creature, and there slumped heavily to the ground. Oliver kneeled suddenly and took its head in his arms, and Ranger saw the wolf look up and its red tongue lick the face of the master. Then it quivered, and all its weight drooped. It was dead.

Oliver Crosson slowly, gently lowered the great head to the ground.

"Blood calls for blood," he repeated.

# CHAPTER TWENTY-FOUR

Even to Lefty Ranger, there was something exciting in the words of the boy. But they fairly drove Peter Crosson frantic. He called out—"Oliver! Oliver!"—two or three times, but Oliver went on into the house without a word.

When he came out, he was carrying a single small roll, too thin to be a pack, thought Ranger, even for a man who intends to journey on foot, and yet obviously meant as an accommodation for a journey. Between two fingers, he blew a whistle that screeched up and down the valley, and in another moment there was an answer—the neigh of a horse. He did not whistle again, but soon a cream-colored mustang came swiftly out of the woods near the river's edge and galloped straight up to him.

Oliver threw onto the back of the horse a battered old saddle, and began to arrange the pack behind it, tying it on with the straps.

The excitement of Peter Crosson grew with the passage of every moment. "Hold on, Oliver," he insisted. "Hold on and listen to me, will you?"

"Yes, sir," said Oliver. But, without pausing, he continued his operations.

"I tell you to stop!" cried Peter, his voice jumping suddenly up the scale, so that one could not help realizing that he was an old man.

"Yes, sir," said Oliver.

But stop he would not.

"Oliver Crosson!" shouted the father.

"Yes, sir?"

"Turn around here to me!"

Oliver turned his head only, for his hands were busied with the work before them.

"Oliver, what's in your mind?"

"I'm going to find him," said Oliver.

"D'you mean that you're going to find Chester Lyons?"

"I'm going to find him," said Oliver.

"What for?"

For answer, Oliver pointed to the big body of the dead wolf. "For that," he said.

"You're going to murder him?" asked Peter Crosson.

"It's turn for turn," said Oliver.

Looking desperately about him, Peter Crosson's glance fell upon Ranger, but there was no help in the blank eyes of the latter. "I'll tell you something!" cried Peter Crosson. "If ever you do that . . . if ever you go on a man's trail . . . you'll never leave it till you've had his blood. And once you've tasted that, you'll have no care for anything else in the world. I've known it these years. That's why I've kept you here. D'you think that I'm a man to enjoy living alone in this blasted wilderness? I've kept you here and suffered for you. But now you throw away the work that I've done for you."

"How do I throw it away?" asked the boy. "Do you mean to say that he doesn't deserve anything that I can do to him . . . Chester Lyons, I mean?"

"You're not the law, and you're not the judge," said the other. "You're a fool, and you're a young fool . . . which is the blackest kind that there is."

It was enough to strike even Oliver silent.

Ranger, seeing that a crisis had come, looked uneasily from one to the other. Oliver was waiting. Peter Crosson plainly had much more to say. But he could not bring it out freely. He was trembling with excitement. There was something that was plainly fear in his eye, together with something very like hatred. Ranger was amazed.

"D'you hear?" shouted Peter Crosson.

"I hear," said the boy.

"I forbid your going."

Oliver answered nothing. But, significantly, he gathered the reins slowly in one hand as he stood at the head of the cream-colored mustang.

Peter Crosson made another effort of a different kind. "Oliver, my son," he said, "in one more month you're twenty-one years old. Let me keep you safe, and in a quiet life for the full legal period. After that, you can be your own master. But now the law gives me a right to your obedience. A month is a short time. It's only a step . . . it's only a step. Wait till the step is finished, Oliver."

Oliver, with a faint frown, glanced over his shoulder. "In a month, he may be a thousand miles away," he responded.

Peter Crosson struck a hand against his forehead. He seemed in despair. Perspiration gleamed on his face. "Oliver, Oliver!" he cried, and actually wrung his hands in the effort to persuade. "Why have I kept you out here in the wilderness alone with me? Why have I lived like a castaway on a desert island? I've denied myself everything. I've tried to bring you safely through. Do you know why I've kept you away from other people and never trusted a gun to your hands?"

"No," said the boy.

"Because there's murder in your blood."

The heart of Ranger contracted a little, but the effect of the words on the boy was amazing. Gray with emotion, rigid as a stone, he stood by the horse and stared at the tall old man.

"You never took a man's life," he said. "Who did, then? My mother?" His voice rose at the last words, and there was a ring and almost a wail in it. But the next moment he bit his lip to master his outbreak.

Peter Crosson was gesturing with both hands, as though in denial. "I've said what I can. I cannot say more," he declared. "But take my solemn oath for it . . . there is murder in your blood. Leave me, and you leave me to start such a life as you yourself don't dream of. And if you leave me now, this day, I swear to you, Oliver, that you never can come back to me."

The boy started again under this bludgeon stroke. "I don't think you mean it," he said. "Whatever there is in me, I don't know. But you can't blot me out of your life like a word on a piece of paper."

"Can't I?" the old man cried, more excited than ever. "I can, and I will. I've given you all that a man could give to a child. I've given you teaching, training. I've been a father and a mother and a brother to you. I've asked you for one thing in return, and that's obedience. If you disobey me now, I cut you out of my heart and out of my life. By heaven, you're more interested in a dead wolf than in your own father. Oliver, Oliver, will you try to use your wits? Will you try to think what it means?"

Oliver, stern and tense, looked down for a moment to the ground. Then he came straight forward to Peter Crosson and held out his hand.

The old man uttered a sharp, high sound of joy and caught the hand in both of his. "Ah, Oliver," he said, "God forgive me for doubting you for a moment. You're staying with me, of course."

"I'm saying good bye," said Oliver. "I want to do what you say, but I can't. There's something pulling at me harder than a wind in a treetop. I'm sick to be gone out after Chester Lyons. I'm starved to be on his trail."

He had raised his voice somewhat; there had been a tremor in it that made the heart of Ranger jump.

"If I tried to stay here another month," said the boy, "it would kill me."

"Let it kill you, then!" screamed Peter Crosson. "I'd rather see you dead here of the bloodlust, than dead in a hangman's noose. That's the branch that you'll ripen and rot on. I wish that I never had put eyes on you. Curse and wither you, brain and body!" He turned his back and stamped off a few paces, and there he threw his long, skinny arms above his head.

The boy looked after him for a moment only. Then he turned on his heel and jumped into the saddle. His face was a blank. If he suffered under the terrible denunciation of the old man, he would not let the trouble appear in his eye; one word sent the mustang galloping away.

At the sound of the hoof beats, old Peter Crosson whirled about. He shouted. But the boy was gone now, among the trees, and Bill Ranger grew sick with pity as he saw Crosson, with terror and rage in his face, throw his arms forward and run in pursuit, still shouting. In that instant, Ranger could see the old fellow condemned to a life of cold loneliness. Well, he would not endure long. He must be near the end of his long span.

It was not mere despair, however, that Crosson showed when he realized that his cries would not bring back the boy. He turned about in a wild frenzy, and, stamping up and down through the clearing, he cursed his luck, his fate, his origin, and all his life. He cursed the house, the trees, the boy who had just left, and the very horse that had carried him.

To this outbreak, the trapper listened in amazement. Anger, disappointment he was prepared to find, but there was something like a blasting hate gathered into the outpourings of old Peter Crosson. He dashed his hands together; he literally tore his hair.

And then, as though he must have some animate object on which to pour out his fury, he whirled upon Lefty Ranger and shouted: "You've brought the pest with you! The evil one was in your pocket. You've come down here to start what trouble you can. Tell me that. Admit it! Come out in the open and admit that Menneval sent you!"

This name struck like a trip hammer on the consciousness of Ranger. "Menneval?" he cried. "What do you know about Menneval, Crosson?"

"What do I know about him?" answered Crosson. "I know that he's a beast, a ghoul. And he sent you down here! Get out of my sight and stay out. If there's murder in the air, I'll do my share of it!"

He looked like a man transported. Lefty Bill, bewildered and unnerved, turned and did exactly as he had been bidden, striding off under the trees and wishing that he had on seven league boots.

He simply wanted to get away from it all— from the mystery of the boy, and Menneval, and Peter Crosson. There was danger in the air, real as fire, and it might burn him to the quick of the heart at any moment.

# CHAPTER TWENTY-FIVE

When Ranger got back to his camp, he did not hesitate a moment. He had learned all that even an exacting man like Menneval could ask from him. He wanted to get straight back to civilization, where he would have the comfort of normal men around him. It seemed to him that his brain was whirling, that he was walking in a dream.

By the time he reached a town, no doubt a rumor would be flying about concerning the death of Chet Lyons. He was as sure of the coming destruction of that outlaw as he was of the setting of the sun. Through his mind went a moving picture of the pursuit through the night, the remorseless speed of the youth, the keen noses of the wolves picking up the trail, and the sound of their hunting cry striking a chill note into the very soul of Lyons and his men.

What would they do? Would they turn back, united, to hunt the hunter? It hardly made any difference, Ranger felt. They would go down, and Lyons with them. Or perhaps the whole group would flee as if from a supernatural power, and, as they fled, the more poorly mounted men would be overtaken, one by one, by that terrible boy and left dead behind him as he pushed forward. What ambush could they make that his wolfish senses and his wolfish allies would not penetrate?

No, Lyons was a dead man, no more and no less, though at this moment he might be cantering securely along, mounted on his fine horse.

With the information that he possessed, Ranger decided, he would return as quickly as he could and, in the great white North, pick up the abandoned trail of his life. Once more it seemed to him that he had come from a land of absolute security and peace, and had stepped into a madhouse here in the sunny southern land.

He made a light pack. It meant abandoning a good many things, but what he wanted was a chance to make good time. He kept his rifle and filled a rough knapsack of his own making. This he strapped over his shoulders and started on his march.

He was a good walker. He had built up the muscle and the talent during the long treks through the snows of the Arctic. Now he hit away through the hills at a four-and-a-half-mile gait, swinging his rifle at the full length of his arm to add to his stride.

He saw the sun slide down the western sky. So great was his haste, it seemed to him that time was running doubly fast about him to shorten this day of his walking. Now and again, he marked the lengthening of the shadows, and then he came into a forest of great pines that jumped up above his head and crowded in a host against the sky. A sort of mild and mellow twilight surrounded him here, but, above, the dying sun touched the hedge of huge branches at intervals. It was a perfect California day; a gentle, warm wind came to him in soft breathings among the trunks of the forest, and the resinous purity of the pines filled the air. Well, let others have this magic land. For him, there was a blight upon it.

He left the forest again for a more open district, where the brush grew as tall as the second-growth trees of a less favored land. Rocks that sloped toward the west were now shining as though they burned; they flashed here and there through the greenery, and he was well into that hole-in-the-wall country that sheriffs hated, and outlaws loved.

Still, as he walked, he canted his ear toward the horizon sounds, a dozen times imagining that he heard the hunting cry of a wolf pack, far away, and a dozen times realizing that the sound was a dream that dissolved in the light of reality. But he was much more content, now, seeing that he had recovered the same trail that he had followed in coming out to this region. He was helped, too, by the knowledge that every stride took him farther and farther away from the Crosson Ranch. The very name Crosson now sent a prickle through his blood.

Going on in this way, he was stopped by a quiet

hail from behind him. He whirled about, amazed. For who knew his name in this part of the world?

He saw nothing but the empty trail behind him. And the heart of Ranger stood still with a superstitious fear.

"Lefty Bill!" said the same voice again.

Then he saw. Through the dense green of the shrubbery to the right and close at hand, he could make out the silhouette of a mounted man. That silhouette now moved and rode a glorious bay mare out onto the rocks of the trail. But what did horses mean to Bill Ranger, then? He was only aware of one thing, and that was the face of the man—a face of a middle-aged man, strangely old and yet strangely unlined, and silver hair so thin and closely cropped that it fitted his head like a white silken skullcap.

He had pulled his rifle to the ready, so that its muzzle covered the breast of the stranger.

"Menneval," said Lefty Bill.

"Yes, it's I," said Menneval. "I couldn't trust everything to your reports, Lefty. You know how it can be with a man. He wants to learn by his own eyes and ears."

Lefty groaned. He shook his head and groaned again. Grounding his rifle, he leaned upon it and took his bandanna out to wipe his face. "I wish that you'd had the idea before you started me south," he said.

"I got it a week later," said Menneval. "Have you had a bad time, Lefty?"

"Bad? I've had the evil one . . . I've had him at my elbow. Do you call that a bad time?"

"It depends, a little," said Menneval. "You've seen the Crossons?"

"I've seen 'em," said the trapper, "as nobody else ever could've been lucky enough to see 'em. I've seen 'em together, and then I've seen 'em break apart for good and all."

"What's that?" demanded Menneval.

"I've seen 'em together, and I've seen 'em break apart."

Menneval suddenly dismounted. It seemed that he wished to be nearer, in order that he might hear more clearly something that was of great importance to him.

"I dunno what it is that makes you take such a lot of interest in the pair of 'em," said Ranger. "One of 'em oughta be in an insane asylum . . . maybe the old one, too."

"Are they both wrong in the head?" asked Menneval. He kept his voice quiet, as usual, but there was a certain tenseness behind his words.

And Lefty Bill, staring at him, strove with all his might to penetrate the secret. He failed. He might as well have searched a mask of stone as to attempt to probe the brain of Menneval.

"I dunno how wrong in the head they are," said the trapper. "I dunno much of anything. I'm kind of stunned, Menneval, to see you step your horse out of that brush. It's like you had taken one step, four thousand miles long, and put yourself from Circle City to here."

"Everyone has a right to wonder once," said Menneval coldly. "But only a fool will wonder twice about the same thing, once it's before him. Suppose you tell me what you found out, and why you're turning back so soon. I thought that you'd hardly got out here?"

"Hardly, but I've had enough of it," said the trapper. "I been trapping varmints for their pelts. I done pretty good at it, too."

"And you saw both of 'em, eh?"

"I saw 'em both."

"Tell me what sort of people they are to look at?"

"The old man's out of a graveyard. The boy is out of a wolf. That's the truth."

"Out of a wolf? What do you mean by that?"

"Menneval," said the other, "I thought that I could tell you, when the time come. But I expected to have between here and Alaska to get my words in order, and you sort of take me a little mite by surprise, d'you see?"

Menneval bit his lip. "Take your time," he said. And he waited impatiently.

"I'm trying to think, but thinking doesn't do any good," went on Ranger. "I'm gonna tell you everything that happened, and just the way that it happened. Mostly you'll think that I'm a grand liar. But if you think so, you go and try to find out for yourself, and you'll soon have enough of it."

"Why'll I soon have enough?" asked Menneval.

The other stared at him. He thought, then, of all the wild and wonderful stories that men told of Menneval and his ways—of his battles, his savageries, his triumphs, his great and impossible achievements of all kinds. But, as he stared, he remembered the wild boy and could only shake his head.

"You're a grand man, Menneval," he said, "but you couldn't handle that boy without burning the palms out of your hands. Asbestos gloves, they wouldn't be good enough to keep him from burning you to the bone."

Menneval frowned almost bitterly upon the other. "It's the boy that you're talking of, and he's a bad one, is he?"

"Yes," said the trapper. "He's too much for me. I reckon that he'd be too much for you or any other man. Or any two men, for that matter."

Menneval pointed with his finger suddenly: "He's been raised with guns, has he?"

Ranger shook his head. "He's only got the instinct for 'em. And he doesn't need guns, and that's a thing that you can't understand until you see him. Look here, Menneval, you're quite a man, but he'd take your gun away from you and make you eat it."

The answer was a faintly sneering smile. "You'd better tell me everything," said Menneval.

"I'll tell you," said the trapper. And that he did.

They sat by the trail until the dusk. Into the dusk they still sat there, and, the longer they sat, the more questions Menneval still asked and the more painstakingly he had to be answered by the trapper. The smallest details seemed to be the details in which Menneval was the most interested.

And sometimes he answered the voice of Ranger with a short, sneering laughter.

It appeared that he was reasonably pleased, and Ranger could guess why. There was something that the man wanted to get out of those two, and, now that the father and the son were parted, get it he would, and with the minimum of effort. For his own part, he lost his feeling of hostility toward the elder Crosson. He merely felt a pang of sympathy for the poor old man, with a tiger-like Menneval prowling on his trail.

# CHAPTER TWENTY-SIX

Then, out of the far horizon, through the dusk, they heard the long-drawn cry of a single wolf, and so patly did it come on the heels of the narrative that Ranger had told, that he started up to his feet with a low exclamation. Menneval turned his head, also, and nodded.

The wolf cry was followed by the sudden clamor of a pack, and on the heels of this a number of rifle shots, one close upon the other, and, following the sound of the guns, the high-pitched death scream of a stricken wolf.

"He's hunting 'em. He's using the wolves," Ranger muttered under his breath.

Menneval laid a hand on the shoulder of his companion and even patted that shoulder lightly. "Son," he said, "if it's really Chester Lyons that the boy's after, he'll get what a fool deserves to get. Anyone who takes mere wolves out after such a fellow as Chet Lyons is going to lose his wolves and his life."

Ranger drew in a gasping breath. "It's the dusk of the day. There's good light for a wolf. There's no light to shoot a gun by. Listen."

A few scattering shots followed, and then the cry of the pack again, the hunting cry, the cry of the blood trail.

"They've found something," said Menneval quietly. "They're on the heels of something."

"They are," agreed Ranger. "There's some sort of vile work going on yonder."

"If that's Chester Lyons . . . ," began Menneval, and paused.

"If that's Chet Lyons and his gang, they're running before the pack!" cried Ranger. "Listen for yourself, if you won't believe what I say."

"It sounds that way," said Menneval softly. "It sounds pretty much that way, of course."

For they could hear the song of the pack, tossed up into the air and now running faint and far away, now flung back more boldly, where there was a sheer cliff of rocks to reflect the cry cleanly.

"Whatever they're hunting, they're following pretty close. No, not so closely now," said Menneval. "They're losing ground, but still they're hunting."

"A mounted man on a decent horse could get away from a pack, until the rough country was come to," said Ranger. "What makes you think that those wolves are losing ground?"

"By the yell of them. There's one song for the pack when it's running in view, and another yell when they've got to trust to their noses. They're running by the nose now, that outfit."

"Likely, likely. But they'll keep on running. I know the look of 'em. They're built to stay like running fire in the wind, and whatever they touch, they'll burn it black. You can trust to that."

"Lyons is drawing the boy on," said Menneval. "That's all. When the pinch comes, Lyons will eat him. I know Lyons."

"I've heard about him, too," said Ranger. "But I've seen the kid at work. And he's a worker, let me tell you."

"Lyons is one of the fastest and straightest men with a gun that ever carried one inside of leather," said the man from the Northland. "He'll eat the young fool, and serve him right . . . going hunting human rabbits through the night like that. Fools are soon out of their luck, and the Crosson boy will be out of his before many minutes."

"I'll make a bet with you!" exclaimed the trapper.

"What will you bet?" asked Menneval curiously.

"I'll bet you a cold thousand that the boy comes out on top. I tell you, I'd bet that if he had you against him. He ain't a man. He's just part wildcat and part wolf, and, if he walks and talks like a man, that's only a mask and it don't mean anything."

"You'll bet me a thousand, eh?" Menneval said thoughtfully.

"Or five," said the other.

Menneval whistled. "But you're not a betting

man, old-timer. Well, I take it that the kid made an impression on you. Do you want to cut across country with me and have a look at that wolf hunt? There's going to be a moon up before long. There's the hair of it blowing up in the east, I guess."

"Man," said the trapper, "if you ain't a fool, you'll keep far away from that hunt."

"They've turned," said Menneval suddenly. "The pack has the view again, or else it can hear the noise of the horses running . . . if mounted men are what they're chasing."

"An elk, that's what it is," suggested the trapper with a shudder.

"Elk? Wolves never sang like that for an elk, my son. Not even in the middle of a starvation winter."

"You know the beasts pretty good, I guess," said Ranger.

"I ought to. I've been out in the winter dark, Ranger, with nothing better than those singers and dancers to amuse me for six months at a time." He pointed. "Let's climb over that hill, Ranger. We ought to have a chance to see some of the fun. And here's the moon for a lantern, eh?"

"I wouldn't go there for a thousand dollars," said the other.

"Then I'll go on alone, and let you keep the thousand dollars, Ranger," said Menneval.

"Unless you're afraid to stay here alone in the dark?"

He laughed as he said that, an ugly ring in his voice, and suddenly Ranger said loudly: "I am afraid to stay alone. I'll go on with you, only I've told you beforehand that you've no sense to go near to the boy and his pack. But if you're climbing the hill, I'll do it with you."

This he did, and, as they went up the slope, the trapper under his pack and the other erect in the saddle, the moon came up over the eastern mountains, shining through the trees and lifting into the steel-blue heavens. There it hung, glowing and floating with a golden face.

They climbed the hills. From the farther shoulder of it, they looked down into a very shallow little valley that had the appearance of a dump yard and unimproved backgrounds of the world, for it was scattered over with trees, big and small, and ragged patches of brush, and great boulders were strewn among the trees, some of them as lofty as the tallest tops.

The pale moonshine did not help to give a sense of order to that scene, and Bill Ranger began to rub his chin with his knuckles. "It looks kind of funny to me," he said, "jumbled and all together. I'd rather get out of here, Menneval."

"Listen," said Menneval. He raised his hand, and out of the distance they heard the cry of the pack again. "They're running in sight

215

again. They've got their view," he said with an odd content in his voice. "I'm not taking that thousand-dollar bet that you offered, though. When a boy can teach wolves to hunt men like that, it proves that there's something in the boy. And men they've certainly got before 'em. D'you hear the hate and the fear in their throats, Lefty?"

"Hear the hate and the fear?" said the trapper, looking wildly at his companion. "Man, are you another one that can talk the wolf talk?"

"Stuff and nonsense," said the other. He laughed as he spoke and stepped farther out on the shoulder of the hill. He had dismounted. He took off his hat and passed his hand over his hair, which flashed like silver in the moonshine. "This is a man's country, Ranger," he said. "This is the sort of place that a man could spend his life in."

"I'd about made up my mind to live the rest of mine here," said Ranger, "but the kid, he put a chill into me. He scared me pretty near to death."

"You didn't like the kid," said the other. "He seems to have bothered you a good deal."

"I liked him," said the trapper honestly. "I wouldn't be able to say that I didn't like him. He has a sort of pull on you. You can't help being interested. You might know how it is?"

"I don't," said the other shortly. "Nobody's ever had a pull on me. You like the kid because he's just a fool, or because he's a dangerous fool? Which is it?"

"I dunno," answered Ranger, thinking the matter over. "I guess it's because I think that he'll have a mighty short life, Menneval."

"So you're sorry for him, are you? And scared of him, too? Well, it won't make much difference to the rest of the world, a couple of Crossons more or less. They've lived out here like wild beasts . . . and with wild beasts. Let 'em die like beasts, too, and be buried and forgotten." A sort of scornful rage was in his voice.

"I wouldn't say that . . . only they beat me. I don't want to think of 'em any more. I don't want to talk about 'em," said Ranger. "Listen to that!" he added with an exclamation.

As he spoke, the sound of the pack burst out between two hills at the lower end of the valley and, with a river of sound, it filled the depression and sent waves of horror shuddering through the brain of the trapper.

A moment later, through the scattering boulders came three riders, pushing their horses with the most desperate haste. They rode as well as they could through the scattering rocks, and, as they fled, the rearmost man twitched around in the saddle and fired once, twice, and again.

Perhaps he hit his target. At any rate, the shooting brought him still farther to the rear of the other flying riders, and now he thrust the rifle back into its long case and gave all his attention to weaving the horse among the impedimenta that thronged the floor of the valley.

In the lead, two of these riders, side-by-side, pushed forward, either better mounted or lighter in the saddle than their lagging companion. As these two passed into a dense tangle of trees and of rocks and were lost to sight for a moment, Menneval touched the arm of the trapper without, however, turning his head toward him.

"Ranger," he said.

"Aye?"

"Wasn't that one on the left a girl? Didn't I see the flutter of a divided skirt, or was it simply the chaps? Was that a girl or an undersize boy? Did you see the one I mean?"

"A girl," said the trapper. "That was a girl, of course. That was a cousin or something of the thug, Chester Lyons. Her name is Nan."

# CHAPTER TWENTY-SEVEN

"How many men were with Chet Lyons?" snapped Menneval.

"There was the girl, and four more men."

"What sort? Soft saps, or real men?"

"The hardest you've ever seen," replied the trapper.

At this moment, through a gap in the bush and the boulders, the same gap through which they had seen the riders first appear, they now saw a pack of five wolves break into the clearing, and behind them, fast on their heels, came a rider. They could not tell the color of the horse, only the silver flashing of the streaming mane and tail in the wind of the gallop.

"Dogs . . . and one man to chase Chet Lyons and four of his best?" said Menneval half to himself. "It isn't likely. It isn't possible. But there it is before our eyes."

He took the spectacle more calmly than did Lefty Bill, although the latter had seen an almost similar picture once before.

"It isn't possible," said Ranger, "but there it is. He isn't a man. He's half wild cat, like I said before. And half wolf. And the rest of him, I dunno what it is."

Striking a hard upslope, the rider was seen to

throw himself to the ground. The horse, relieved of that weight, ran on easily, or trotted, while the lad bounded beside him, sprinting like the wind, only sometimes catching hold of a dangling stirrup leather to help him over a smoother spot where the horse ran with more ease. But he continued on foot at such a rate that the rearmost man of Lyon's party was drawn back to the pursuer. Rapidly, almost as though his horse were carrying a double burden, he was pulled behind, and the pursuer came up, hand over hand.

"A fine thing," said Menneval with an unexpected enthusiasm. "I never saw a better thing in my life. He's saving his nag for the level going, and running like an Indian in between. Why, a fellow like that could run down a relay of race horses in twenty-four hours. He's made of rubber and watch springs. Look at that!"

Coming to a rougher patch of small rocks and brush, the lad sprang here and there and, like a rabbit, came onto the easier footing beyond, where, without stopping the horse, he flung himself into the saddle and went on at a rapid gallop.

By this time, the two leaders—Lyons and the girl—had swept on into the shelter of the higher woods, and the trailer behind them was still in plain view. As the pursuer came nearer, this man turned and looked behind him.

"One left out of four," said Menneval under

his breath. "How's it done? How can he do it?"

"You'll see, pretty *pronto*," suggested Ranger. He breathed hard and sighed. "It ain't human," he commented through his teeth.

He who was being hunted now checked his horse to a walk and turned. And the moonlight threw a long beam along the barrel of the rifle as it was leveled.

Then, clearly up the slope, came the voice of a man yelling for help.

"He's too late . . . they'll never come back to him. They don't know how far he is behind," said Menneval.

"They don't care," said the trapper. "They've seen the evil one, and they don't want to feel his teeth."

The shout was repeated. As if in answer to it, out from among the rocks sprang a volley of the wolves; their master had disappeared behind the same screen. They did not come in a single, headlong charge. They had first encircled the rider, and now they rushed him from all sides.

He was not witless with fear, though he had been shouting for help the moment before. He fired, and the watchers saw one of the wolves bound into the air, double up, and land in a shapeless heap even before the death yell rang in the ears of the two up the slope.

"Come on," said Ranger. "Come on and help. They'll murder him."

"He'd be dead before we got there," said Menneval sternly.

He laid a hand upon the shoulder of his companion. It was only a touch, but the effect of it ran like liquid ice through the blood of Ranger. It was true. They had not time to intervene. They might have opened fire on the brutes, by daylight, but in this treacherous moonshine their rifles were as likely to strike down the man at bay as to drop his enemies.

The next instant the wolves were in and at their work. The horse reared, then went down, hamstrung by deadly teeth from behind, and, as it went down, another timber wolf was at its throat, slashing.

"They'll tear him to pieces before our eyes . . . they've torn the other three," groaned Ranger, turning sick.

A keen, piercing whistle rang up the side of the valley. And into sight came young Oliver Crosson. It was too dim a light to enable Ranger to recognize the features of the boy, but there was something unmistakable in his carriage and in his step. He was on foot, the horse from which he had dismounted, again trotting dog-like at his back. In his hand was the gleam of the revolver, like a spark of fire.

The whistle, which must have come from his lips, scattered the wolves at the very moment when the horse fell, and the rider rolled on the ground, almost among their teeth. They bounded back as though from a grizzly bear, fallen, but doubly dangerous in his fall.

The youngster ran straight in on the fallen man.

"He's going to pistol him where he lies," said Menneval through his teeth.

"He won't do that," said Ranger. But he doubted, even as he spoke, for he saw young Crosson lean over the prostrate body. In another moment he was up and away again, springing into the saddle on the horse, and the four wolves cantered easily ahead. All the troop disappeared in another moment among the trees.

"He's gone," said Menneval. "He's knocked that poor devil on the head in cold blood, and he's gone. What has happened tonight? Is that the fourth man he's murdered because a wolf was killed? An infernal stealing, throat-cutting timber wolf?"

"Not a wolf to him," said Ranger, in instinctive defense, although he was shaking from head to foot. "Not a wolf, but more like a friend would be to you . . ." He checked himself. Had this man ever had a friend? Tradition and rumor said that he had not.

Menneval was already hurrying down the slope.

And he was right. For perhaps it still was not too late for them to render some aid to the fallen man.

Among the rocks they raced down into the

hollow. When they came there, Ranger was greatly relieved. He had not known how much he was horrified until he had the relief of seeing the fallen stranger stagger to his feet. They were beside him instantly, and found him looking about in a dazed way at his dead horse. He was trembling violently; his eyes were forced so wide open and the pupil so dilated, he had the look of a madman.

"Take a jolt of this," said Menneval, and gave him a metal flask. But the hand of the other was too unsteady. Menneval himself had to hold and tip the bottle, while Ranger studied the stranger. Of course, this was one of the men who had ridden with the outlaw, Lyons, but he was unrecognizable, now, his face was so distorted by the aftereffects of a great terror.

With the whiskey under his belt, he recovered rapidly. Menneval got him to sit on a stone, furnished him with another drink, even rolled a cigarette and lighted it for him. He seemed to Ranger to be ministering like a doctor to the needs of a patient in whom he had no great personal interest, but who might prove a useful man.

"What's happened?" he asked finally.

The other rolled back his head and stared up at Menneval.

"What's happened?" he repeated. "I've been

through . . . Oh, I've been . . ." His voice had risen to a half-hysterical note.

"Take it easy," said Menneval. "There's plenty of time. There's all the time in the world for you. Steady up, now, and make yourself at home. You're with friends. Nothing can happen to you, now."

"He didn't want me," said the other. "I says to myself that it's for me that he's hunting the whole pack of us. But it wasn't me. You see that he tripped me up, and then went on. I thought that I was going to be wolf food for the . . ." His voice shuddered away to a silence.

"It's Lyons that he's after," said Menneval. "There's no doubt of that. It's Lyons that he wants, and not you. Now, tell me, if you can, how five men and a woman ran away from a single hunter and a pack of wolves?"

The other passed a hand over his face. He shook his head violently—like a dog trying to clear water from its hair.

"We were up in the hills when we heard the wolf song beginning," he said. "We knew something about young Crosson. We were ready for trouble all right. Lyons was laughing. He said that we'd pick up a few lobo scalps, and give the boy a spanking to teach him sense. But going through the dusk with the yell of the pack behind us was kind of hard on the nerves.

"Then, all at once, the baying stopped off short.

We didn't hear a thing . . . Lyons said they'd turned back . . . but some of the rest of us figured that trouble was sneaking up on us. We were going up a pretty narrow ravine and Pug Morris was riding last when I heard a screech out of him, and looked back and saw a shadow run at him on horseback out of the trees and knock Pug off his horse. The mustang went swift out of that and up the side of the ravine, and Pug went after it, yelling. I emptied a six-shooter at the shadow, but it was gone again into the brush.

"Well, we went on. Even Lyons had stopped joking. He got us together and told us to look sharp, but the next place where the trail narrowed and pinched out, that shadow and half a dozen wolves swarmed out and took Bunny Statham off the tail of our march. Lyons turned us around, and we charged. But the wolves and the shadow had gone out, and Statham was away off through the brush . . . hiding out, I guess, or dead with his throat tore open. I don't know which.

"After that, we kind of lost our nerve. The moon was up. A sneaky kind of a light for us, but good enough for young Crosson and his pack. Lyons wanted to stay in one place and fight it out, but me and Wully, we held out for a quick run to get to the town of Shannon, where we'd have some humans around us and no werewolves. Lyons had to buckle in. I guess he was feeling kind of sick himself. So we hit across country. And that sneaking ghost and his dogs, he picked off Wully first, and then he got me here and . . ." He stopped with a groan and covered his eyes with his hands.

# CHAPTER TWENTY-EIGHT

"You come with me to Shannon," said Menneval.

But the other stared at him as though he were a madman. "Go to Shannon?" he said. "Why, that's where Lyons has gone, and that's where the kid will be hunting him. I'm not going north to Shannon. I'm going south to any place that comes along. Wherever Lyons goes, I'm gonna be the farthest possible away from him. If you go to Shannon, you're a fool."

"I'm going to Shannon," said Menneval. "You want to come with me, Ranger?"

Lefty Bill looked yearningly at the rascal who had so frankly declared his fear. He would have liked to make the same decision. For there was no place in the world where he so little wished to be as in the town of Shannon, or wherever Lyons and young Crosson were to meet. But as he saw the steady, keen eye of Menneval, he knew that he would yield and that he'd go.

He said: "You know that there's going to be a grand lot of trouble, Menneval . . . and you know that I'm not very much with a gun. I'm no hero, either. I don't pretend to be."

"Let me tell you something," insisted Menneval. "I'm going to Shannon not to take part in the trouble that may come up there. I'm going to try to prevent that trouble from breaking, if I can. I'm going to try. And an honest man like you can do more than anybody else to prevent a fight. I see in your eye that you're coming along with me, Lefty."

And Lefty, with a sigh, was forced to nod his head.

They left the broken-spirited gangster behind them and started across country. Menneval would not ride. He forced Lefty to take the saddle, and Menneval himself walked on at a brisk pace. One would not have expected such endurance and such lightness in a man deep into middle age. Uphill and down, over rough and smooth, he led the way by the shortest cut to Shannon, and in the middle of the night they reached the town.

They came out from the verge of the great pine forest and looked down on the town. Most of the lights were out; there was only a red glimmer of lamplight, here and there, a mere stain on a window, seen through the brilliancy of the mountain moonlight that, almost like a sun, cast deep black shadows beside the rocks and printed on the open ground the silhouette of the huge trees.

It was a wild little valley in which Shannon stood, and the people who lived in it were as wild as their surroundings. Not only on the upper Shannon, but on half a dozen of the creeks that flowed into it, gold had been found. They were not great and rich strikes, but there was enough color to bring the enthusiastic prospectors out of the desert to the south, out of the mountains to the north, to try to find the mother lode. And there were always a number of claims working, yielding usually a little less gold dust than the cost of working. However, gold is not only money, but an enchantment and an enchanter. And a good many of the bewitched were generally to be found in Shannon.

Shannon Creek itself went with a bound and a roar through the center of the town in the season of the melting snows. In full summer it was a mere pleasant trickle. In winter its headwaters were locked in white frost, and not a drop came down its channel. It was at a midway point now, and, instead of filling the valley with the ominous roar of the flood waters, its voice dwelt in the air like an echo from some undiscoverable source.

Ranger looked down on the little, shapeless, ragged town that lined both sides of the creek, and he could see the shadowy skeleton of the bridge that crossed it.

"Look here, Menneval," he said. "I'd like to know what you're really up to."

"In coming here?" said Menneval.

"Aye."

"I'm coming here to prevent trouble. I told you that before."

"Menneval," said the trapper, "I don't call any

man a liar, but you haven't been famous for stopping fights before this. Mostly they kind of say that you've given them a boost along."

"Do they?" The other smiled. "Well, whatever they say, I've told you the Gospel truth. I've come in here to keep young Crosson from running amuck, if I can."

"They're friends of yours, are they?"

"Well, I'll tell you," said Menneval. "I'm under an obligation to old Peter Crosson, such an obligation as mighty few men ever have been under. And he's under an obligation to me . . . such an obligation as mighty few men ever have been under. And that's the reason why I say that I'm going to stop young Crosson from making trouble, if I can."

The trapper looked oddly at him. "Menneval," he said, "maybe it ain't my business . . ."

"It is your business," said Menneval. "It's your business because you've come here and taken the trouble on your shoulders."

"Then I've gotta say, it seems to me you're holding something back."

"I am," admitted the other. "I'm holding a lot back, and what I'm holding back nobody in the world, but two, knows about . . . and nobody more ever will know, if I can keep it from 'em. Now, will you stop asking questions, and go down into the town with me, to take potluck?"

"I'll do it," agreed the other. He dismounted.

They walked down the last steep slope into the town, side-by-side. They saw the small house grow out of the distance into a larger size. Cows rose out of the slanting, dewy pastures and shook their heads at the interlopers. A young colt jumped up beside its mother and went off with a snort and a squeal.

"Seems kind of peaceful," said Ranger.

The other replied: "Why, Lefty, don't you know that this is a sort of a mining camp?"

"Oh," said Ranger. "That's what it is, eh? Well, that listens a lot more like it, just now."

As though just issuing through a doorway, a song exploded upon the open air of the night, a song already in the middle, and sung powerfully by half a dozen voices. The mere melody was not enough for them. They added variations and flourishes, largely in the form of tremendous whoops.

"Yeah, it sounds like a gold town, all right," said Lefty Bill. "And that sounds like an easy place for a fight to happen."

"It won't, though," insisted Menneval. "Ranger, I'm going to count on you. I'm going to lean on you in every way I can. You'll have six thousand of my money for doing the first part of your job."

"I only did half the job," said Ranger. "I didn't go back to Alaska."

"We don't split hairs when you work for me," answered Menneval. "You get that six thousand,

and another thing . . . if the fight doesn't take place here between Lyons and young Crosson . . . I'll tell you what I'll do. I'll round out the six and make it a full ten thousand. Does that sound to you?"

"Sound to me?" cried Ranger, and his voice was alive with anticipatory joy. "I'll tell you what it sounds like to me . . . it sounds like a bit of grazing ground, and some cattle on it, and a shack to live in, and a pair of horses to fork, and me able to sit on my doorstep and thumb my nose at the world as it goes down the road. That's what it sounds like to me."

"You'd be willing to work hard and take a chance at that?"

"I'd be willing to die, friend," said the other with emotion. "Yes, willing to die."

Menneval held out his hand. They shook. And then Menneval said such a thing as no other human ever had heard from his lips: "Lefty, will you tell me how I feel?"

"You feel pretty good, I guess," said Ranger. "You mostly do, they say."

"Lefty, I'll tell you the truth. I'm scared cold. I've got to go on with this business, but I'm covered with an inch of white frost. I'm a lump of ice. There's no heart in me."

Ranger gaped at him. Suddenly his mind flashed back to the great white North and the tales of this man who traveled among the mining camps, the snow-besieged towns, and went flickering like fire along the obscure trails. They had attributed all manner of evil to him. They looked upon him as something inevitable, something poisonous. It was no disgrace to flee from Menneval, for the simple reason that they said Menneval would as soon live as die. But other men wanted only to live.

Ranger halted. The horse stopped behind him, with a grunt. Menneval also paused and turned toward his companion.

"Up in Dawson, once," said Ranger, "there was a fire, and a three-story building went up. While it was burning, a dog ran out on the roof, a no-good little fool of a house pet, and stood there crying and yapping. And you bet five dollars that a man you hated in that watching crowd wouldn't bring the dog down, and that you would. Is that right?"

"I was a fool in those days," said Menneval carelessly. "I remember something about that."

"And you climbed up the side of that house when the wall was rotten with fire, and you got hold of the puppy and brought it back, all for five dollars."

"Not for five dollars, but to make Jim Torry feel a little sick."

"You did that, for five dollars. You did a lot of other things. The boys talk about the things you did. They talk about 'em while they sit around in the evening, before turning in, while they're drinking tea. But now you say that you're scared?"

"I am. I'm icy. I said so before."

"Is it young Crosson that you're scared of?"

Menneval hesitated. "Old-timer," he said finally, "I hate questions . . . I hate to ask, and I hate to answer 'em. But I'll tell you that it's on account of young Crosson that I'm scared. Down here in Shannon is going to be the showdown. That is the place where he'll be made or broken. He's come out of the wilderness. When he first meets with other men, there's likely to be an explosion. And I tell you what I want you to do."

"Go on," said the other uneasily.

"I want you to be the damper that keeps the fuse from burning down to the powder. I want you to help keep that explosion from happening. You understand?"

The trapper sighed. "Well," he said, "I'd rather try to handle a full-grown lion. But I'll try what I can. Maybe he's not here in Shannon, after all."

"Not here? Tut, tut," Menneval said carelessly. "He'd follow Lyons around the world, and through the world, but Lyons he'll eventually find in the end . . . and then God help him unless he's stopped from murder."

# CHAPTER TWENTY-NINE

When Bill Ranger got into his bed at the hotel, he balanced two great ideas in his mind. One was the thought of $10,000, and the other was the thought of young Crosson. Between the two he felt that he would never be able to close his eyes, but, as a matter of fact, the fatigue of the strangest day in his life crushed him instantly under a great burden of sleep.

A flare of sun striking from the east through his window wakened him. He got up, took a sponge bath with icy water, shaved, dressed, and went downstairs. He wanted to be a little careful of his appearance while he was in town. In the wilderness, of course, it did not matter, but he was away from the wilderness now. A town of so much as five houses was enough to make him feel more than a little self-conscious. The roughness of his boots, the ragged, patched state of his clothes disturbed him, and he hoped that there were few critical feminine eyes in this town to fall upon him. He blushed at the very prospect.

When he got to the dining room, he was relieved to find that it was already pretty well filled. People who breakfasted at this early hour could not very well be more civilized than he was himself. And it was a great pleasure to see that the serving of his guests was in the hands of a Negro and a Chinaman. No women—there was not a woman in the room.

He managed, also, to get into a chair at a corner of the long table, where he would have his back to the wall and from which he could keep an eye upon the door through which guests entered. There were plenty of reasons for such vigilance. For one thing, Menneval himself might be coming in at any moment. For another, Lyons might appear, if it were true that he had come to Shannon for refuge from the wild man who had hunted him across the mountains. It was true that Lyons was an outlaw, but the law had not reached as far as this little mountain town. Men took care of themselves in this part of the world.

There was not much talk for some time after he entered. There had been a rattle of voices as he came in, and, following this, there was a general pause during which men frowned at their plates and looked askance at him, when they were sure they would not be noticed. People kept their eyes to themselves. A man was supposed to deserve a certain sanctity of privacy until it was proved that he was beneath such consideration.

Ranger knew what that pause meant. He was being sized up by the others, his outfit and general looks and manner considered, and, according to their approval or disapproval, they would open up general conversation once more or, else, the talk would change to quite private mutterings, here and there, barely audible even to the persons who were addressed.

For his own part, he apparently paid no attention to anything but his food. But when he lifted his eyes in reaching for the platter of cornbread, or, when he stretched his hand for the sugar bowl, he allowed his glance to whip rapidly over the faces along the table.

They were such men as live on every frontier. They were the frontier. He had seen the same faces in Canadian lumber camps, far north, in the Alaskan wilderness, in the mountain camps of the mines. And here they were again. He had expected exactly this. He could have sighed with relief to find that he was not mistaken. There might be more cultivated and finer people in the world, but Ranger was used to this type of humanity and he preferred it, just as the rancher can eat bacon and eggs three hundred and sixty-five mornings in the year, or the Scotsman is never dismayed by the appearance of a large bowl of oatmeal porridge.

In this case, the preliminary survey to which he was subjected did not last long. A little down-faced man, whose jowls bulged with what looked like fat but what was really muscle, remarked that it looked like a good day, and he responded that he thought it was and that he was up in Shannon "to look around a little."

"With a hammer?" said the little man, grinning.

"Yeah, I might chip a rock or two," Ranger said frankly.

This turned loose the flood of conversation at once. They accepted Ranger as one of themselves.

"You were saying that old Lyons had come to town," said one of the men.

The man addressed was a red-shirted individual, his entire face blackened and swollen with beard, so that he looked like a man in a mask. He was big. His chest arched out before him. He had the look of a draft horse among men.

"Lyons is here. He's in this hotel," he said.

"Come on!" said one. "Lyons wouldn't be coming into a town. Not where there's so many guns."

"All right," said Red Shirt. "I seen him. That's all I've got to say."

"Hold on! You seen him?"

"I seen him. What's more, the girl was with him."

"What girl?"

"The girl that came out here to see Lyons. The girl that come all the way out from the East."

"I've heard about her. Is Lyons vacationing her up here in Shannon? Showing her the sights?"

"Now," said Red Shirt, "I ain't one to gossip, but him and the girl didn't arrive like they wanted to see sights . . . they arrived like they'd seen plenty. They was both plastered with mud and dust. They had a look like they'd been through a mud storm and a sandstorm. They was all wore down."

"What could've wore down Lyons? He ain't the kind to wear down. Not even on a grindstone."

"I'm telling you what I seen. You can make up your own minds."

"Go on."

"There ain't anything to go on about. They got rooms. I was in late, and sat still in the corner of the room and didn't peep. I seen that something was up."

"They say the girl is a beauty."

"She's all gold and blue, all right," said Red Shirt, "and don't you make no mistake. After they got signed in for their rooms and went upstairs, I saunter over to the stable and look things over. There's two horses in there that've been rubbed down and blanketed, but the work they done had started them sweating again. Their knees were trembling. They stood in their stalls with their heads hanging. Not even the barley in the grain boxes could get their eye. They was done in, the two of 'em. And Lyons, he must've been done in, too, or he would've showed up for breakfast before this time of the day."

"Shut up," whispered one of the men.

At this, Ranger looked up toward the door, and in it he saw Nan Lyons standing and her cousin behind her. They paused in the entrance to the room for a moment, and then they came in slowly. Lyons stepped in front of the girl and said to the Chinese waiter: "Sam, put a pair of plates on that little table in the corner, will you? And be lively, boy. Ham and eggs for two. Put three eggs on my plate, and brown them on both sides. You can bring a pot of coffee before the rest of the breakfast."

Sam was not well trained in the ways of the world, but he knew enough to bow to this superior being until his pigtail flew up over his shoulder. Then he hurried to fill the order. In the meantime, there was not an eye lifted from the main table to scrutinize the two newcomers closely.

A second later, Menneval entered the room and sat down beside Ranger.

# CHAPTER THIRTY

Menneval was hardly seated before Lyons got up from the corner table and approached the big one. He paused before Ranger as he nodded to Menneval.

"Will you two gentlemen finish your breakfast at my table?" he asked.

Menneval stood up at once. "Come along, Lefty," he said. "Bring your things. I'll carry your coffee for you. Very glad to sit with you, Lyons."

As they were going across the room, Ranger could feel the sudden outpouring of silent curiosity behind him. There was even a faint rustling, as those whose backs were turned, twisted about to stare. What were the thoughts of the men of Shannon? Why, something was about to happen, to be sure. The arrival of Lyons was enough to fill even a hardy town like Shannon with rumors and murmurs. The coming of the girl with him was sufficient to brim the cup of gossip. But, in addition, Menneval was there. They could not be expected to know who Menneval was, but he had with him the air of a man of consequence. In a crowd of ten thousand, even a child would have been able to pick out Menneval.

They reached the table.

"Nan," said Lyons, "this is a man I've talked

to you about. This is Menneval. You've seen his friend before."

Nan stood up and shook hands with Menneval. Then with Ranger. She had a curiously direct way of meeting a glance. And Ranger noted that she bore with her no real signs of fatigue. Her color was fresh, her eye was as clear as the evening sky. But Lyons looked decidedly worn. There were shadows beneath his eyes and an uneasiness about their shifting expression.

They sat down together.

Lyons rested his knuckles on the edge of the table. He looked straight at Menneval.

"Ten years, Menneval," he said.

"Ten years," said Menneval. "I'm surprised that you knew me, since that . . ." He stopped.

"Since that little Wells, Fargo business, eh?" said Lyons. "You can talk right out before Nan. I've told her everything. And she has come all the way out here to save my soul." He smiled a twisted smile. "Does your friend, Ranger, know as much about you?" he asked.

"Ranger," said Menneval quietly, "knows more than that. He knows everything that's said in Alaska about me. And they talk in Alaska. When an evening lasts six months, there's need for something to talk about."

He smiled faintly and, like Lyons, there was a twist of his mouth that suggested that the mirth was only lip-deep.

"Now, then," said Lyons, "suppose that I cut down to business."

"Do that," said Menneval. "Though this isn't a business trip, with me."

Lyons looked fixedly at him for a moment. "We're being honest?" he said.

"I am," said Menneval.

"I saw Ranger with the Crossons," said Lyons. "Do you know the Crosson tribe?"

"Yes."

"I half thought that you did. There's a strange thing in the air, Menneval, and, when I saw you here, I couldn't help connecting you with it."

Again Menneval smiled a little.

"Just what do you know about the Crossons?" asked Lyons.

"Crosson was an old schoolteacher. I met him a long time ago. The boy seems to be a different cut. I don't know much about him."

This answer from Menneval caused Lyons to frown a little. "Menneval," he said, "I'll tell you a strange thing. Last night I had four good men with me. The sort of men that even you would approve of. We were hunted across the open country by a boy and a wolf pack. The boy was Crosson. The wolves were his pack. He cut off my men, one after another. When I tried to get at him, he melted away into the brush or among the rocks. Finally I couldn't take any more chances. I had Nan with me. I had to get her to shelter. I brought her here. Now I want to find out about young Crosson. If he's a madman, I'm through with him. I go on. If he's sane, I'll make him pay for the three men of mine he murdered."

This brief tale caused not the slightest change in Menneval's expression. He simply said: "Crosson didn't kill your men. He merely cut them off from you. And what he did to them . . . well, I don't think they'll ever ride with you again . . . not if they know that the boy is on your trail."

"You say that he killed none of them," said Lyons. "How do you know that?"

"Because I saw the last one of the four."

"You saw Eddie Hare?"

"That may be his name. His nerve was gone when the boy was through with him. That's all I know. But not a tooth or a bullet or a knife had touched him."

Lyons closed both eyes tight. "It's not possible," he murmured.

"Cousin Chester," said the girl, "don't you think you've talked enough about it?"

"She's afraid that I'm weakening," said Lyons bitterly. "Perhaps I am. But I've never been driven before. Last night I was hunted like a rat. Today is a new day. Menneval, tell me more."

Menneval looked down at his plate. Food had come. No one had touched it. "Ranger," said Menneval, "finish your breakfast. Then take Nan

245

Lyons for a walk. I have to talk to Lyons alone for a while."

Not one more word was spoken among them. Menneval and Lyons, lost in thoughts, ate like people in a dream, hardly knowing what they did. Ranger, as he watched them with side glances, felt, for all that Lyons had gone through, that it was Menneval who seemed to be affected by the greatest emotion. Now and then his lips would compress and a sudden frown darken his forehead. It even appeared to Ranger that the very color of his employer altered from moment to moment.

All of these things were incredible, for Menneval was a man of iron and famous for his lack of nerves from Dawson to the sea. But there he sat, as obviously uneasy as a child confronting its first day at school.

Ranger finished his breakfast hastily but, quick though he was, the girl was through before him.

"Be back in an hour," said Menneval to Ranger.

And the latter went out with the girl.

They went into the good, warm sunshine. The brightness of it dazzled him. The warmth of it relaxed his taut muscles, his taut brain. The girl took off her soft felt hat and swung it in her hand, so that the brightness of the morning flashed on the golden tints of her hair and her unshaded eyes were as blue as blue water. Ranger would have been glad if she had kept that hat on her head. He told her so in another moment.

"You're worrying a lot about something, Mister Ranger," she said.

"It's about your bare head," he said.

"I won't catch cold," she assured him.

"It ain't you," said Ranger, "but somebody else is going to get a terrible chill."

"What do you mean by that?"

He looked askance at her and then up the long, crooked street. It followed the snaky contortions of the creek. "Well," he said, "there's all of Shannon up and awake, right now, and getting out into the street. And along you come. Mind you, there likely aren't more than about three women and a half here in Shannon. It has the look of a man-made town . . . kind of dusty and ragged, you see? And along you come, and . . . and . . ."

He looked down to her, and found her studying him with a faint, grave smile. Her eyes were as clean as a wind-swept sky; she was as simple and direct as any young boy.

"Well?" she prodded.

"Nan," said Ranger, "ma'am, I mean to say . . ."

"Nan is the right name," she said. "Go on, Lefty."

He thanked her with a grin. Suddenly he was at ease. "Your hair will be gold enough and your eye will be blue enough even under the

247

shadow of a hat brim, Nan. Don't you reckon?"

She put on her hat again without a word. Then she made a gesture that included the dancing light on the waters of the creek, the dark and shaggy forest beyond, the hills, the ragged mountains, the houses up and down the street.

"People are all right, out here," she said. "The men are all right. They make me feel at home. They're not like . . ." She stopped at a point difficult of explanation.

"Sure they're all right," Ranger broke in hastily. "They're too much all right."

"Why do you say that?"

"Well," he explained, "it's like this. Suppose that you take a young chap that's said good bye to his folks three, four years ago and since then hasn't shook hands with anything friendlier than a pick handle or a red-hot forty-foot rope . . . and his Sunday-school time, it's spent in washing the shirt that he wore all week, or playing poker with a greasy pack, or riding on a half-broke mustang forty miles to get a newspaper . . . suppose you take a young chap like that, he's just a stick of dynamite with a lightning cap. And the kind of lightning that sets him off is the golden kind, Nan. You follow my drift?"

"Not quite," she said, frowning.

"I say," said Ranger, "that these young fellers can fall in love quicker and easier than they can fall out of their saddles, and, when they fall, they hit harder and make more noise and trouble than big guns. They'll trail a girl across five states and set down on her pa's front doorstep and scare all the nice boys away. They'll go mooning and bawling around her like a calf around its ma, when there's a fence in between. You've got the lightning of gold that slides into their brain quicker than moonshine, and easier. That's why I say . . . keep your hat on your head."

She settled it more firmly. "Not that I believe a word you say," she said. "But . . ."

He lost the last of her words, for just then a wild procession dashed past them up the street, whooping, yelling, swinging hats.

# CHAPTER THIRTY-ONE

They were in front of the blacksmith shop just then, and the blacksmith came hurrying into the open double doorway, tongs in one hand and a short-handled eight-pound hammer in the other. Not all of yesterday's soot had been washed from his face or from his hairy forearms, the tan intensifying rather than diminishing his reddish complexion.

"There goes Winnie Dale," the blacksmith said. "Oh, Winnie, you're gonna raise a big wind someday that'll blow all your boys to perdition and yourself after them!"

There were five men in the procession, which went by in single file, not because that was the natural order but because each man was wringing from his mount all the speed that could be got out of it by whip and spur. At the head of the line, a good distance before the rest, flew a tall youngster whose bandanna fanned out behind his neck and snapped like a flag from a flagstaff. He rode with a very long stirrup. He seemed to be standing, rather than sitting, and the size of him made the horse seem small.

"He can fork a horse," said Ranger.

"He can fork a horse all right, and he can break a man," said the blacksmith. "There he goes back

250

to the cattle ranch to play around and pretend that he's working for another couple of months, and then he'll roll back into Shannon and blast us loose."

"Hold on," said Ranger. "He's found something to play with up there."

Winnie Dale had disappeared around the next corner of the street, and now he reappeared, riding in a circle, swinging his hat, sending out piercing Indian yells. One half of his revolution continually carried him out of view.

"Yeah, he's got some trouble on hand," said the blacksmith, grinning and yet shaking his head. He added: "Come along and we'll see what it is. A greaser, most likely."

"No," said Ranger. "I'm not going where there's trouble."

The blacksmith saw the girl for the first time, and his mouth opened for an instant before he continued. "No," he agreed. "You've got trouble enough on your hands, I guess." And with this, he hurried up off the street with great strides.

The girl started after him.

"Don't you go there," said Ranger. "Don't you go up there. The crowd's gathering. Don't you go up there. You stay here with me." He caught her arm. It was round, firm, almost hard with muscle. She made no effort to pull free.

She simply said: "I intend to go, Lefty. Don't you try to keep me here."

"Well," he answered, breaking into a sweat, "I don't like it, Nan. But I ain't your father, nor your cousin, neither. If you have to go, you have to go."

They hurried up the street together. Ahead, at the corner, they could still see half the circle that the riders made, for the followers of Winnie Dale had strung out in a line behind him, and every man was swinging a rope and yelling like a fiend in imitation of his employer and master.

"A greaser," said Ranger.

"They've likely got a greaser or a poor Chinaman who is two-thirds scared to death."

The girl said nothing. Head up, stepping with a good, free swing, she set a pace that made her companion stretch his legs. When they reached the corner, where the dust was flying up under the hoofs of the circling horses, a small crowd was already gathered on the fringe of the circle, and that crowd was growing as fast as running feet could bring more of the curious.

Loudly they laughed; still more loudly arose the yelling of the riders, and then through the dust Ranger had a glimpse of the new victim with whom Winnie Dale was toying. It was neither a Mexican nor a Chinaman, but a young Indian, in appearance, with long, black hair sweeping below the shoulders and held away from the face by a headband. He stood with folded arms and behind him was a cream-colored horse.

The color of the horse opened the eyes of Ranger to guess the truth, and a moment later, through a rift in the dust cloud, he saw clearly.

The girl saw at the same instant. She caught the arm of Ranger. "It's Oliver Crosson," she said.

"Yes, it is." Ranger nodded. "Now the mischief will be to pay. Why in heaven's name did Winnie Dale have to pick out that dynamite bomb?"

"He's not even on his horse," said the girl. "Why doesn't he get on his horse? He might break through them, then." Then she added, fiercely: "But I hope he doesn't. I hope that they rope him and drag him through the street. What else does he deserve?"

The flinging nooses of the ropes, now and then, darted out from the hands of the riders and threatened to catch over the head and shoulders of Crosson, but he would not stir. He kept his eyes seemingly straight to the front, his arms remained folded, and one might have thought that he was unaware of all the turmoil and the dust clouds sweeping around him.

It was not strange that they had picked him out for their game. He looked as wild a human as ever came out of a wilderness of forest or desert. His home-made clothes of deerskin, patched and ragged, his long, sweeping hair, his sun-blackened skin, and, above all, something untamed in his face and his whole bearing made him an outlander in a whole crowd of outlanders.

He was a freak among freaks. And Winnie Dale had taken him up for sport.

What would happen? The boy carried a revolver and a knife, as Ranger knew, and, at the first hostile gesture, either the one or the other might come into play. If there was such a gesture made, who could doubt that the young blades with Dale would instantly have their own weapons out? It would be death to Crosson—death to one or more of the others, before they had done with that young wildcat.

"Look," said the girl, breaking out into instinctive admiration, no matter what reasons she had for hating and fearing this youth. "He's not a whit afraid. Look at his eyes. They're straight ahead. See how his lip curls a little. He's a panther. They're only house dogs and they don't know what he is. I never saw such a man. I never saw such a face."

Ranger hardly heard her. His own heart was not swelling with any reluctant admiration; it was turning to ice, because he felt the overmastering urge of his conscience, driving him on to interfere. What could he do, if he slipped through the circle of the yelling riders, through the rim of the laughing, whooping crowd, and stood at the side of the boy? Yet he felt that his place was there. Perhaps if he merely got in there beside the lad, his presence would make the tormentors relent when they saw that a man of their own kind knew and sympathized with the stranger.

Ranger drew in a quick breath. "Nan," he said at the ear of the girl, "you get yourself together and go straight back to the hotel."

"I won't budge till it's over," she replied.

"You've got to budge," said Ranger. "You've got to do what I tell you. Your cousin trusted you to me. You've got to go back, because I've something to do here that maybe might . . ."

"You?" exclaimed Nan Lyons, looking quickly up to him. "You are going to do something here? But what can you do, Lefty?"

He looked desperately about him, in the hopeless chance that he might recognize some face. But all were strange to him. He was alone, in the playing of this hand.

"I can get myself into the same puddle with him," said Ranger. "That's all that I can do." He set his teeth. "Nan, go home," he said, almost groaning.

Then, straight before him, he saw a gap in the rim of the pressing crowd and a gap, beyond that, between one rider's horse and the outstretched head of the next. For that gap he raced and got through under the very nose of the animal.

A yell went up from the spectators, from the riders who circled the place as Ranger came to the side of the boy. The latter flashed at him a side glance of utter amazement and of something like admiration, as well.

They could not speak together, for the crowd had broken into an uproar now. There was only time for that single interchange of glances, which meant more than words could have done. And Ranger felt that perhaps he had acted like a madman.

Whatever was to happen, he certainly had precipitated the climax. Winnie Dale had risen still straighter in his stirrups. Daylight showed between him and his saddle. It was as though this touch of opposition had maddened his headstrong young nature. The rope swung faster in his hand, the noose opened a little. Then, with a screech, he cast.

Ranger was watching, but he was watching for the sake of young Crosson, rather than himself. Therefore, he was unprepared to dodge until he saw the thin, shooting shadows of the noose fly just above his own head. Then he started to the side, with an exclamation. He was too late. A throw that even an active-footed calf could not have avoided was much too fast for Ranger to jump clear of in the last fraction of a second. Over his head whipped the noose, and, catching an arm against his body, while the other arm remained free, he was jerked from his feet with violence and skidded into the dust of the street.

This action brought from the watchers and especially the riders a wild uproar of applause, as if it had been a deed of courage and matchless skill. The rougher the jest, the merrier, to the eye of that crowd.

Twice over, Ranger twisted. Then he found his knife and drew it, only to have it knocked flying from his hand as he whirled over a third time. He skidded on his back. The flying heels of a horse seemed about to smash into his face. And rolling his eyes upward, away from this sickening danger, he saw young Crosson leap into action at last.

Now he came across the radius of that circle. He made straight at the running horse of Winnie Dale. No circus performer could have cared to jump at a horse running at such speed, but Oliver Crosson jumped not for the horse but for the man in the saddle. He bounded higher than seemed credible. The force of his leap and the speed of the galloping horse smote him against the rider with an irresistible force, and the saddle was instantly emptied.

# CHAPTER THIRTY-TWO

The moment that the hand of Winnie Dale was removed from the round turn on the horn of his saddle, the rope flew freely out. Ranger skidded to a halt through the dust, and, rising, half blinded, he saw Dale's mustang galloping furiously away up the street, and the whole of Dale's company thrown into the uttermost confusion. The crowd was likewise disturbed.

There was a reason, for straight on under the feet of the onlookers tumbled the bodies of the two, head over heels, until, as Ranger got to his feet, he saw Winnie Dale, practical joker, lying stretched on his back, his arms thrown out crosswise, his face streaked with the blood of a cut that he had received in falling, his body limp as a rag.

Over him rose the form of Oliver Crosson, erect, white with dust in which he had rolled, but smiling, and in one hand he held a revolver, not aimed at any of the members of the Dale band, but in readiness to cover any one of them. And they, in turn, did not put hand to weapon.

It was a very amazing thing to Ranger. In his turn he had drawn his Colt .45, and he hurried to put himself beside young Crosson once more to face the crisis.

But the crisis was gone. There remained some dust flying in the air and the limp body of Winnie Dale upon the ground, but that was all. There would be no further action. He knew it as he glanced at the scowling but uncertain looks of the Dale followers.

And he was not greatly surprised. They had seen themselves holding a pair of men in the hollow of their hands, so to speak. The next instant, at the very moment when Dale began to play his rough joke, the ring had been broken and the strangers were gone.

Not gone, perhaps, but standing side-by-side, armed, in readiness, while their leader lay helpless upon the ground.

The situation was clear to Ranger after the first instant. It was clear to the crowd, also. What an uproar rose from the onlookers. How they shouted and whooped. They called on the Dale band to charge and rescue the fallen leader. They complimented the riders on the jest that had just been consummated. And those miners, cowpunchers, lumbermen, gamblers, wildsters of all sorts, shouted with laughter until the tears ran down their cheeks.

Young Crosson was the last to understand that the action was ended. He exclaimed to Ranger, without ever taking his eyes from the horsemen before him: "Are they going to back out, Ranger? Do you mean that they're going to pull clear of this after they've started it and got in so deep?"

"They didn't know the kind of claws you wore," said Ranger. "That's all. They didn't understand, but they'll never try again."

"Well," Crosson said, and sighed, "I suppose that this is the best way with it."

Yes, actually with a sigh he gave up the prospect of a fight with all of those hardy rangers. He leaned over. He took Winnie Dale by the hair of his head. With the strength of his single arm he raised Winnie to his knees.

"Stand up," said Crosson.

In all the babbling of the crowd, there was no sound like his voice. It differed from the other noises as, in a host of confusion, the trained ear detects the clang of the rifle bolt driven home.

"Stand up," Crosson repeated.

And Winnie Dale, reaching his hand vaguely before him, blinking, gasping, more than half stunned, stumbled the rest of the way to his feet. He was taller than Crosson. The result was that, since he was still held by the hair of the head, his head was bent backward a little. He looked like a helpless body about to tumble on its back.

"Get that horse and bring it here," young Crosson said to Lefty Bill.

One of the Dale men was bringing back the charger from which the leader had fallen. Ranger, understanding, went and took the horse by the bridle. When he brought it up, still the followers of Winnie Dale hung back a little distance. They had seen their master knocked out of the saddle as though by a cannonball, and yet it had been only a human projectile that sent him sprawling. They still hesitated to approach this strange youth, who leaped like a wildcat and struck like a bear.

As the horse swung alongside, there happened a stranger thing than ever was seen by all that fascinated crowd. Even Ranger, though he knew a good deal about the cunning physical mechanism of the boy, was amazed. For he saw Oliver Crosson, bending, pick up two hundred pounds of solid muscle and bone and throw the weight easily into the saddle!

A gasp of admiration came from the watchers.

Big Winnie Dale, landing half in and half out of the saddle, sprawled forward upon the neck of the horse, and the horse reared in great excitement, striking out at the empty air with its forehoofs.

"Now," said Oliver Crosson, "if I come across you again, or any of your pack, I'm going to hunt you like deer. I'm going to chase you until I've found you and peeled off your hide as I'd skin a blacktail. Get out of my sight, and get fast."

A quirt was hanging at the pommel of the Dale saddle. This the boy took, and, giving it a good swing around his head, he brought it down with a loud crack upon the quarters of the horse. Off went the mustang. He scratched like a frightened cat to get his footing in the slippery dust, and then away he went, scooting. Big Winnie Dale, topping first to this side and then to the other, his head flopping, his brain stunned, was like a helpless drunkard. Luck and some traces of the normal riding instinct kept him in his place. But he furnished the comic touch that he had tried to provide at the expense of the stranger.

A yell of joy went up from the crowd of Shannonites. Two of Dale's followers, heading frantically after their master to catch his horse before he had a bad fall, were presently followed by the rest. Perhaps they were riding to catch up with Winnie Dale, but it had all the appearance of the most ignominious rout, and the whooping of the crowd filled the very zenith of the sky.

Under the cover of that confusion, young Crosson turned to Ranger and took his hand. He stepped very close. His face was only inches away, and, as with his hand, so with his eyes he held Lefty Bill Ranger.

"Ranger," he said, "you stood by me in the pinch. If I ever fail you, if I ever keep you for anything but the best of friends, may I rot like a weed. Ranger, I'll never forget."

And he would not. No, it seemed to Ranger that he never before had heard any man speak so solemnly as the boy did now.

Then the crowd, forgetting the Dale outfit, swarmed about them. They were full of congratulations, amusement, joy. A good many of them had suffered from the pranks of Winnie Dale. A good many had been forced to laugh, at one time or another, because they dared not offer resistance to such a known young ruffian and hoodlum. Now they could laugh in earnest, and they were full of praise for the conqueror.

He endured it calmly, but with a faint frown. He was busy shaking the dust out of his long hair, and knocking it out of his clothes, and, while the others spilled about him, he ran his eye over them with deliberation.

Ranger was used to that cold and deliberate regard. He knew how it checked the easy flow of the blood. And now he could afford to be amused as he saw the temper of the crowd dampened and chilled. One or two hands had reached to slap the strange youth on the shoulder, but in each case a quick turn of the head and a single glance had made the rough congratulations hang suspended in the air.

"Let's walk on. Let's get out of this," said the boy to Ranger. He whistled, and his cream-colored horse came trotting to him, head high, gay and light of hoof. No matter how far he traveled, his master gave him such care, it appeared, that he was ever in fine fettle. But Ranger could understand this. He had seen Crosson leave the saddle and run on foot over the steep of the valley trail. And now, as he watched the horse come up, with the most speaking thrust and brightness in the eye that met its master, he could not help smiling with pleasure.

But Crosson merely turned his back and walked off through the crowd. And the crowd did not follow.

They slipped away from Oliver Crosson as water slips away from the back of a duck. And so they came through the verge of the mob, and there was Nan Lyons before them.

She came hurrying up to Ranger. "That was a mighty fine, foolish, useless, brave thing that you did, Lefty," she said. "That was a grand thing. Shake hands on it. I'll bet you were quaking when you went in there."

"Oh, I'll bet I was," said Ranger. "And I got a quick roll in the dust for my pay, right off . . . but it's all right. It's all behind us. Nan, you know Oliver Crosson? You've seen him before?"

She stepped back a little. She was as calm, as cold, as hostile as a stone. Ranger was amazed by her lack of perturbation.

"I've seen him," she said. "I've seen him in the moonlight . . . at a distance. I never saw him as close as this, before."

"Have you seen me?" said Crosson. "I don't remember you, though. I ought to. I would remember you, I think, if I'd seen you as far away as one of those pines on the rim of the mountain shoulder. I'd remember you, if you'd as much as spoken to me in the dark. No, I never saw you before."

"Hold on, Oliver," said Ranger. "You've seen her before, all right. Oh, yes, you've seen her."

"You're wrong," said Crosson. He came closer to her with a stealthy, imperceptible movement. His eyes never left her face. He stood entranced, his lips a little parted, bewilderment and joy seeming to choke him.

It was the very thing that Ranger had prophesied would happen in that town. But to have it happen to Oliver Crosson. Who could have foreseen such a coincidence?

"You're wrong," went on young Oliver. "If I ever had seen her, I don't think I could have left . . ." He paused and went on: "Why are you sneering at me, Nan? Why are you looking as though you despise me? Is it my clothes? I'll get a fresh lot. Is it my long hair, like a woman's? I'll cut it off. I'll wear store boots and spurs and bells. I'll do anything you say. Is that why you're sneering at me, Nan?"

She looked for one dismayed moment at Ranger.

The latter, half startled, wholly amazed, began to grin a little, biting his lips to keep it back.

"Lefty," she said, "you'd better tell him who I am."

She turned on her heel and went quickly up the street toward the hotel.

# CHAPTER THIRTY-THREE

The boy hesitated for a moment, and then started to follow her, but Ranger caught him powerfully by the arm and stopped him. Then, giving up his will, Oliver Crosson looked at his companion with a sort of mute agony.

At last he said: "Why did she hate me so, Lefty? She couldn't hate me like that for nothing. I've never harmed her. I've never touched her. Do you think that she hated me, Lefty?"

"The way of it is . . . ," began Ranger.

"The way of a woman. They say that's a lot different from the way of a man," said Oliver Crosson. "Tell me, Lefty. You've been out into the world a lot. Did you ever see a woman like her before?"

"No, not exactly," the trapper admitted.

"I didn't dream that there was ever such a thing," said the boy. "She was as fresh as the morning. There was dew in her eyes. She was beautiful, Lefty."

"Now you hold on and wait a minute," said Ranger. "Don't you go getting excited too much about this girl. She's pretty. She's mighty pretty. But there are others that are prettier."

"I don't believe it," said the boy, plainly incredulous. "I don't think that there could be another woman in the world at all like her."

"Couldn't there?" muttered Ranger. He let the eye of his mind look back into his past, and in that past what he saw was framed between a row of poplars going up a hill and the quick turn and flash of a surprising little stream in the heart of the valley. Down the path to the stream, down the steppingstones carrying a bucket of water, a girl came slowly, singing—a mountain girl, straight and strong. Her head was tilted up to the sky, and her throat rounded and filled with music.

"I've seen a girl," said Ranger, swallowing hard, "that would've made this one look like nothing at all."

"I don't believe it," answered the boy instantly. "I mean," he explained, "she may have been very lovely. But this girl, this Nan, touched me, Lefty. She touched me at the hollow of my throat. She took my breath away." He added: "I don't know her last name. I've got to know that. Can you tell me, Lefty? And where does she live? Does she always live in Shannon? Who is her father? Has she any brothers? Will she be here long? Is she poor like me? Or is she so rich that that was why she sneered at me? Why don't you say something, Lefty? I can't wait to know. I'm on fire to know all about her!"

"I can see that you're all on fire," said the trapper. "But how can I answer when you don't give me a chance to speak? Before you finish with one question, you start in on another."

"I won't do that any more," said the boy. "I won't interrupt you for a second. Only . . . tell me what you know about her."

"I'm afraid that I know mighty little about her."

"Then tell me where I can go to find out more. I want to know everything about her. I would like to read all about her in a book, so that I could memorize it."

"What I know will be enough for you, I'm mighty afraid," said Ranger. "Why, you don't remember a lot that you might know, son. Who was it that you chased across the hills, last night?"

"You mean Lyons and the boy with him? I missed them in the rocks above Shannon. I was coming up fast, but the last upslope stopped me a little. I would have had to kill my poor horse to catch them. And even the killing of Lyons . . . that wasn't worth the death of the horse, was it?"

"No, of course, it wasn't," said the trapper, looking oddly at the boy.

"And when I started down the slope, I saw Shannon below me, flickering in the moonlight, and I saw that they were so close that I wouldn't have a chance to catch up with them." He snapped his fingers impatiently. "But what has that to do with her? I'll finish off Lyons. He ran away from me once. He'll never get away the second time.

He'll have no men to delay me. I'll catch him. And what he gave to the black wolf I'm going to give to him. Isn't that justice?" He seemed on fire with the idea. His eyes flashed. He walked on tiptoes of eagerness.

"Maybe that's justice in your sense of it," said the trapper, "but, mostly, other folks say that animals are worth money when they're killed . . . but him that kills another man gets hanging."

"Why should he?" the boy asked sharply. "An animal can't fight back. But a man can. It's ten times as bad to kill a helpless animal as it is to kill a man. But that has nothing to do with the thing. It's the girl that I want to know about. Won't you please tell me everything about her?"

Words flowed from him like a river in the spate of spring. He trembled with his emotion, as a flame trembles in a strong draft.

"I was going to tell you only one thing. I was going to tell you that the boy, the second rider that you chased last night, was not a boy. It was a girl, and the girl's name was Nan Lyons."

The fire went out of the boy at a stroke. He no longer walked on his tiptoes. Instead, he sagged weakly and supported himself with one hand against a hitching post that they happened to be passing at that moment.

"Nan Lyons," he said. "Nan Lyons? God be good to me. Of all the names in the world, it had to be that one." He was so hard hit that he remained there for a long moment with a sick look of pain on his face. Then he stood up, and idly, mechanically put out his hand and laid it on the shining, silver mane of his horse.

"I feel blasted . . . like lightning had struck me . . . as if a lightning of gold had struck me, Lefty. She was like that. Sky blue, and golden lightning that went right through me."

The trapper was startled and amazed. The very phrase that he had used had come back to his ears upon the tongue of this lad. He looked at the boy with a curious feeling of brotherhood and understanding.

"A girl like that," he said, "she's going to strike through and through a good many hearts of men, before she's caught like a bird out of the air and held in some man's hand. And the worst of it is, when she's caught, she'll likely feel that the man is God Almighty . . . and the man himself, he'll think that she's just no more than any of the other little birds in the air. That's the way of it. You never like nothing except what you ain't got. And her . . . well, you ain't likely to have her for yourself, are you? You don't see your way to that, I suppose, Oliver."

Oliver Crosson walked on again. The agony had made him pale. It made him sweat. It doubled him forward a little, as though a hand of ice or fire were gripping his vitals.

"I don't know," he said. "My brain is full of

smoke. I can't think. I don't seem able to see my way through this trouble. Will you try to help me, Lefty? Show me the way through the woods, will you?"

Lefty Ranger laid a hand on the boy's shoulder. They went on at a snail's pace. It was the most beautiful of brilliant mountain mornings, and only in the mountains are the mornings really beautiful. In all other places they are dull things comparatively. The windows flashed; smoke went up in translucent silver streams above the tops of the houses; the trees gleamed on the western hills, and to the east the poplars were glittering like fluttering bits of metal. A glorious morning, and yet there was such a shadow cast from the boy's suffering, that the trapper saw little of all that was around him. He yearned over the lad as if over his own flesh and blood.

"I'll try to show you how it stands," he said. "I suppose that you like the girl better than almost anything else in the whole world, don't you?"

"Ah," said the boy, "if everything else were to be rolled into one, all the mountains and trees, the beautiful deer and the wolves, the hunting lions and the birds in the air, the fish in the streams and the streams themselves, with all the gold that is washing in their sands, I'd not change the whole of it for five minutes of sitting and looking at her. Do you hear me, Lefty?"

"I hear you."

"But believe me, too. Only to sit and look at her. She wouldn't have to talk. She wouldn't have to know that I was near her. If only I could be where I could watch her. Did you notice how she walked, Lefty?"

"She steps out good and free," said Ranger.

"Why, she steps over the ground the way that a swallow steps over the air . . . with a dip and a swing to it."

"Well, you see her that way, and so she's that way to you," said Lefty Ranger. "But then it'll be easy for you to go and make up with her cousin, and tell Lyons that you're sorry you treated him like a wild beast, chasing him through the hills."

"Tell him I'm sorry? Make friends with him?" echoed the boy, a separate breath of astonishment to every word. "Why, I've sworn an oath to God Almighty that I'll do to him what he did to the timber wolf. Ah, I see what you mean. You think that it was only to me like the death of a dog. But you weren't with me to see the thousand days I worked over him. He was a sick puppy. I got him well again. I trained him. He could read my mind. He could lie at my feet and read my face. If I frowned, he dropped his head. If I smiled, he raised it.

"Once when I closed in on a puma, my foot slipped and the big black fellow went in and slashed the mountain lion and turned it on himself. He was cut to pieces before I could get

272

up and finish the thing. It took me three months to make him whole again. But he saved my life that day. So he was all to me that a man could be. What more can a man do than offer to die for you? And then he was murdered . . . and you ask if I can shake hands with the man who murdered him?"

He laughed, a sudden, short, broken laughter. And the heart of Lefty Ranger stirred in him.

"Well, son, you see how it points," he said.

"I don't see. Only that it's like a thundercloud ahead of me. That's all that I see. Nothing but a lot of blackness."

Ranger sighed. "Try to look at it this way, too," he said. "From her side, I mean. Suppose that she even likes you a lot and forgets that you're the man who hunted her with wolves through the mountains, even suppose that she forgets that, how would she feel toward the man who killed her own blood . . . Chet Lyons?"

"Would she feel it so much?" said the boy, his mouth twisting, his eyes dim with pain and with fear.

"So much? She'd want to see you hanged. That's about all, I guess, that she would want of you." He turned suddenly on Oliver Crosson. "Son," he said, "you've got to give up this murder idea. You've got to step off the trail of Lyons, and then you can try to get the girl. Maybe you'll succeed."

The other drew a groaning breath, but slowly he shook his head. "I've sworn it," he said. "I couldn't change. I've sworn it higher than the sky and deeper than hell. I've got to do it, now."

# CHAPTER THIRTY-FOUR

At the corner table in the hotel, Menneval and Chester Lyons, when the other two had left, remained for a moment watching one another. Then Menneval smiled a little and nodded slightly.

"You're about the same, Chet," he said.

"Do I look the same?" asked Lyons curiously.

"Yes. You look about the same."

"I'm not the same," said Lyons.

"Tell me how that is?"

"I don't know," answered Lyons. "I don't know that there's much good in talking about it. You're here today, Menneval, and you're gone tomorrow. Why do you care to hear about me?"

"Why, for old times' sake. And for the new time, too. Young Crosson is on your trail. And I'm interested in him."

"You are?"

"Yes."

"What's he to me?"

"I knew his father when he was a schoolmaster in the hills. I knew the boy when he was a baby. The Crossons have struck a root in my mind. That's why." Then he added: "But I can guess why you think that you've changed."

"Tell me, then."

"I'll tell you," said Menneval. "You were always one of the fellows who thinks that he's going straight. Bad today. But tomorrow, you'll wash your hands as clean as clean. Eh?"

He smiled, but Lyons remained grave.

"There's where you're wrong. I've always wanted to go straight. And now I've done it."

"With a price on your head?" asked Menneval.

"There's no price on my head. That's been taken off. It's not murder that they want me for. It's other things. Plenty of other things. But I'm working. I have a pull, here and there. I have some money. I think that before long I can go down and stand trial and clear up my record, in the eyes of the law."

"You were always an optimist, too." Menneval nodded.

"Perhaps I'm foolish. I don't think so," replied the other. "I have a decent stake saved up."

"Decent stake?" Menneval said, and smiled.

Lyons frowned. "I know what you mean. Dirty money. I tell you, man, that I've spent the dirty money. It went as it came. But what I'm talking about is honest stuff, made by honest work. I found a rift of pay dirt up in the mountains. I worked it with my own hands. I took three hundred pounds of dust out of it. Nuggets, a lot of 'em. Three hundred pounds of red gold. That's what changed me, that and the girl."

"How could it change you, that much easy money?"

"I got to thinking . . . you may call me a fool . . . that when God gives so many chances to a worthless ruffian like me, He wants him to change."

"Aye," Menneval said, sneering. "And you always have had your religious streak, too."

"You can sneer," said Lyons calmly. "Why are you here, Menneval? To pick a fight with me?"

"I'm here to save your life," Menneval answered with equal quiet.

His companion started, even glanced over his shoulder, as though danger might be approaching stealthily behind him at that moment.

"No, he's not in the room. But he'll be here before long," said Menneval. "So you're going straight, Chet? Going to pay half your money to a foxy lawyer and have him give you a clean slate?"

"I'm going to try to manage it. I think that I can. For two years, there's nothing chalked up against me. People have been yammering a good deal against me, accusing me of this and that. Some of the boys have stuck to me, hoping that I'd lead them. But they've led themselves. I've only been a name and a figurehead, waiting for the time when I could make my move, and that time has just about come. I've got to go. The girl wants me to."

"That's pretty Nan, of course?"

"That's Nan. More than pretty. That's skin-deep. She's the sweetest soul that ever was called a woman, Menneval."

"But, still, a woman," Menneval said with his habitual sneer.

At this the lips of Lyons twitched and a frown darkened his forehead, but, when he looked straight into the face of the other, something stopped him. It was like the touch of a cold wind. He shivered a little and looked down at the table.

"I've told you what I'm doing and intend to do," said Lyons. "I don't know why I've been such a loose-tongued fool. I know that you don't care a whit."

Here a great hubbub broke out up the street of the village. It grew so loud, such a roar of shouting, such Indian cries and whoops of distant laughter, that it drew from the dining room every man who had barely begun his breakfast. But Menneval and his companion paid no heed to it whatever. They continued to face one another across the narrow table.

"First, I'll be a prophet, and then I'll tell you why I care," said Menneval. "To begin with, I'll tell you exactly what will happen to you. Young Crosson is going to track you down. Probably in this very town he'll find you, and he'll kill you out of hand."

The head of Lyons went up a little. "He's a strange youngster," he stated. "I've seen the proofs of that. Maybe you know him better."

"I do," said Menneval shortly.

"I know him well enough to see that he's dangerous. But I'm able to take care of myself. I ran from him last night . . . that was because of the girl. I'll never take a back step before him again, in all the rest of the days of my life. I never have taken a back step."

"Except once," Menneval commented coldly.

Lyons flushed. "It's true," he said. "I took a back step before you one day. But I'm a harder man now than I was then."

"Let me tell you," said Menneval soberly, "that, if I was a fighting machine, in those days I was nothing to what this lad is. He has the cunning and the skill. He has the strength. More than that, he has the will. He could jump over mountains . . . he could swim over oceans. He has the will to do it."

Lyons shrugged his shoulders, but he listened intently.

"If you stay here," went on Menneval, "you're no better than a dead man. You're surrounded by people. But he'll manage to get at you someday. And two seconds later, you'll lie dead, with your three hundred pounds of red gold, and all of that."

He pointed at the floor, and so emphatic was

his manner that the other instinctively looked down and changed color a little, as though he saw himself already stretched lifeless there, his eyes glazed, his powerless arms thrown wide.

He swallowed with a decided effort. "You say what you think. It's not what I think. And even if it were true, even if I'd seen my death warrant signed, I tell you that I'd never shame myself by running away from any man."

Menneval leaned forward across the table. "You will," he said softly, insistently.

"Never in my life."

"Listen to me, Lyons. Frankly I don't give a damn about you. The Crossons are the people I take an interest in. I have a reason to. There's something between me and old Peter Crosson that the world doesn't dream of. You might die and rot, and little I'd care. But I want to keep the hands of the boy clean. So I say that you're going to leave this town and leave it at once. You are going to do as I say. Do you understand?"

Lyons shrugged his shoulders; slowly he shook his head. But he was fascinated by the fire in the eyes of Menneval and, to his amazement, the combination of authority and pleading in his voice. He knew much of Menneval. He knew enough to swear that he never in his life had condescended to plead before.

"I'll tell you what you'll do," said Menneval.

"You'll saddle fresh horses. I've already bought some. They're ready for you this minute. You and the girl will ride straight across country. You'll hit the railroad. When the boy picks up your trail . . . and nothing in the world could keep him from doing it . . . you'll probably have enough of a head start to distance him. Anyway, if you haven't, I'll follow on behind you and turn him off the trail, if I can. And I think that I can. I know that you're not persuaded yet. Am I right?"

"Leave this country? It's the only place where I'm safe. Away from here . . . leaving out the shame of running away before that boy . . . I'll be lost. This is my only country. I've not been a world rover, like you."

Menneval went on: "I'll give you everything that you need. I have friends in the shipping business in San Francisco. You get the train to the city. You go straight to the Rixey and Parkhouse offices. You ask for old man Parkhouse. I'll give you a note to him, and the minute he sees the writing, everything that he has is yours."

"You've made friends, too, in your way around the world?" asked Lyons curiously. He seemed almost as much interested in this revelation of character as he did in the import of Menneval's persuasions.

"I've made a few friends," said the other briefly. "You'll find them good friends as well.

Don't doubt them. They'll take you and the girl away to Honolulu. Better, they'll cruise you through the South Seas. You'll stop off where you please. You'll be treated like a king and a princess. It'll be an education for you."

"And the whole thing will be given absolutely for nothing, eh?" said Lyons.

"In the meantime," Menneval said insistently, "I'll have two lawyers that I know work up your case hand in glove with your own man. Graham and Steele are the men I speak of."

Lyons said with an oath: "Have you got those fellows in your pocket?"

"I have . . . absolutely in my pocket and in the hollow of my hand." He paused. "As for the cost of traveling, it's pretty high, I know. But I'll pay the way. I'll give you fifty thousand dollars if you'll take my advice, save your life, give your girl a cruise that will open her mind and add to her culture. When you come back home, you'll be safe from young Crosson . . . I'll guarantee you that . . . and I'll also guarantee that I'll have the way for your return to the ways of legal life made as smooth as silk for you."

"If you can do that," said Lyons, "why don't you do it for yourself?"

"Because I can't," Menneval said, again sneering. "The marks against you are little streaks of mist, here and there. The marks on my slate are blood. Now give me an answer, Lyons.

Look me straight in the eye and let me have your answer right now."

A long, long moment did the silent stare pass between them.

Then Lyons shook his head. "No," he declared.

# CHAPTER THIRTY-FIVE

As though to mark the importance of this crisis in the conversation, the uproar in the street sank away to a confused babbling that was hardly audible in the dining room of the hotel.

"That ends it, I suppose," Menneval said bitterly. He stirred in his chair, as though he felt the prick of the decision to the core of his being.

Lyons merely nodded. "What staggers me, Menneval," he said finally, "is that you're making this effort for the Crossons. I never would have guessed that anybody in the wide world . . ."

Menneval lifted his hand, impatiently, to stop the comment. "All that we're able to guess about one another," he said, "is surface stuff, rot, driftwood. Tell me, Lyons. The crux of the thing is the girl, eh?"

The other nodded once more. Then he explained: "I've liked the wild life well enough. But I wanted something better than that, something more real and lasting and solid. Something like a chance at permanent happiness. I can have that, looking after Nan."

"*Bah!*" exploded Menneval. "In two years, she'll be married and gone from you."

"She'll be married, perhaps," said Lyons, "but

she won't be gone from me. She's not the kind that chucks old friends overboard."

In the manner of Menneval there was at all times an essential ferocity that was never hidden very far beneath the surface. It came out in a flash now. "Sometimes I think," he said savagely, "that the only great fools in the world are the optimists."

"I won't fight with you," Lyons answered calmly. "But look at yourself. What is it other than optimism that makes you want to spend fifty thousand dollars on the Crossons?"

Before he could get an answer to this, Nan came hurriedly back into the room. The emptiness of it seemed to frighten her for an instant as she paused at the door, but then she located Lyons at the table and came hastily toward him. She was very altered. They stood up to meet her and saw that her face was pale, her lips a little pinched, her eyes blazing with excitement.

"What is it, Nan?" asked Lyons.

"Where's Ranger?" Menneval demanded angrily. "Did he leave you in the lurch? That's not like him."

"Lefty Ranger is a splendid fellow," she said. "He didn't leave me in the lurch."

"Sit down," said Lyons. "Sit down and tell me about it, will you? What's happened? Did it have anything to do with that hurly-burly up the street?"

"Yes. It was the hurly-burly. I'll tell you what I saw . . . half a dozen men trying to make a fool out of one . . . half a dozen of them trying to bully him . . . and Lefty Ranger jumped into the circle and stood with the single man, because he was a friend."

"Did Lefty do that?" Menneval asked curiously, almost sadly. "Aye, there's always more courage than you expect in an honest man."

"They roped Lefty, and then the other fellow went for the bullies like a panther. It was a wild thing to see. He knocked a big fellow out of the saddle . . ."

"With a bullet?"

"No, with the weight of his own body. He jumped like a wildcat, I tell you. I never saw anything so beautiful, and horrible . . . and the lot of them scattered. And do you know who Lefty's friend is?"

"Well?" said Lyons.

"I can guess," muttered Menneval.

"Yes, it was young Oliver Crosson. And he's coming down the street toward the hotel this minute. He's . . ."

Someone came into the doorway and paused there, half seen. All the three turned tensely, in that direction. But it was only Lefty Ranger who came into the room.

He walked like a man who is overburdened by a great weight. His head and shoulders hung. When he came up to the group at the table, he looked them over with a dull eye of worry. Then he said, with an unexpected authority: "Nan, you'd better go up to your room. I've got to talk to Lyons."

"I want to hear," said the girl.

"You can't hear," said the trapper. "You go up to your room. I've gotta talk some hard things over with Lyons, here."

"Yes," said Lyons. "Go up, Nan."

She stepped to him and took his hands. "You won't go outside?" she pleaded.

He hesitated a minute before answering.

"You'd do it to prove that you're a brave man. But I know how brave you are. Everyone does. And this fellow is not like other men. He's not human at all. It was terrible and horrible to see the way he handled those 'punchers."

"I'll do what's right, Nan," said Lyons. "And I won't go outside unless I let you know beforehand. Now, you go upstairs."

She went, reluctantly, pausing at the door to smile back at Chester Lyons.

Then the three men sat down again.

"She's told you what happened?" said Ranger.

They nodded. They hung on his words, both of them, with a sort of desperate eagerness.

"I've been with young Crosson," said Lefty Ranger. "He wants you, Lyons. He wants you pretty bad. But there's something else that has happened. He's lost his head about Nan."

287

"That fiend . . . that human wolf . . . he's looked at Nan?" said Lyons fiercely. "I'll . . ."

"Wait a moment," broke in Menneval. "We'll have some more of this. Go on, Lefty."

Said Ranger: "She hit him hard. I'll tell you what he said. He said that she was a lightning of gold . . . he's on fire about her. He's blazing. Then I tried to tell him that if he got off your trail, he'd have a chance to see her."

"I'd rather see her dead," Lyons hissed. "What put such an idea in your head, Ranger?"

"What else was I to do?" said Lefty Bill. "Otherwise, he'd be here now."

"I'm to shake hands with him and turn Nan over to him, is that it?" said Lyons, white with anger.

"I wish it could be as easy as all that," answered Lefty. "It ain't, though. The fact is, nothing will put him off your trail very long. He's taken an oath, he says, that he'll have it out with you and do to you what you did to the wolf."

"It was Wully who shot the wolf," said Lyons.

"I tried to say it might not be you. It doesn't make any difference. You're the man who led the gang. That's all he'll think or remember. He wants blood for blood. He's going to have it . . . and God help your unlucky soul." He paused. He had spoken so solemnly, so hopelessly that the other two exchanged glances. The pallor of Lyons was not caused by anger, now.

Ranger continued: "I tried to argue. You can't argue with a man like him. He has his idea. It's kind of sacred to him. That wolf saved his life once. He feels that the way to pay back, now, is to get at you. There's only one thing in the world that can get him off your trail."

"What's that?" asked Menneval.

"Why, something that makes him hate another man more than he hates Lyons, and I reckon that ain't possible. But he's waiting down the street in the Wayfarer's Saloon. He's in the back room of it, sitting in the shadow."

"Drinking?" asked Menneval sharply.

"He doesn't know what drink tastes like," said Ranger. "I don't suppose that he ever tasted it in his life. He ain't like other people in any way. He knows that I'm up here talking to you, Lyons. He hardly knows why. Neither do I. But he's a friend of mine now. And so I persuaded him. And now I want to persuade you to get out of town and get fast and far. That's the only way to keep your neck safe, and keep murder off the hands of the boy."

"Aye," Menneval broke in. "You see how it is, Lyons. Even Ranger sees right through the matter and has come to the only conclusion. Are you going to let your pride kill you, man?"

The Chinaman, clearing away the dishes from the long table, was making a great clattering.

Menneval turned and silenced him with a glance that made him cower.

Chester Lyons, stiffly erect, his eyes fixed upon empty space straight before him, was like a statue for a long moment. Then he moistened his lips a little. Breathing seemed hard for him.

"Don't be ashamed, man," said Menneval. He leaned forward and spoke softly, as though he hoped that the words he spoke would sink into the brain of the listener and become a helpful part of the processes of his mind. "There's nothing to be ashamed of in back-stepping before a fellow like Crosson. You've seen that he's not like other natural men. There's a different strain in him. He's a new cut and another way. Get out of Shannon. Do as I've advised you and as Ranger tells you. Or you'll be a dead man before another day's out. Then where are your plans, and what happens to Nan?"

The breast of Lyons rose and fell quickly. At last he said: "I've made up my mind."

They waited with breathless interest, as if to an oracle.

"I have some affairs that I need to arrange and I'll have to spend some time in my room, writing. There are some things that have to be put in order. About noon tomorrow I'll be able to move."

Menneval closed his eyes and leaned back a little in his chair, so great was his relief as he heard this promising beginning. But Lyons did not so much as glance aside at his companions. He went on: "You'll be able to see the boy, Ranger?"

"I'll see him. Yes. He's waiting for me now."

"Back there at the saloon?"

"Yes. I'll talk to him. I'll hold him for twenty-four hours or a little longer. I'll manage to keep him there somehow, until you get away."

"Then go back and give him a message for me. Tell him that tomorrow, at noon, I'm going to walk out of the front door of this hotel and straight up the street through Shannon, and, if I see his face, I'll pull a gun and shoot him down if I can."

# CHAPTER THIRTY-SIX

All that Nan Lyons could learn was that her cousin would stay in Shannon for another day. She had tried in every way to get something out of him, but he was taciturn for the first time. And the thing began to madden her.

If there had been an officer of the law in Shannon, she would have gone to him for help. Sometimes she thought of appealing to the big, rough men of Shannon and begging them to give Chester Lyons protection against that fierce and uncanny lad. But she knew that she dared not do this. Lyons himself never would forgive her, for he would far rather be killed out of hand than to ask help against any single man.

And the nerves of Nan began to tauten to the breaking point. She would not talk to Chester Lyons. There was no confidant to whom she could turn. She seemed stripped of all help.

The very shadows of the clouds sweeping across the window of her room made her start violently and lose color. She was finding Oliver Crosson like a ghost in all things. Suddenly she decided that she could endure it no longer. She would have to leave the hotel. And leave it she did.

There was a slope below it, where the truck

garden was laid out on a sort of upper terrace, and below this extended a region of bush and second growth, the bigger trees having been felled for firewood. And then the forest itself began, still sloping away with the fall of the valley level. It was not one of those vast, dark growths of evergreens, shoulder to shoulder, so that a perpetual twilight and damp evening reigned under them even in the midst of the brightest August day. It was, instead, a cheerfully open woodland where one could wander pleasantly back and forth, where natural clearings appeared and springs came piping out of the ground, with little green meadows about them.

From her window in the hotel, she could look down over some of these clearings. Now she remembered them and the brightness of the sun, and the cheerfulness of that woodland made her yearn to be there, walking by herself, escaping from her thoughts. So down she went.

She passed the truck garden. She wound by a narrow path through the borderland of thickly massed shrubbery and second-growth trees. And so she came into the forest itself. It was better than she had hoped for even. It was not all evergreens, but here and there were deciduous trees, their more delicate and yellowish green foliage looking like a mist against the dark and shadowy heads of the pine trees that towered above them.

Almost at once she heard a musical bubbling and rippling of water and she located the source of it. It was a good spring that leaped a foot from the surface of the ground and then spread out in a pool, from which the current flowed softly along, with green margins, very silent and pleasant underfoot. It was the most casual of streams. Sometimes it danced and rippled over a little cascade that would have made a child clap its hands with pleasure; sometimes it idled in swinging curves; sometimes it spread into still pools that showed only a faint stir at either end, where the water entered and left it.

She began to walk along the course of this stream. She felt like wandering, and the course of the water was like a companion and a careless guide, taking her to the easiest place. She had barely started down the waterway, when she heard, distinctly, the sound of a breaking twig. Of that she was sure; furthermore, the sound was a little muffled, as it usually is when a softly clad foot, say, presses upon the fallen wood.

In an instant she was on the alert. She looked carefully about her. She stepped this way and that. But she could see nothing suspicious. Moreover, a wind had come up, not strongly but in little gusts, and it might have been that two boughs had touched together, and a dry little branch had broken at the contact. Such things were continually happening in woods. Indeed, such a thing as a silent woodland is a term, not a possible fact. Above all, she was reassured by the sight of the roof of the hotel, which was plainly visible through a cleft between some of the larger trees. So Nan went on.

After that, she gave most of her attention to the stream itself. Looking into it, she could see the forest, the sky, even glimpses of the sun in the sky, blinding bright as a falling bolt of golden lightning.

She began to have a fancy that human lives were like that. In places they were full of sound and white water, taking the attention, making one frown. But at times they spread out placidly, and then the deep images of thought and of beauty fall into the mind and are held there so lucidly that others can pause and feel the grace and charm of that life, and then go on smiling and content.

She would like to have a life like that, she told herself, without too much excitement, a quiet life with a pleasant home, children, and a garden, not too large, but something that her own hands and thought could cherish and care for. Other people wished to go rushing through the world like great rivers, bearing boats, bearing ships, smashing through to the distant ocean. But, for herself, she would rather have the quiet way, like this stream with the blue and gold of heaven falling into it.

She stopped to look at a little brown water dog,

stretched on a mossy-topped stone. The tip of its tail was in the water. She kneeled to look at it more closely, when suddenly it vanished into the stream.

The water was very still here. When she leaned still farther, she could see her own face as in a mirror whose back is not very well silvered. But there was the glint of her hair, the shadow of her hat brim, and even the glow of the reflection that fell upon her cheek. More distant objects were reflected more closely, like the intense and shining whiteness of one towering cloud in the central sky, the gleaming leaves of the trees, and the blue of the sky, with all its suggestion of nearness and yet of impalpable distance. So crystal clear was this standing water, that she could see the pebbles on the bottom, the water weeds and grasses, standing straight up, with never a wavering of head or of stem. She could see a twig, thoroughly massed over, and the almost invisible shadow of a minnow swerving through the shallow depths.

She leaned there until the stones began to hurt her knees, and she was about to rise when the image of a wolf's head appeared in the water close beside her, the wicked little bright eyes, the puckered brow of diabolical wisdom, the lolling red tongue, and the glitter of the long fangs. She had not had time to leap to her feet before, on the opposite side, she saw a second image, and this was of a man. He was leaning a little, so that she could see his face clearly, and on it there was a smile, either of mirth or of contempt.

Nan jumped up, with her hands gripped, ice on her lips, ice on her heart.

And there was Oliver Crosson of the wolves.

There was not only that one that she had seen in the water—now it squatted, watching her intently and with a savage interest—but on either side of the boy was another of the monsters, each lolling a red tongue, each wrinkling its bright eyes at her.

She drew in her breath to scream. But, from a corner of the eye, she saw the hotel again, the blink of an upper window, and she restrained the impulse to cry out.

She wondered why he did not speak. He was only smiling, watching her, and mute. She tried to edge away down the stream a little. With an idea of bolting, was it?

One of the wolves, a lean, gray female, came and sat down before her and dared her with eyes of a shameless boldness to move another inch. So she stood still.

"They could hear me at the hotel, if I yelled," she said. "You know that, I guess."

"If you shouted?" said the boy. He opened his eyes at her. It was like the naïve way of a child. "Why should you shout?" he asked her.

She did not speak until she was sure that her

voice would not tremble. But even then she was wrong. There was a decided quake in it as she said: "Do you think it's an easy thing to be here like this . . . and have wolves . . . and . . . wolves, I mean, come out at one?"

"Oh, it's the wolves," he said. "They're nothing. They wouldn't touch you. I'll show you that they wouldn't touch you, if you'll let me."

"Show me, then," she said.

"Well, it's an easy thing. Just give me your hand, will you?"

She looked blankly at him. And then curiosity mastered her as it often masters the young and the foolish. And she thought of the gay grand story she would make of this when she returned to the hotel and told Chester Lyons how she, alone and unafraid, had stood there with the wolf-man and talked to him in the woods. It would be something worthwhile.

She held out her hand and he took it gently with the lightest of touches.

"It's like this," he said, explaining. "They don't like strangers. Lots of dogs are that way, you know. Now you see this one. She's the fiercest. She's really a sort of demon. But she's going to be introduced to you, and after that she'll never harm you. She'd be a friend to you, in fact, I think."

He spoke softly. The sound did form a word, so far as her straining ears could make out. Or was it some soft, guttural Indian tongue? It seemed wordless. It was not unmusical, but rather something between a deep growl and a whine.

The gray female, when she heard it, threw herself back as if about to attack. Her eyes turned green. She showed her set of needle-sharp teeth.

"She'll jump," said the girl, jerking back involuntarily.

He did not close his hand around her wrist. The gentle touch, however, fitted her like a glove, and she could not get away. "She won't jump an inch," he said. He spoke again, and suddenly the wolf skulked forward, tail between legs, still with the silent sneer, and came straight under the hand of Nan Lyons.

# CHAPTER THIRTY-SEVEN

Now Nan Lyons was as one who stands on the brink of danger, but feels impelled to take the risk on account of the audience that watches. It seemed to her that the whole body of the big wolf was trembling with a virulent hatred and that the naked teeth fairly dripped a poison of resentment. But the man smiled down on the female wolf steadily, and suddenly the eye of the lobo turned from the girl to the master and clung there. She no longer trembled with hatred. She stood erect. Her lip no longer writhed back hard from the glitter of teeth. She was more like a house dog about to be petted.

"Now she's safe," said the boy, and Nan, with a vast effort, let her hand fall and fall until it touched the head of the wolf, which shrank down a foot or more from the contact. Its glance was now swerved back to the face of Nan herself, but there was more fear than enmity in the look. The hand of Nan descended again. What a vast power of will it cost her. And she found herself stroking the fur of the brute, whose eyes closed at each touch and, opening again, surveyed her with the look of one who has been hypnotized.

"You see," said the boy. "She's safe enough. I

can make the rest of 'em do the same thing, if you wish."

Nan straightened. Her hand was freed, she blinked and shook her head a little to assure herself that this was not a dream. "One is as good as a crowd," she said.

She saw the gray wolf leap backward, stiff-legged, as though out of a trap, and to it slunk the other two wolves, half snarling as they sniffed at the head of the mother, as they detected upon the fur the evidence of a dangerous hand.

"Why, they hate humans," she said. "They'd like to cut my throat, every one of them."

"Why not?" explained Oliver Crosson. "You see the way they're born and the way they live. They hunt, they find fresh meat on the ground, and they eat it in spite of a little scent of man about it, and they die in an hour or so, poisoned. Then there are some of them that escape and remember. They tell the rest, and they go playing over the open country. Men come on horses and hunt them. Then again, they're simply sleeping in the sun, and they hear thunder when there's no cloud in the sky and die as they wake up, with lightning through the brain." He looked fixedly at her. "You can understand that, I suppose?" he said.

She had been accustomed, all her life, to look every man in the face except those who stared at her in such a way that the only thing to do was to be unconscious of their glances. The eye of the boy was not insolent, however. It merely burned with his question, and a sort of unspoken demand that she should see as he had seen.

She made a vague gesture toward the three brutes. "I don't quite know," she said. "You understand better than I do. They love you, I suppose."

"Of course, they do," said young Crosson. "But we've grown up together. It's a different thing for all of us. If one of 'em has a thorn in his foot, he comes limping to me naturally. If they're hungry, they come and sit down around me as though I were a dying elk in the snow." He broke off with a laugh.

"Then you go hunting for them?" she asked.

"What else should I do?" he replied. "Of course, I go hunting for them just as they go hunting for me."

"You don't mean to say that they go hunting for you," she said, incredulous.

"I never lie," he said with a gentle and rebuking dignity.

She flushed. It was as if, in a sense, she had questioned the word of an innocent child. He seemed to be sunning himself in the pleasure of her company and in utter belief in all that she would seem to be. Then how could she doubt him?

"I only mean," she said, "that I don't see how they could hunt for you."

"Well," he said, "sometimes I go hunting and spot a place where I know that a deer is lying. You know how it is. You see that the trail is only an hour or two old, and that it points out of water into covert."

"How would you tell that the trail is only one or two hours old?" she asked him, beginning to feel with a little pinch of anger that perhaps after all he was deceiving her.

He hesitated. "You can tell that yourself, I suppose?" he insisted.

"No. And how can you, really?"

"Well," he said, "there's the way that grass comes up after you've stepped on it . . . slowly, in the spring, when the ground's soft and the grass is growing . . . faster in the tough days of the summer, when it's wiry. You can tell from the way that the grass is rising about how long since it has been walked over."

"But suppose there is no grass?" she demanded, determined not to be convinced.

"Well," he answered readily, "then you lie flat on your face near the hoof print in the ground. If it's wet ground, there's a trace of water in the bottom of the hole or there isn't. If it's dry ground, then from the edges of the hole there are grains of the sand or the dust still sliding off, one by one, and spilling down into the hollow. By the time you've looked a few hundred times you begin to know just about how old a trail may be."

She took a breath and nodded. She began to feel as if she were passing through easily opened gates into a new world.

"Well, then," she said, "we've got to the place where you know that there's a deer in a covert?"

"How the wolves hunt them for me?"

"Yes."

"Why, that's pretty easy. First, you take four or five wolves. Then you lay off a course about a mile from the covert, and you turn on that point and lay a trail around the covert."

"You run for three miles, you mean?"

"Yes, for three or four." He went on briskly, as though the matter were quite an ordinary thing for a child to know. "Every now and then, where the covert's good and the space about right . . . every mile, perhaps . . . you leave a wolf behind you and point out the direction to be watched."

"You tell a wolf to wait there, and he does it?"

"Oh, yes. You can teach a yearling in three lessons. Especially if you have a wise old she-wolf like Bianca to help you out. She gives them a couple of taps a good deal harder than I'd have the heart to do. Well, then, your wolves are down there, waiting, and they lie in a circle all around the covert. Then you go down yourself into the covert and rouse the deer out. Sometimes, if you're very careful, you'll come right up the wind to the very spot where the deer is lying, and half a dozen times there's only been need of a jump and a knife thrust to end the thing.

"But usually the deer's up and away. And then the nearest wolf runs and cuts it off. It swerves, but the wolf keeps the outer side of the circle. The deer can't run back to the covert, because the scent of man is in there among the woods. Sometimes the man is on the rim of the woods, running along, keeping the course on the inside. And the wolf runs until it's winded, or at least until it comes to the next wolf. Then it drops down into hiding, and the fresh wolf is up, ready to sprint another mile, and the deer runs around that circle with a new wolf jumping up every mile and running at full speed."

"The poor thing," the girl murmured.

"Well, we have to eat," said the boy, and added a little guiltily: "Besides, there's a sport in it. But that's the way the wolves hunt for me."

"And eat what they kill, too, I suppose. What good does it do you?"

"Why, I whistle them off when they've pulled the deer down."

"Come, come!" she cried. "Will they leave the good red meat of a kill just because you whistle to them?"

"Yes, they'll leave it," he said. "That sounds pretty impossible, perhaps. But a wolf can be taught. And not with a whip, either. I make them discipline each other. All they know is that the commands come from me, and the punishment comes from each other." He made a little gesture, as though inviting her to see how simple it was. "There's nothing strange about it at all," he said.

She looked fixedly down at the ground. Then she looked up at him. She had thought of him as a young fiend in human form. After her look at him in the street, she had thought of him as a handsome, lithe, young fiend. But now her opinion was changed. She hardly knew what to say, but she knew that she was fascinated, that most of the horror had disappeared from her conception of him. She had to think and consciously remember that this was the man who had hunted her and Chester Lyons through the mountains only the night before.

He was saying now, in the gentlest and most conciliating manner: "But you don't like them? They look dangerous . . . mostly tooth and claw to you? I'll send them away."

"No," she said. "It's all right."

But he shook his head, and, whistling a thin, shrill, piercing note, he waved his hand. The three wolves started to slink away. Once or twice they paused, crouching a little, their wild, bright eyes fixed upon the master. Then they galloped away on a single impulse and were gone from sight in the woods.

"There they watch you out of shelter, I suppose?" she asked.

"No. They'll only stay within scent and hearing," he said. "You notice that they're down wind from us?"

She had not noticed. But before she could pay any heed to another thing, a water ouzel flew up the stream and sheered wide to avoid them. The next instant it was snared in the whistle of young Crosson. It was an amazing thing to see, as though he had thrust out a long, invisible arm and caught the bird, for it began to flutter in a rapid circle about his head. He turned slowly on a pivot, his face lifted, mischievous, delighted, the whistle trilling repeatedly from his lips, the bird making darts toward him and shooting off again, lured, incredulous, frightened, and yet fascinated again and again by the sound.

Now and again he glanced at Nan, to invite her to an understanding of the sport, and suddenly there was the bird perched upon his shoulder, and the whistling trilling softly, continually, while the wild little ouzel canted its head quickly first to this side and then to that in a manner absurdly like that of a musical connoisseur pronouncing judgment upon an important performance.

A finger was held up. It hopped upon the proffered perch. It spread its wings as though to fly when it was held directly before the face of the musician. But still the whistle persisted, and still it was forced to cant its head to listen. At length he was silent, and the bird, after a moment, darted off.

"But the next time," said Oliver Crosson, "it will come at the first call."

# CHAPTER THIRTY-EIGHT

"How do you learn to do that?" she asked.

"It's a hard thing," he answered. "You have to lie and listen for hours. Sometimes there are other birds striking in . . . but you glue your ear to one song. You keep following it in your mind. You keep pursing your lips to make the same sound. Afterward you go off, and for a few minutes you practice it aloud until you know that you've gone wrong. Then you come back and start over again. Sometimes it takes a month, working every day like that, before you've learned the whole song.

"And still there are the single whistles and the trills, and that sort of thing. You know the noises they make, sleepy noises, at the end of the day, or when the dawn starts, before the full song is started. You can make a sound of nesting and bring a mother bird dropping right out of the middle of the sky."

He laughed at the thought. But she was filled with wonder.

"You like to do it," she suggested. "Because you like the birds?"

"They're beautiful things," he said, "and there's never a one like the other. Take the jays. Some of them are more green than blue, and some of them are more blue than green. Jays are demons, but they're entertaining. They're up to tricks. There are some at home who steal things from me." He laughed.

"Important things?"

"Not often," he responded. "And it makes no difference. I know where the nests are, and I can go and get them again whenever I wish. Terrible thieves, though, the jays are. Terrible thieves!" And he laughed. Then, turning serious, he pointed to a fallen log. "Sit down," he said.

She sat down. She was entranced by the new door that he had opened to her, and through which she was seeing the world. That other thing—that monster with wolves at hand that hunted men through the mountains and struck them down one by one—that other thing like a disassociated phantasm was pushed away into the shadowy corners of her memory.

He took a place facing her, on a low rock that stood at the verge of the stream.

"You're not comfortable there," she observed.

"I can see you better this way," he said.

There was no cause for her to flush; he was stating a fact, not a mere compliment. He went on, enlarging his thought.

"I thought at first that standing beside you was very well. But this way is better. You turn a little aside now and then when you think. So I see you from every angle. Ha!" he cried so suddenly that she started. "It makes me remember a day."

"What day?" she asked.

"The first day that I caught a solitaire. I made it sit on my finger like that water ouzel. It listened to my whistle, and then it seemed to shake its head and say no. And it would ruffle its throat feathers and lift up its head and thrust out its wings in flurries, so that the light shone through the feathers. Then it would give me a singing lesson. But a lesson like that I could never learn. I could do the whistling of the other thrushes, some of them. But never the solitaire. It's a poet. It makes up as it goes along. And that's the way with you."

She did flush, then—suddenly red hot with embarrassment and with shame. For she began to have a guilty feeling. She had no right to remain here with this lad. But it was hard, very hard, to leave him.

"Come, come," she said. "I've hardly said a word."

"Look," he said, pointing.

"Well?"

"What do you see?"

"I see the still water in the pool."

"Is that all?"

"No, not all. I see the blue of the sky in the water and the trees shining. Why?"

"Well," he said, "has the water of the pool said a word, either?"

She was amazed at the turn he had given to the talk.

"So with you, also," he said. "Words would be foolish things for you to use. Or even to sing would be foolish, too. Because, by yourself, you are . . . you are . . . the lightning of gold that comes from nearest the sun."

She stirred. If another youth had begun to talk to her like this, she would have told herself that it was high time for her to go home. To him she merely said: "How many times have you talked to . . . to women before?"

"Never once," he answered.

She opened her eyes. "Not once?" she cried.

"I have seen them a good many times. Once there was a big hunting party in the hills. There were women with them, too. I used to go out and follow them through the evening and come up to their camp at night and lie on the horizon of the firelight. Then I'd look at them and listen to them. Most of them had squeaking voices. There was only one who had a voice a little like yours. She was golden, too, but not the gold that lies nearest the sun."

"You see," she said, "that's what I wish that you wouldn't do."

"What?" he said. "You tell me only what it is and I'll never do it again."

"I mean, to talk to me, like that. I mean, I hardly know how to put it, only you mustn't think out loud or pretend to think out loud about people, because it embarrasses them."

"Are you embarrassed?" he asked.

"I would be, soon," she said.

"I'll stop," he said, "if I only know exactly what I should stop. Will you try to tell me more clearly?"

"Why, when you speak of me and the blue sky in the pool . . . and of me and the golden light nearest the sun . . ."

"I was trying to reach out for ideas that were most like you," he said. "I've been a fool. I should try to use my brain better and find clearer words. I should try to say that you are . . ."

"Don't say what I am."

"Ah?" he said, fell silent, and stared sadly at her. "Well," he said finally, "my father always said that I would do a great many wrong things when I came to know people." His eyes grew sadder still. He pressed a hand over the hollow of his throat, as if there were a pain that touched him at that place.

She was amazed that she could hurt him so easily. She said, trying to explain: "Suppose that I were to talk about you?"

"Ah, well," he said in a melancholy tone, "I know that I'm as sun-blackened as a crow."

She stared at him at that. He was a dark bronze, with a patina and sheen of perfect health. His black hair shone, also, but, most of all, she was struck with the intense blue eyes, unlike any she ever had seen in a human face except one. She could not remember, just then, where she had seen an eye like the boy's. And an odd, dizzy feeling came over her, so that she felt, if only she gave her tongue way, it would find words, many of them, to speak to him as he had spoken to her, in a language and with such images as never had come to her mind before.

She forced herself to stand up. He leaped to his feet.

"You act as if . . . ," he began. Then he stopped himself, as though dreading to name his suspicion.

"I have to go back," she announced.

He stepped before her, with his arms extended, barring her way, but, when her head went up, in half fear, half anger, he stood aside.

"Look," he said. "It has only been one moment."

"It has been a long time," she contradicted. "I must go back."

"The shadows have only gone from here to here." He drew a line on the ground to show how far the shadow beside the log had traveled. "From there to there," he said, "and that is the only time in my life when I have been perfectly happy. Is it all right to say that?"

She avoided his curious and pleading eyes. "Why," she said, "of course . . ." And then she hesitated and stopped.

"But I'm used to trouble," he said. "This is some more. You are going back. I may walk with you to the edge of the trees?"

She could not speak. Her tongue was leaden, and as she started back up the course of the stream, he walked beside her. They entered the woods again. Behind them, silent shadows moved, drifting here and there. They were the wolves, she knew, but she gave them no more heed than she would have paid to leaves blowing down the wind.

At the outer verge of the forest he stopped. "I have to wait here," he said. "There may be guns watching for me from the windows of the hotel. Unless you wish me to walk up the slope with you?" His eyes shone. He invited her, he begged her to challenge him even to that desperate game.

She merely shook her head.

"Will you tell me where I can find you a second time?" he asked her. "If it is a thousand miles away, I shall get there and wait before you."

"You'll never see me again," said the girl.

She watched his eyes wander wildly for a moment. He drew himself up and bowed a little to her.

"As my father said," he replied. "And I have made you angry and you despise me."

"You know that I'm Nan Lyons," said the girl. "You know that you're hunting down my cousin. What else do you expect me to say?"

"You love him, then?" he asked her.

She could hardly face the intolerable anguish of his look. "Yes," she said, "with all my heart I love him."

She could not, being what she was, plead with him to leave that blood trail. She could merely wait for an instant with a blinding hope that she could turn him aside. But she saw his head bend, and knew that it would not lift again while she was before him.

So she went hastily away through the brush. And when she was almost at the outermost verge of it, she turned and looked back, and she could see vaguely, through the mist of foliage, that he remained as she had left him, looking down at the ground, dumb with misery, turned to a stone.

She hurried back to the hotel and up to her room. When she came in, she passed in front of her mirror, and what she saw there made her stop short to look again, for her face was pale, her lips pinched, her eyes staring with pain.

# CHAPTER THIRTY-NINE

It was the brightest time of the day in Shannon. The shadows, which had been shortening from west to east all the morning, were now standing straight under the objects that cast them. Under the trees there was a steep downdropping of the shade.

It was, in fact, exactly half past eleven, when young Oliver Crosson, seated in the back room of the saloon, saw Menneval enter the place.

Oliver had come to Shannon, a person totally unknown. Overnight he had become famous. There were a hundred purses willing to buy his liquor. They knew what he had done in the street the day before to Winnie Dale.

It happened that Winnie was a famous man in Shannon. Just as a champion is rated by the strength of the champion who he has dethroned, so young Oliver Crosson was judged by the worth of Winnie Dale. And Winnie was known as a man of bone and sinew, of might, of courage, of a sort of reckless willfulness for which he was loved by the town of Shannon, and for which Shannon was right to love him. But he was also a danger. And just as one likes to see a big, overbearing dog disciplined, so Shannon enjoyed the thought that Winnie Dale had been put in his place, that the next time he rode in with his followers they would not follow him quite so blindly, and that the lights of Shannon would not be shot out so soon.

On top of this, they knew that the famous Chester Lyons was in their village. That in itself was enough to thrill every heart. In addition, they also understood that young Oliver Crosson was to meet Chester Lyons that day, and that he would fight with him until one of the two was dead.

In thirty minutes, to the second, Chester Lyons would walk out of the hotel and cross the hotel verandah and walk up the long, crooked, winding street of Shannon. The entire town knew that he would do this thing, and it had gathered to stare. At the windows, by the doors, and posted at the corners of the houses, every man, woman, and child in Shannon was at some chosen spot, waiting.

How the people knew that the duel was to take place no one could say. Some said that Mr. Lyons himself had admitted it, scornfully, bravely. Some said that a waiter at the hotel was blessed with ears that were oversharp. But however it came about, the fact was that the entire town understood exactly what had taken place.

To another city such an affair would have been terrible, no doubt. To Shannon it was simply delightful and enthralling. They had seen countless gunfights, those men of the town, and they were ready to see another. But this one was posted, declared, and established beforehand. It was advertised, so to speak, and would surely take place.

Therefore the men, the women, the children were in their places.

Some of them had chosen posts near to the hotel, because they felt that Oliver Crosson would rush out and meet his man as soon as he appeared through the door of the hotel. Others had taken posts at the first bend of the street, because from that position they could look to the hotel and well up the way to the place where the street made the next bend. Still others were beyond this corner, and more were at the farthest end of the street, thinking that Oliver Crosson would probably wait until the very end before he fulfilled his promise of an encounter with the great Chester Lyons. There were still others who waited for the battle just outside of the saloon.

And these were the best guessers. For there young Crosson intended to stay until the word was brought to him that Lyons had left the hotel. Afterward he would walk out to the door, and, when Lyons appeared, strolling up the street, they would have the matter out.

He had a curious lack of doubt about the thing, though he knew that Lyons was much more practiced with firearms than he. It might be, very possibly, that the first bullet would fly from the pistol of Lyons, and that that bullet would strike him down. But unless he were killed, he knew that he would turn as he fell, and level his own weapon and shoot to kill.

What were mountains lions, even when they were braved in their dens? They were as nothing compared with a brave man. And Lyons was a brave man. He was famous for his courage. Every man here in Shannon knew all about him, it seemed.

Had they not come to Oliver Crosson and said: "Look out for him if his back is turned. He can whirl and draw and shoot all in a second, and he never misses."

"Look out for him if he's looking down and away. He can get out a gun like a thought, and he never misses."

"Look out for Lyons when he seems to be joking and laughing. He can change in a second and pull a gun, and he never misses."

They had given him such warnings, as he sat there in the little, dark back room of the saloon. It was not empty, that room. There were others in it. They were pretending to play cards. That was merely their excuse. They had to have some reason for being back there in the shadows of the house. So they sat, at four tables, playing poker. The betting was small. No man had his eye on the deal. Each was looking at the youngster who sat there in the corner, his hands folded in his lap, silently waiting. They looked at him, and they ventured to smile on him, and he smiled back absently. They could see that he was merely waiting.

And they respected him all the more for his quiet pose. Which one of them could have endured that dreadful interval without growing impatient, terrified? Which one of them would not have welcomed talk, even from a Chinaman?

But the boy wanted nothing, it appeared. He sat there with his hands folded in his lap. When they spoke to him, he said nothing. When they smiled at him, he smiled back absently, as though he sympathized with their mirth, but knew not the cause of it.

So, exactly at half after the hour of eleven, Menneval stepped into the saloon. They did not know him. It mattered not that the first part of his career had been passed in the same state. Long years had passed since that time, and he had become a legend, and then the legend had died. There was nothing remembered now except that somewhere in the vague past there had been a Menneval, and he had done certain strange things. No man talked of those things. Very few knew of them. And those who knew did not talk. They had learned discretion in the course of the years, and there was only a head shaken, now and again, and a secret twinkling of the eye.

When the youngsters said curiously—"Well, who is this Menneval?"—the older people would look at one another. They would perhaps wink. They would say: "Well, you'll find out someday."

And then the youngsters would perhaps say: "Who is he? What is he? Is he a crook, like Lyons?"

And one old man, white-headed, stern, an old prospector, had said: "Don't make fools of yourselves. There's a thousand Lyonses. There's only one Menneval."

Such comments were sure to make talk. The youths gathered together and made a thousand conjectures. But they could not hit on the truth, ill-guided as they were.

Therefore they built a mountain of imagination that hit the sky. They had in the town, at the same moment, Lyons, his lovely cousin, Oliver Crosson, and Menneval. The other three might be interesting, but there was a special mystery about Menneval.

When he came in, the oldest man in the town was standing there at the bar. And he looked at Menneval, and Menneval, in passing, looked at him.

He was walking straight on toward the inner room, the little room where the four tables of poker were going and where young Crosson was sitting in the darkest corner. When he saw the oldster with his white hair and white beard, he went across to him and stood with him at the side of the bar.

"Your name is Adams," he said.

"My name is Adams," said the old man. And he smiled a little, as though his name amused him, or as though he were philosophically amused by the fact that Menneval remembered him. Those who stood by and heard this talk were not impressed at the moment. But they remembered it afterward.

"You were in Frisco when the *Golden Arrow* burned at the docks," said Menneval.

"Hello," said Adams, "how come that you remember that?"

"You were working on the forecastle head," said Menneval. "And you had on a blue shirt, and you were handing parcels over the bow to the men in the boats."

"Well, well," said Adams, beginning to laugh, "you got a memory on you, I must say."

Menneval had been reciting as from a book, with his forefinger extended, pointing to the other, and the old man had been nodding and smiling. Now Menneval straightened suddenly, like a man who has cast off a load. "And you're still here," he said.

"Not in Frisco. It's a long way from Frisco," said Adams.

"You're still here," repeated Menneval. And his air seemed to say that it was wonderful to find the other in the same world, in the same form, in the same existence.

"You're a strange kind," said Adams. "I would've thought that you remembered me, maybe, from the time when the Wells, Fargo Express came into Carson City and the express box was . . ."

Menneval raised his finger. "Sometimes," he said, "things drop out of a man's mind. Sometimes they ought to drop out." He turned to the bartender. Old Adams was silently looking at the floor. "Here," said Menneval. "Take this twenty dollars. If you spend more than five of it on yourself, I'll come back here and have a talk with you. The other fifteen you spend on Adams as often as he wants a drink."

"Yes, sir," said the bartender.

"Will you have a drink yourself, sir?"

Said Menneval, a thing remembered afterward: "I never drink on working days." Then he nodded to the bartender and smiled almost affectionately upon old Adams.

"Thank you, Mister . . . ," said Adams.

He swallowed the name, and Menneval smiled again and went on through the length of the barroom, into the darkness of the back room where poker was being played at the four tables, and where young Oliver Crosson was sitting in the darkest corner of the room.

# CHAPTER FORTY

When such things happen as happened there in the obscurity of that little back room of the saloon, the memories of men are sharpened. The trouble is that their imaginations are stimulated, also. Therefore, of the twenty-five people who were within the walls of the room, there were not two whose accounts of what followed agreed in every detail. No more easy, to be sure, is it for witnesses in a court of law to rake the truth out of the hot embers of established fact. One remembers one thing, and one remembers another. None of them recalls the entire train of events.

So were the testimonies of the men who were in the little obscure back room of that town of Shannon in California.

Afterward they tried desperately to remember, but where they left off remembering and began to think there were always peculiar combinations of mind and memory that were added to one another, and finally made a story that was quite fictitious.

But what actually occurred was this: Menneval, coming into the back room of the saloon, paused for a moment just in front of the window, though by standing there he cut off half of the light that fell upon the cards of the gamesters. Some of them were rough men, and they would have protested, ordinarily. They would have protested, anyway, had they been actually interested in the fall of the cards.

But they were only passing the time. When they looked up at the strange face of Menneval and the silver hair that covered his head as though with a thin cap of silk, they changed their minds about speaking to the stranger.

So Menneval was left unmolested, to look over the room and watch the faces of the gamblers— the way they picked up their cards casually, as men who have no interest in what they are doing.

He looked at their faces, and an odd sneer curled the corners of his lips. He was like an arch-demon who looks in upon the tiny affairs of men who are worth neither a blessing nor a cursing. He seemed to be reading and despising them. Finally his glance rested upon young Oliver Crosson.

The latter had not stirred, though there had been a little commotion and a casual readjusting of people after Menneval came into the room. He remained with his hands folded in his lap, looking somewhat like a child that is troubled by being in the presence of strangers. On the other hand, he seemed chiefly absorbed in his own thoughts, for his eye had an inward look, and there was a faint smile on his lips, very like that of a woman who is striving to be polite and has forgotten why she wishes to seem so. In this manner he sat in the corner, when Menneval walked over and accosted him.

"You're alone here, young fellow?" said Menneval.

Oliver Crosson looked up, startled. "Alone?" he said. "Yes, I suppose I'm alone." He said it in a strange way, as though he were always alone, and found it odd that the fact needed any commenting upon.

"I'll sit down," said Menneval. And he pulled up a chair beside Oliver Crosson.

How many of those present wished, afterward, that they had strained their ears and jotted down every item of the words that followed, but, as it was, they could remember only bits of the conversation that, at first, was pitched in a low voice, and continued in that manner for a few moments. Two or three other men sauntered into the back room of the saloon after a time, and these, in turn, took note of the fact that Menneval was there and with young Crosson.

Suddenly Menneval's voice rose, and it became a sharply ringing challenge as he stood up. "Then what brought you here?" he was crying out.

"A thing I had to do," said the boy almost gently. "That was why I came."

"You came for murder," Menneval insisted. "You came for murder, because there's murder in you. There's murder in your blood. You're as detestable as a wild beast, and there's my opinion of you."

As he said this, he leaned forward a little and flicked the open palm of his hand across the face of Crosson. It was a stroke so light that it would not have stung the delicate skin of an infant. It was not a blow, but simply an insult, and Oliver Crosson seemed to realize the distinction instantly. A blow he would have answered with a tiger leap that would have landed him fairly on the stranger. And what man was there who could have resisted him for a moment? Not even Menneval, perhaps, for Menneval was no longer what he once had been.

But it was not a blow. It was simply the insult that stung, and Crosson, springing up, drew his revolver at the same instant. He drew, but he did not fire.

For Menneval, the instant that he had struck the lad, turned deliberately on his heel away from him and made for the doorway. He did not go with haste. He certainly was not fleeing, but, with a calm and ordered step, he left the room and passed into the front of the saloon. There was an old clock fixed there upon the wall, above the swinging doors, and in the face of this clock he saw that the time was ten minutes to twelve. He looked up at the clock and nodded a little, satisfied. Then, passing through the swinging doors, he stepped out into the blinding white light of the midday.

Dignity and slowness of gait left him now. He ran like a bounding cat to get his horse. He had not tethered it at either of the long racks that fronted the saloon. Instead, he had tied it around the corner of the saloon. There he found it, mounted it, and at the same instant had his spur in the side of the stallion. He flew it over the fence, rushed through the back yard of the place, winged loftily across another fence, and then down the free open fields of the valley of the Shannon.

In the meantime, young Crosson had stood for the first few seconds, amazed. Some thought that he was waiting for Menneval to turn and come back for the battle that had to follow. Others imagined that the purplish color of his face and the tremor of every fiber of it betrayed a numbing fear that made him incapable of movement. But they were wrong.

It was intolerable rage that numbed the body of Crosson for a moment. Whatever had happened to him in the way of wild life, his personal dignity was now affronted for the first time. It was a thing that he could not have imagined, and that he could not now understand. In the place of understanding, there arose merely a blind resentment.

Like a torrent the fury ran through him. He

forgot the purpose that had brought him the long distance to Shannon. He forgot lovely Nan Lyons. He forgot Lyons himself. There was no problem, no fact in existence, except that he had been insulted in public, and the offender had walked calmly away, as though he had struck a mere child that was in need of a bit of disciplining.

Then a low moan grew in the throat of Crosson. He looked wildly about him. Finally he leaped for the door. He went through it and into the front room without pausing. His quick glances, flashing from side to side, showed him that his quarry could not be here.

He leaped out to the front of the saloon and passed into the glare of the sunlight. Still the other was not there, and the ranks of the horses tethered before the saloon showed no gaps. The cream-colored horse with the silver mane and tail was there among them, for one thing.

He bounded around the corner of the building, half bewildered, and there in the distance he saw a great black stallion plunge over the rearmost fence and sweep from sight in a grove of poplars. It was too far for more than a blindly chance shot with the revolver. Yet his fury was so great that he actually made a few steps forward, as though ready to hunt down his newly made enemy on foot. Then he thought better of this.

The men who had poured out of the saloon,

watching him agape, saw his face transformed with rage and hatred, and watched him run back to the hitching rack. There he untethered the cream-colored horse, leaped into the saddle, and drove the animal straight at the fence. Over they skimmed. They crossed the yard. They soared above the second barrier and twinkled out of view in the silver flashing of the poplar grove, on the trail of the fugitive.

Then the bystanders could afford for the first time to turn and look at one another. They did not make any comments, however, for just then there occurred in rapid succession two things almost as fascinating as the insult, the flight, and the pursuit.

First, out of the door of the hotel, straight down the street, appeared Chester Lyons, trimly dressed in his tailed coat, and walking with a cane, which he carried in his gloved left hand. The right hand was left bare, for reasons which all who saw him understood. There came Chester Lyons at the appointed hour, but the danger had flown out of Shannon town, for the moment, at least.

In the opposite direction down the street, with its fringe of curious, tense watchers, came a man who seemed to be hurrying to meet an engagement. He was a very old man, his hair flowing and white, his clothes of ragged deerskins, and his mount a shambling, knock-kneed mule. Eagerness and haste were in the face of the veteran. He looked wildly about him, to either side of the street, and, when he came to the front of the saloon, where the crowd was thickest, he halted.

Ranger, coming up at that moment, was in hearing distance, and recognized the old man at once as Peter Crosson. Looking down the street, he saw Lyons approaching. Hurrying, half running in the rear of her cousin, was Nan Lyons, desperate of face, bent on intervening before the duel should take place. All these came up as the old man said in a hoarse, weary voice: "Gentleman, may I ask you if a lad with a cream-colored horse has been seen in this town? Shannon, I think you call this place?"

The bartender had come out and had planted his fists on his broad hips. Now he called over his shoulder: "We've seen a lad on a cream-colored horse, stranger. We've had him here for a day, and he's warmed us up like a fire. You want him?"

"It's his father," said Ranger in a hasty muttering. "Don't say another word."

"His father?" growled the bartender, nevertheless lowering his voice. "They're no more alike than a crow and a hawk."

He made no direct reply to Crosson, who was saying: "I have to see Oliver Crosson at once. I must see him at once."

One of the crowd, who had not heard the warning of Ranger, pointed toward the poplar trees. "There's his trail going out. You foller it and you'll soon find red."

# CHAPTER FORTY-ONE

Old Peter Crosson groaned audibly. "Has he been hurt? Have they driven him out from the town?"

"He ain't hurt, but he's gonna be soon . . . unless he kills the other one," added the bystander. "He was due to meet up with Chester Lyons, yonder, at twelve sharp. And then in steps this other gent . . . this stranger, Menneval . . . and slaps the kid's face, and then runs out of Shannon with the kid on his trail."

This explanation struck old Crosson like a bullet, or, rather, like a club, for he reeled heavily in the saddle, with his hands thrown up before his face.

One would have thought that he was striving to keep out a new impression and additional details of horror. Yet the added burdens seemed to be falling upon him, for he swayed more sharply in the saddle. He actually fell forward and rolled off the neck of the patient mule.

Several arms caught him before he struck the ground. His foot was disentangled from the stirrup. He was in a dead faint, with pale face and closed eyes. And they carried him into the shadow of the saloon verandah. There they put a folded coat under his feet to raise them higher than his head and forced a choking dram of brandy down his throat.

He coughed. His eyes opened. "Oh, Oliver," he muttered. "Oh, Oliver. My poor boy."

"Look here," said the hearty bartender. "The kid ain't dead yet. And from what we've heard and seen of him around here he's more likely to kill."

Old Crosson staggered to his feet. "Who of you have the fastest horses?" he cried. "Go after them as hard as you can gallop. Overtake them. Stop them in the name of God. It is most horrible murder. Menneval has drawn him away, but he'll never fight back against him. It will be parricide. Do you hear me? Why do you stand like stones around me? Parricide! He is the true father of Oliver!"

It went through the mind of Ranger like a thunderclap. As he stood there, immovable, remembering all that had gone before that pointed toward and justified the truth of what the old man had just said, he heard out of the woodland distance the weird and blood-chilling baying of a wolf pack, gathering on the trail. He knew what wolves they were, and the human leader that urged them on, and the fugitive who fled before them.

A most magnificent horse was that black stallion that Menneval rode, but suddenly Ranger knew with profound conviction that no horse, no man, could escape from the boy and his pack in that rough wilderness of mountains and wooded ravines.

And still he was stunned and more stunned as he thought of the thing that had happened. The life of Lyons was saved for the moment; the price might be the murder of Menneval by his own boy.

There was a sudden response.

Those who had fine horses rushed to get them. Someone must overtake young Crosson, or young Menneval, if that were his name. Someone must tell him his true identity. It was a thing to drive one to madness. It was an incredible thing.

Old Peter Crosson was saying: "Menneval will never tell the boy the truth. It's the one purpose he's had in making me act like a father to the boy. He'd have me be the father and give him my name because he said that the name of Menneval was too black, and there was a curse on it. Aye, aye, there's a curse on it, and today the curse begins to work, and I've wasted twenty years of my life for nothing. He's gone. He's wasted, he's thrown away, and God forgive the miseries and the wretches in this world. Oh, Oliver, poor lad, poor lad. What man will ever look you in the face?"

He sat down in one of the chairs that lined the wall of the verandah, and, swaying slowly back and forth, he gave way silently to his sorrow.

Those others, in a frenzy of horror, were doing their best to get away on the trail as fast as they could. But Ranger was in no such haste. It was likely to be a long hunt, considering the qualities of the horse of Menneval. If only he could keep away until the darkness fell, then the danger might be evaded for a time. But could he keep away?

Gloomily Ranger faced the danger and considered it with care, while he tightened the cinches on his horse. It grunted and rolled back an eye reddened with evil thoughts and malice. Then he mounted.

A dozen hard riders on chosen mounts were making thunder over the rocks or dashing up the dust as they fled in pursuit of young Crosson. Well, might they have luck—might they have luck. But Ranger doubted this very much.

The pack was silent now. Without a sound the wolves were hunting forward through the woods.

Lefty Bill Ranger did not leave Shannon with the explosive, gallant rush and roar of the other mounted men. He took things easily. He opened gates and even lingered to shut and bolt them behind him. Then he put the mustang to a steady canter, and it rocked smoothly forward over the level, dipped down the slopes at a trot, and, when it came to the upgrades, it took them at a trot, with its rider running beside.

He had taken one leaf from the infinite book of

Oliver Crosson, and the wind and strength of the mustang that were saved would be well used later on, he had no doubt, when there was a chance to close on the boy in a final spurt.

The trail seemed simple enough at first. There were keen eyes among those mountain hunters. Besides, half a dozen heavy-footed wolves, a horse, and a rider do not get over the ground without leaving some imprint behind them.

So for three hours Lefty Bill Ranger followed the way, slugging in the blinding heat, pushing through choking dust clouds now and again, and toiling through difficult tangles of brush in other places. For three hours he saw neither horse nor man. Then he began to go by some of the gallant volunteers from Shannon.

One man was down and halted by a bad fall. He sat nursing a twisted ankle, and gave Ranger no more than a single black glance as the latter went by.

Then he passed another whose horse had pulled a tendon and stood with a foreleg delicately, painfully raised. The man loved his horse. He stood, lamenting beside it, shaking his head in utter grief. His eyes were blank with trouble as he looked at old Ranger. And the latter went riding silently by.

He was more pleased with his mustang every moment. When he picked out that ugly-headed roan the day before from half a hundred sturdy range horses, he had trusted its strong legs and the demon in its eyes. It had a gait like the thudding of a springless dray cart over rough cobblestones. The gallop of a mule would have been the sweetest music compared with the gallop of this beast. But it went on through the three hours of drudgery until the sprinters from Shannon town began to come back to it by degrees, and still it showed not the slightest signs of faltering.

Old Lefty Bill himself was far more troubled than the horse. Dismounting and walking at the upward slants when they were really steep—this was by no means a mere joke or a flourish. It was a constant drag that turned his face purple and filled his lungs with fire. It was a lug that brought a black mist over his eyes. But every time he came to a grade he got down and struck up it like an Indian runner, and the mustang drifted lightly behind him on the lead rope.

Well, it cost Ranger much to make those efforts, but the horse was being saved, and that terrible three hours of labor saw the mustang comparatively fresh, while the best and the costliest mounts in Shannon came back one by one.

He found a group of three sitting beside a stream, bathing the legs of their horses, swearing softly, disgusted with their labor and the failure of it. They eyed Ranger sourly as he went by on his $100 misfit of a mustang.

Said one man: "I raised that brute myself and sold it for fifty bucks. And it's passed up this seven hundred and fifty dollars' worth of trouble."

Ranger was soothed as he overheard that speech faintly echoing behind him in the distance. And the rest came back, all of those fine flyers. If they had joined him in taking that leaf from the book of young Oliver Crosson, they would not have been there, lagging in the rear.

Then, though he was not sure, he felt that he was alone. He had been riding for five hours steadily. He thought that the last of those brilliant young riders from Shannon was behind him, and still he was going ahead, the good mustang working with the patience of a mule.

It was at the end of five hours that the trail went out completely. He cut for sign in a circle. Before he had made one round, well ahead, in the far distance to the north and west, he heard the cry of a wolf, a single cry, cut short in the middle. He closed his eyes, analyzed the direction from which he was sure that the sound had come, and then pointed with his right hand. When he opened his eyes, he sighted along his extended arm and found that he was pointing straight at a sheer wall of rock. He shook his head. The floating echo of the wolf's bay might, of course, have deceived him. But he had to trust to a trick that he had used more than once before with accuracy.

He rode up to the bottom of that wall, and suddenly it was no longer sheer. It gave back in unexpected small ridges, like steppingstones, irregularly laid. It was a perilous bit of work. Only a daredevil, in the first place, would have tried to get up the face of such a rock—at least, with a horse under him. But Ranger put his mustang on a long lead and made the effort, and, like a mountain goat, it followed him up, stepping wisely where its master had put down foot, studying its way with the most consummate care. They had to zigzag from side to side, but finally they came to the top, and amid plenty of sign that had disappeared on the face of the stone, he saw the tracks of two horses. He saw the places where the wolves had scampered through the grass, and the trail pointed straight up a mountain ravine. He was in the saddle at once. He gave the word to the mustang, and it struck out at a good clip.

The going remained fairly level, but it grew so rough that they were forced to proceed at a walk. But the horse worked well, dog-trotting where it could, coolly making the best of every difficulty until they came to a thing that stopped their way, and that almost stopped the heart of Lefty Bill.

# CHAPTER FORTY-TWO

What he saw was a ravine, narrow at the lips, with sheer walls of rock spotted green and brown with moss and lichens, dead and living. In the bottom the water ran with a sound that was hollow and far off, like the sounds that come up from the shaft of a mine. There was a three- or four-hundred-foot drop to those walls, but at this point they leaned in, and the distance from edge to edge was only maybe forty feet. Looking down, it seemed a vast distance, and the stream was contracted by perspective and ran white and brown, alternately. It ran with a terrible speed. If one should fall down from that height, even if there were a little life left in the bruised and beaten body, the stream would quickly devour all that was left of the mortal spark.

Ranger had dismounted. He stood at the edge of the chasm now and looked down at the picture and shivered a little. Then he looked at the bridge. It was not really a bridge. It looked more like an accident. A great tree trunk had fallen across the ravine. Or had some man purposely felled it, making the cut deep on the stream side of the tree, and then watching for the favorable wind to topple it? And someone had leveled off the trunk of that tree for a width of perhaps two feet. That was the bridge.

Ranger took hold of the edges of the log and shifted it back and forth from side to side. It was so uncertainly poised that it stirred in either direction. Then he stood back and looked at his horse, and the ugly roan mustang pricked its ears and seemed to consider. Ranger faced back to the stream once more. He wondered why he was there. He had been hired by Menneval, but not for such a purpose as this. He had been hired to go up the trail to Shannon with him; he had no orders to march across country on a death trail, in this fashion. And then he remembered.

It was a son who was pursuing a father, and the father would not strike back in self-defense. Old Crosson had said that, and old Crosson must be right. He had spoken with the dreadful assurance of a man close to death. Crosson was right, and Menneval was fleeing from the boy merely to lead him away from Lyons—offering his own life so that Oliver Menneval would not kill Lyons, and therefore become a victim of the law or an outcast from the ways of law-abiding people.

And he thought of Menneval as the white North thought of him—the stranger to the ways of other men, the lone wolf, the secret malefactor, the utterly daring and contemptuous desperado. Men said that Menneval could do such terrible things because he cared not a whit about two things.

One was his own life; the other was the life of other men.

And yet here he was offering his life to the boy and for the boy.

Then it seemed to Ranger that he remembered, not accurately but dimly out of legend, out of hearsay, other stories of men who had slain their children or had been slain by them. He could recall nothing clearly. He only knew that these terrible things had been, and here it was about to be again. Even with all his best will, how could he get to them in time to avert the tragedy? Even with all of his straining, he would surely be late.

So he told himself, shaking his head. As he stared at the bridge, it seemed to narrow, like the edge of a knife blade. But then he knew that he would make the venture. He had not given his word for this. He was not hired for such a thing. It was beyond and above hire. But he grasped the lead rope in his hand and advanced to the edge of the log. He mounted it and felt it tremble beneath him. He went on. He came to the end of the lead rope and pulled upon it. He could not pull hard without running the redoubled danger of casting himself into the void beneath him. Into that void he dared not look. He dared not think of it. Its voice, the imprisoned roaring of the waters, rushed up and thundered wildly about his ears.

The bronco held back against the rope. It gave a jerk of the head, and Ranger staggered. He sank down, his knees weakening, growing unstrung, but, when he pulled again, he felt the mustang yield.

Then he ventured a backward glance, and he saw the horse mounting the end of the log, carefully, nimbly like a dog or a wild goat. Suddenly an emotion of kindness rushed out from his breast toward the dumb beast. It could know none of his impulses, none of his reasons. Its mind must stop with the mere knowledge that its master commanded, and therefore it would obey. It came onto the top of the log and went along, putting its hoofs down carefully, one by one, feeling its way along like a creature in utter night.

The man went before it, still crouching, looking sometimes ahead toward the distant ledge. The log trembled and wavered with tenfold violence under the massive weight and the less yielding step of the animal behind him. Then he found himself in the very center. He thought that the tree bent under him. It seemed a limitless distance to go, a limitless distance to return. He glanced down involuntarily. And so far did his eye fall to the white bottom of the cañon and the angry rushing of the waters that he felt he was losing balance and toppling. The uproar made him dizzy, also.

*I am going to die,* Ranger thought to himself. *I've got to try to die fighting.*

He forced himself to go ahead. The bridge

wobbled more uncertainly behind him. Suddenly he had a picture of how young Crosson must have crossed this bridge, running lightly across it, with the horse, perhaps, trotting behind him, until the long log bounced and jerked through all of its length.

Poor Menneval. How could he escape from such a creature as this son of his? But Ranger forced himself on. He stood upright. When there were such men and ways in the world, it was a folly to deign to fear. He strode firmly across, with a long, elastic step, and he felt prouder and stronger when he stood safely on the farther bank. The horse followed him, making a jump of it at the end. Then it turned its head and looked back, snorting at the danger that was behind them.

Whatever came of this venture, Ranger told himself that he would not return as he had come. He mounted. The floor of the upper ravine grew smoother. The trees receded. He was riding over a gently rolling terrain, and the mustang was making good time of it, holding gallantly to that soft, chopping stride of the lope, which Western horses learn by instinct.

As he went on they began to climb again. The trees were diminishing quite rapidly in height. Sometimes, through gaps in the foliage, through openings in the ranks of the evergreens, he could see the naked upper mountains rising beyond timberline.

It was beginning to grow dusky in the woods, but in those loftier, more naked regions, a rosy light began to glow. The sun was out of sight, but it had not yet sunk below the rim of the world. Its color had changed, its fierce whiteness was dimmed, rose and gold were pouring over the world. It seemed to Ranger as though God were fiercely rejoicing in the tragedy that must be impending before him. Perhaps the man was already dead there among the high places.

The climbing grew so difficult that he dismounted again. He was very tired now. He felt as though he never had done such work in the white North, certainly never at such a speed. But he forced himself forward. He told himself that he had not much strength left, but that he must burn it up to the last ounce in order to give himself a proper chance of interfering in time. He could speak two words that would wither the fury in the boy's nerves: *Your father*. He gulped in a deep breath as he thought of this. It was not merely Menneval that he was serving. It was all humanity that would be his debtor if he should be enabled to come up to the two in time, for he would save the world from the blackest of crimes—a thing not to be thought of.

He had labored up a sharp, steep slope. Above him he saw the trees dwindling, thinning, and at that moment he heard from behind the snort of a horse. His heart jumped. Had he, by some chance, worked ahead of the fugitives? For some time he had been journeying not by trail, but by instinct, taking it for granted that they would have gone in this direction, the pursuer and the pursued.

He looked back, staring into the dimness of the ravine, and he saw a rider mount, a slender and boyish figure, unwearied, jaunty. The horse was of the best. The rider was of the best, also. Perhaps it was some youngster pushing across a short cut, aiming to descend into one of the western valleys before the night closed its icy hand over the upper mountain passes?

A thin, sweet-voiced call reached him from the rider. He shook his head and rubbed his eyes. He stared until his eyes started out of his head as he remembered the fierce labor of that march, the precipitous wall of rock that he had climbed, and the peril of the log across the chasm. But then he no longer needed to doubt. There, beyond a doubt, came the girl. There was Nan Lyons, riding straight up to him and holding out her hand with a smile of quick welcome.

He took the hand. He held it with a long pressure while he wondered up at her. "Nan," he said. "Nan, how in heaven's name? Nan, how did you get here without wings?" He looked more closely. Her clothes were rent and dust-covered. The horse was scratched and cut to bleeding in twenty places.

"We've had a couple of tumbles, but here we

are," said the girl. "That bridge is no highway, eh? Come on, Lefty. I've been praying all the way. Let's see if there's going to be any answer." And she rode straight past him, forcing her fine horse up the remaining distance of the slope.

He followed her as fast as the mustang would go. But it was badly spent, and in the other horse fine blood and a light burden were telling the story.

The ravine ended. The trees stopped at the same time. Before them was the last rosy-gold of the day, the incredible beauty of the mountain tops before the actual setting of the sun beneath the horizon of the sea, far to the west.

They were now well above timberline, but for certain scrawny, wind-blown hedges of low-leaning willows and such hardy trees. They scanned the heights above them with quick, eager eyes.

"There!" called the girl.

But her hope had been surer than her vision.

"There!" called Ranger.

He pointed, and far above them they could see a stream of wolves running across the shoulder of the mountain, and behind the wolves a rider on a horse whose mane and tail flashed like silver metal.

# CHAPTER FORTY-THREE

It was the last upward push to the top of the pass. Once the ridge was gained beyond, the fugitive would be able to make better time, and the boy would not gain so much. In spite of all his power, his speed of foot, his matchless way of covering country, it was marvelous that he had been unable to gain more on Menneval. Aye, but did not Menneval still make such trips through the wastes of the Arctic that some men considered him a wizard, in touch with the unclean spirits who accomplish magic?

But there they were, struggling on the mountain, and he, Ranger, had overtaken them both. He became like a madman. Success was here before him. If only he could gain a little more, a precious distance from which his voice would carry to young Oliver.

With all his might he forced himself. And still the girl was with him, shoulder to shoulder. And the light gilded the rocks. The mountains burned with it. From their heads the blowing mists turned to sheets and masses of purest fire, golden fire stained with red. There was something unearthly about this. It was like riding through an upper world. Only there was always that hideous, human toil of climbing, ever climbing.

Nan gained. Suddenly, as she was ten yards ahead, her horse slipped on the treacherous, rolling rocks. Down went horse and rider, and the trapper groaned, closing his eyes. But when he came closer, he threw the noose of his rope over the pommel of the saddle of the fallen animal. It lay perfectly still, rather from exhaustion than the hurt of the fall, it seemed. The girl was pinned among the rocks, under its side, and she lay still, her face upturned, looking at the sky, making no complaint. The heart of Ranger stirred and leaped in him. Here was one woman in a million. Was her delicate body bruised, crushed, ruined forever?

With the rope made fast, he urged the roan ahead. The good little horse pulled until it grunted, and the fallen gelding stirred, then pawed and stumbled up. It stood with hanging head, utterly beaten, its knees trembling, and Ranger, leaping down, leaned above the girl.

She did not stir, but lay on her back and looked straight up at him. "I'm all right. I'm a little flat, and that's all," she said. "The rocks kept most of the weight from reaching me. I'm all right. Don't you worry. Maybe I've a sprained ankle. That fool of a horse . . . but go on, Lefty. Go on, and God help you to go fast."

He could hardly have left her, but suddenly, from close above them, he heard the clamor of the wolves commence loudly. And that sound washed all concern for other things out of his mind. He left her without a word. He mounted the roan. With quirt and spurs he tortured the gallant little horse forward. But even the mustang stopped.

So Ranger threw himself down, and he rushed forward on foot. He came through high boulders. Before him the outcry of the wolves rang savagely terrible. And then he could see them, in a little flat plateau ringed around with massive stone. They sat in a circle, four monsters, and, pointing their noses at the fiery sky, they loosed their savage wails. They were giving tongue for the kill.

Then Ranger saw the rest. In the very center of the group, fenced in by the wolves, two men lay writhing, twisting, wrestling on the ground.

Why would not Menneval speak? Would he rather die by his son's hand than let the boy know his true name and their relationship? It curdled Ranger's blood. It gave him a new and sudden strength to run in.

The battle was ending as he came up. He saw young Oliver twist himself on top, saw his hand jerk suddenly upward with the sheen of a knife in it, flashing like a bit of silver fire.

Then Ranger, with both hands, grasped that poised arm and jerked it back.

The face of Oliver turned toward him, savage as the face of a hunting animal.

"Your father!" screamed Ranger. "Your father! You murderer!"

He had grasped what seemed the body of a writhing snake, a body hot with power, hard as a steel cable. But his shout took the power from that young arm. He was able to drag Oliver away, and he saw Menneval come to his feet and stand there, staggering.

There was a streak of crimson down one side of his face. That was where the stunning power of Oliver's fist stroke must have gone home. Half blank of eye, aghast, reeling, he stared at Oliver and the boy at him.

Ranger, looking from one to the other, saw one thing in common between them, the intolerable blue brightness of their eyes.

"My father," said Oliver in a gasping, groaning voice, and he covered his face with his hands.

Menneval drew himself up, took a breath, and with a handkerchief wiped the blood from his cheek. "It's the whining fool of a schoolmaster. It's old Crosson," he said. "He weakened in the end and told. Is that it, Ranger?"

Ranger could make only a sign; he was incapable of speech for the moment. Then he saw the silver-haired man go to the boy and draw down his hands from his face. Almost sternly, almost fiercely he looked at the son.

"Oliver," he said, "I would rather be dead than to have you know. I wanted you to grow up clean

353

and have your chance in life. I wanted to keep you from weapons and from men until you were fixed and sure of yourself. I wanted you to live and die and never know that Menneval was your father. But the evil one I've served all my life has waited for this moment to run a knife into my heart and twist it. I'm your father. Now you know your heritage. The stain is on me, Oliver. I've done what you'll learn from other men before long. I've done such things as God Himself could never forgive."

It seemed to Ranger that the boy was as one rousing out of a long trance. Now he wakened. The knife was still in his hand. He dropped it among the rocks, and, stepping on it, the blade snapped and sprang to a little distance with a shivering, tinkling sound.

Then he said quietly, but in such a voice that Ranger never after could forget it: "I know. Peter Crosson used to speak as if there were a curse on me. But I've seen the curse, and it's no curse at all, but a blessing. You were ready to die for me. I'm ready to live for you. I'm ready to do all I can . . . with my hands empty."

And he looked down at his hand, from which the knife had just fallen, and Ranger, watching, was suddenly inspired. He knew that no weapon would ever fill the grasp of those fingers again so long as the boy lived.

"Oliver, Oliver," said Menneval. "If you knew

what I have been." There was a tremor in his voice that struck Ranger to the heart.

"I don't know," said Oliver. "I don't care. To me it's like being born again, and it's the first day of life. Well, if I could take your hand and we could say to one another that the old life's dead and that there's a new one for both of us . . ."

Ranger found Nan Lyons without even a sprained ankle. She was standing beside her horse, gathering the reins. She started like a guilty thing when he came hurrying, scattering the stones under his blundering feet. She tried to mount, but he stopped her.

"They know you're here, and they'll be coming down the hill together in a minute," he said. "I've seen Menneval. Aye, and I won't say it."

"You stopped them? You got there in time?" the girl asked anxiously.

"I did, thank God."

"Thank God," she said. "But it's almost dark, and I have to get home."

"Maybe you'll be home by a short cut," said Ranger, smiling. "I've got a sort of an idea. Stay quiet. I won't let you go. When I told young Oliver about you, I could see the lightning of gold hit him all over again."

And then they came down the side of the mountain together, arm in arm. As they came, suddenly they laughed together and paused, looked at one another without unlocking arms, and then they laughed again.

"There's a man happy for the first time in his life," said Ranger.

And suddenly he looked into his own life and wondered—had he ever been happy really? All the riches he had mined for, hoped for—if they were his, could he really be happy? He looked up. The sky was brilliant; it dazzled his eyes with an untold wealth of yellow in the zenith, softening to amber, then to rose and purples that filled all the mountain ravines. There was the wealth there, the impalpable thing, the gold that never could be gathered in the hand. And what was happiness except the knowledge of having served others? He who gives shall receive.

A hand fell on his shoulder, and, looking down, he saw in the little distance Oliver and Nan, close together, she looking up to the boy's face. But it was Menneval who had touched him.

"Lefty," he said, "God bless you. What can I ever do for you? For here are three lives that you've made happy . . . happy forever. I begin to have a crazy hope. What shall I be able to do for you?"

"Why, there's nothing you can do for me," said Ranger. "It's been done for me. I've seen the lightning of gold, and I've seen it strike, and that's enough for me."

# ABOUT THE AUTHOR

Max Brand is the best-known pen name of Frederick Faust, creator of Dr. Kildare, Destry, and many other fictional characters popular with readers and viewers worldwide. Faust wrote for a variety of audiences in many genres. His enormous output, totaling approximately thirty million words or the equivalent of five hundred thirty ordinary books, covered nearly every field: crime, fantasy, historical romance, espionage, Westerns, science fiction, adventure, animal stories, love, war, and fashionable society, big business and big medicine. Eighty motion pictures have been based on his work along with many radio and television programs. For good measure he also published four volumes of poetry. Perhaps no other author has reached more people in more different ways.

Born in Seattle in 1892, orphaned early, Faust grew up in the rural San Joaquin Valley of California. At Berkeley he became a student rebel and one-man literary movement, contributing prodigiously to all campus publications. Denied a degree because of unconventional conduct, he embarked on a series of adventures culminating in New York City where, after a period of near starvation, he received simultaneous recognition as a serious poet and successful author of fiction. Later, he traveled widely, making his home in New York, then in Florence, and finally in Los Angeles.

Once the United States entered the Second World War, Faust abandoned his lucrative writing career and his work as a screenwriter to serve as a war correspondent with the infantry in Italy, despite his fifty-one years and a bad heart. He was killed during a night attack on a hilltop village held by the German army. New books based on magazine serials or unpublished manuscripts or restored versions continue to appear so that, alive or dead, he has averaged a new book every four months for seventy-five years. Beyond this, some work by him is newly reprinted every week of every year in one or another format somewhere in the world. A great deal more about this author and his work can be found in *The Max Brand Companion* (Greenwood Press, 1997) edited by Jon Tuska and Vicki Piekarski. His Website is www.MaxBrandOnline.com.

Books are produced
in the United States
using U.S.-based
materials

Books are printed
using a revolutionary
new process called
THINKtech™ that
lowers energy usage
by 70% and increases
overall quality

Books are durable
and flexible because
of smythe-sewing

Paper is sourced
using environmentally
responsible foresting
methods and the
paper is acid-free

**Center Point Large Print**
600 Brooks Road / PO Box 1
Thorndike, ME 04986-0001 USA

(207) 568-3717

US & Canada:
1 800 929-9108
www.centerpointlargeprint.com